# OH MY GODS

# OH MY GODS

## Alexandra Sheppard

SCHOLASTIC

Scholastic Children's Books
An imprint of Scholastic Ltd
Euston House, 24 Eversholt Street, London, NW1 1DB, UK
Registered office: Westfield Road, Southam, Warwickshire, CV47 0RA
SCHOLASTIC and associated logos are trademarks and/or
registered trademarks of Scholastic Inc.

First published in the UK by Scholastic Ltd, 2019

ISBN 978 1407 18873 7

A CIP catalogue record for this book
is available from the British Library.

Printed by CPI Group (UK) Ltd, Croydon, CR0 4YY
Papers used by Scholastic Children's Books are made
from wood grown in sustainable forests.

1 3 5 7 9 10 8 6 4 2

www.scholastic.co.uk

*For Peggy and Liz*

Dear Mum,

Dad said he wanted to spend more time with
me. Translation: he needed a hand selling a
load of rusty antiques from his old house in
Edinburgh. So, instead of spending my Sunday
doing normal Sunday things (washing my hair,
unpacking my boxes, freaking out about starting
at a new school tomorrow), I was in a muddy
field with people fifty times my age. He even had
the cheek to complain that I wasn't ready and
dressed at seven a.m.! On a Sunday!

   Sometimes I struggle to believe that my dad
is Zeus, ruler of the gods. Because, seriously,
how can someone go from striking people down
with lightning bolts to getting excited about car
boot sales?

   I hope he doesn't think I'll be spending every
weekend helping him shift his dusty relics. I
lived with Grandma Thomas for five years, and
she never once forced me to get involved with

her (many) dull hobbies. I'll never forget her knitted-finger-puppet phase – Gran couldn't give them away. (I miss her already.)

Dad said that leaving Edinburgh and moving into our new house here in London was the perfect time for a clear-out. But he's lived there since I was a toddler! Collecting junk the whole time, no doubt. I predict we'll be shifting it for many more Sundays to come.

This new hobby will make it impossible to make friends at school. Who wants to befriend the girl who spends her Sundays grubbing about with rusty antiques? I certainly wouldn't. Here's hoping that his new job as professor of anthropology at SOAS will keep him too busy for car boot sales.

Why he doesn't sell it online is beyond me, Mum. Maybe he's confused by technology? It annoyed him that I was on my phone the entire drive from Grandma Thomas's in Derby to London.

"It's remarkable, Helen, that you haven't looked up from your phone for longer than three minutes at a time," he said. Then he muttered something about it being antisocial, which made absolutely no sense. What could be more social than catching up on Instagram gossip?

I hope that being the half-immortal, half-human daughter of a god gets more exciting than car boot sales in the rain. The only so-called perk of being a demigod so far is never catching a cold. What kind of superhuman power is that? Everyone else at school gets to spend a few days at home with a runny nose, but my loser self has never even pulled a sickie. You always put my robust health down to your organic natural remedies, but I don't think lemon and manuka honey tea is that effective.

There is a chance that some godlike powers could kick in eventually. Dad said they might still appear, and I'm crossing my fingers that they do. But in the meantime, can I at least get an invisibility cape? Winged trainers? Heck, I'd even be happy with Dad doing a few neat tricks with lightning bolts from time to time.

But I suspect that won't happen any time soon (something cool or exciting happen? To me? Get real). Since I was little, Dad has droned on about the gods being strictly forbidden from using their powers outside of Mount

Olympus. But I've seen him use his powers to reluctantly set up the Wi-Fi router (after I begged for internet) and hold off the rain clouds at the car boot sale. And that was in the last week alone. One rule for the head of the gods, it seems.

Still, I'm clear on the rule that no mortal can know that he is a god. This is why he's masquerading as an average (if slightly eccentric) middle-aged professor. I wonder if Aphrodite will be yawn-inducing, too?

I almost forgot to tell you, Mum! As well as moving to a new house and starting a new school, I'll be getting to know my half-sister Aphrodite. She moved into the attic room a few days ago. I reckon Dad thinks I need a feminine presence in the house, in case I'm overcome with the urge to talk about my feelings, or tampons, or something.

Did you ever meet Aphrodite? She came to a couple of my school assemblies. I thought she was the most glamorous thing I'd ever seen (like a real-life fashion doll – the type that I begged you to buy but you never would, because they "promoted unrealistic beauty standards").

I've barely seen her since we moved into this new house. She's a make-up artist on some breakfast TV show, so she's up very early and out most of the evening. Probably at some swanky bar surrounded by her equally swanky friends.

My fingers are tightly crossed that I'll make friends at this new school. But I don't have high hopes. I'll be joining nearly halfway through a term, after all. Everyone is bound to have their friendship circle sorted already. I wish I had something to set me apart, like an interesting scar or exotic accent. When Jamie Atkins joined my old school, he showed half the year his eyelid flip trick and made new friends by the lunch break.

The fact is, I do have something that sets me apart – a family of super powerful, super beautiful beings that are Greek gods in disguise. It would make a good ice-breaker, right? It's a shame that telling people a) is strictly forbidden and b) would make me sound like a pathological liar.

I should stop moaning. I'll focus on the positives, like you used to. It's not all bad. I'm excited to be back in London, even if it did mean leaving Grandma Thomas and all my friends in Derby. I know Gran loved having me around, but raising a teen involves energy she doesn't have any more.

So far it's good to be back, even if the area has changed loads. The Algerian butchers you liked (they always gave me cherry bubblegum, remember?) isn't there any more. Vintage boutiques and organic grocers have replaced the greasy spoon cafes on the high street. I hope that soon I'll be ready to walk past our old flat and see if the shrubs you planted in the front garden are still there.

It might not sound like it, but I'm making progress. At one point, anything that reminded me of you had me crying into my pillow. Now, five years later, I can think of your favourite Al Green song, or wear one of your chunky wooden bracelets, and not feel my heart break all over again.

I'll be honest, Mum. At first, it was hard writing letters to you knowing that I'd never get a reply. It felt pointless. Now I don't know what I'd do without these letters. I can write things to you that I can't tell another living soul. Sometimes it's the only thing keeping me sane.

You're the only one I can talk to about my immortal family. Isn't that weird? Not that I know much about them. I can literally count the facts I have about this side of my family on the one hand:

## ALL I KNOW ABOUT THE GODS:

1. They live for ever. I still can't get my head around this one.
2. They have powers, but they're not allowed to use them on earth. Dad hasn't told me exactly what he can do yet, but it's got to be more exciting than household chores.
3. They can manipulate their appearance, which is why they all look like real-life Snapchat beauty filters (smooth skin, sharp cheekbones and they don't know the meaning of a bad hair day).

And what I know about half-mortals (i.e. ME) is about the same:

1.  We don't live for ever, but Dad said we could
    live a longer life than most mortals "with
    healthy lifestyle choices." I'd better stop
    skiving PE then.
2.  Some of us have powers, and some of us
    don't. Hercules had strength and Achilles
    was a badass warrior (apart from the dodgy
    ankle) but for me, Helen Thomas? Nada on
    the powers front.
3.  If I had ANY control over my appearance,
    you can bet I would never have to pluck my
    eyebrows again.

I hope I get used to living here. This new
house is so different compared to Grandma
Thomas's. My room is bigger, and I don't have
to share a wardrobe with Gran's church hats.
But the mouth-watering smell of fried plantain
doesn't linger in the air on Saturday mornings,
and it's so quiet. I used to get annoyed at my
little cousins Shara and Chantelle following me
around after school, but now I'd welcome the
background noise.

Will it be like this every night? Dad is always
marking essays in his office, and Aphrodite has

barely talked to me since she moved in a few days ago.

I'd better go now, Mum. It's time for me to wash my hair (and yes, I'm still using organic coconut oil on it every week).

Love for ever,

Helen xxx

# ONE

I wrapped up my letter to Mum just as Aphrodite barged into my room. Not only did she waltz in without knocking (am I going to have to put up a DO NOT DISTURB sign?), she had nothing on. And I mean nothing.

She was totally naked!

Even though *she* was the one treating our house like a nudist beach resort, I felt mortified. My cheeks flushed, and my eyes shot to the floor – to Aphrodite's perfect ankles.

Seeing her up close, I realized that there was no way I could introduce Aphrodite as my half-sister (clothed or not). We don't even look like we're from the same planet, let alone share the same parent.

We may both be tall with dark brown hair, but the similarity ends there. Hers falls in waves and mine is in tight coiled curls that defy gravity. My brown skin is closer to Mum's than her and Dad's olive glow. And I have freckles like someone dipped a paintbrush in coffee and splattered it over my face. Aphrodite's face is completely smooth, like a toy doll. No moles, birthmarks or visible pores. She didn't look real.

I couldn't find a flaw if I tried. And boy, I tried. I glared at her feet, but there wasn't even a crusty toenail or bit of flaky skin. Of course even her toes were perfect.

Aphrodite was stunning. And not in a "she could be a supermodel" sort of way, but in a "one flutter of her eyelashes and she can bewitch any human into adoring her" sort of way. Dad can pull off being a bumbling middle-aged man, but Aphrodite? No way can she pass as normal. How was I meant to invite new friends over when I'd turn invisible next to my *Vogue* cover star of a sister?

"Helen, I was unpacking and found this Turquoise Shimmer eyeshadow. Do you want it?"

The little eyeshadow palette floated in mid-air above Aphrodite's outstretched palm. I blinked. Once, twice, three times. But my vision was fine. There really was an eyeshadow palette levitating in my bedroom.

Aphrodite noticed the shock on my face and laughed.

"You haven't seen this little trick before? I thought even half-lifers could levitate at will," she said.

I didn't know what a half-lifer was, but I could tell from her crooked smile that it wasn't a compliment. It was so annoying that she could tease me about a million things and I had nothing on her. I ignored it.

"I thought that you weren't allowed to use your powers here?"

She shrugged. "This is no more effort than you tying your shoelaces, Helen. Are all half-mortals so easy to impress?"

Wow. Rude. But I still wanted Aphrodite to stay and talk, even if her sentences dripped with sarcasm. I was curious about her, and she had this magnetic pull. But before I asked any more questions, she had to put on some clothes.

"Did you want to borrow this?" I held up my dressing gown, throwing it in her direction.

She watched it land on the ground before stepping over it to get to the full-length mirror. My eyes stayed on her kneecaps. It wasn't eye contact, but it was progress from her ankles.

"Helen, do you want the eyeshadow or not? The teal would work wonderfully with your brown eyes."

Aphrodite didn't say this to me, by the way. She conducted the conversation in front of my floor-length mirror, piling and twirling her long chocolate-brown curls around her face, trying out various updos. I was surprised she didn't blow her reflection a kiss and a cheeky wink. She was far too absorbed in the mirror to notice me rolling my eyes.

"No thanks. I don't bother with make-up," I said.

That got her attention. She reacted as though I said I didn't bother with having showers.

"You don't? How extraordinary. You really should."

I tried not to take it personally. After all, why should I be surprised that the goddess of beauty values appearances more than anything else?

Aphrodite, finally bored of her reflection, turned her attention to the clothes I was halfway through unpacking. She ran her fingers over my folded jeans and hoodies with disdain. Did she have to wrinkle her nose like that?

"It's such a pity that you and I don't have the same style, Helen. A live-in sister would come in handy for wardrobe swaps and the like."

"Well, you're welcome to my Air Max collection anytime," I said.

Aphrodite snorted in response. I could tell from her

manicured toenails that she wouldn't be caught dead in trainers.

"My, how times have changed. Don't boys these days like it when a girl makes an effort for dates?"

"I wouldn't know."

It's true. I wouldn't. I've never even been out on a date. And there would be no chance of anyone asking me out if they saw me with Aphrodite. I'd look like a garden gnome next to her. I made a mental note to avoid being seen with Aphrodite outside of the house.

Anyway, even if I had been on a date, in my old school that meant going for a milkshake in the shopping centre, or if he was really into you, a trip to Nando's. My trainers would work fine there, thank you very much.

Would that be the same in my new school? What if I'm the only girl not wearing any make-up? London girls might be more like Aphrodite than I thought.

"I've changed my mind. I'll take the eyeshadow," I said.

Aphrodite handed it to me and sat on the edge of my bed. Did she want to chat with me too? I cast around for something to say. Somehow I knew that Aphrodite would jump at the chance to talk about herself.

"Dad said that you're a make-up artist?" I asked with my eyes fixed over her left shoulder. I felt like such a prude.

"That's the day job. If I must work, then beautifying humans seems like a natural fit. It's what I'm best at, after all."

How on earth would this mannequin fit in amongst normal people? "Is it hard? Pretending to be mortal?"

"Nothing about being mortal is hard, Helen. I can tone down all this if I need to." Aphrodite pointed to her face. "When I'm among mortals I look rather ordinary," she said, looking at me haughtily.

Ordinary like me, I guess? I smiled extra-wide to show that her snootiness didn't bother me, and pressed on with the questions. This was my opportunity to pump her for as much information as I could get. Who knew when she'd bother to talk to me again?

"And when you're not around mortals?"

Aphrodite's cat eyes flicked up to meet mine. "What do you mean?"

"Well, I know that Dad can control the weather. I've seen him do it. What can you do?"

She leaned in close, mouth curling into a smile. "I can make any creature on this earth do what I want. And they would do it. Gladly."

Now that sounded like a power I wanted. Imagine it! Starting at a new school would be an absolute breeze if everyone fell at my feet. I definitely wouldn't be sitting alone at lunch.

"Anyway, Helen, that's quite enough questions for now." Aphrodite's smile disappeared. "I didn't just come down here to give you old make-up. I wanted to lay down some ground rules."

Ah. I should have known Aphrodite had an agenda. Why else would she finally acknowledge my existence?

"As you know, I have the entire attic for storage of my things. I'm in possession of many beautiful and valuable clothes. You're not to touch them unless I've given you express permission."

So she did have clothes, then? Good to know.

I nodded. "Fine by me. Something tells me we don't have the same style, anyway."

Aphrodite smiled and got up. "I agree," she said, sauntering out of the door. "Oh, and Helen? Just in case you had any ideas, I have the power to make life quite tricky for you. Look in the mirror, and you'll see what I mean." Her laughter floated down the stairs as she made her way up to the attic.

Why did I need to look in the mirror? Did I have

something in my teeth? I turned around to face my mirror, and. . .

I gasped. My brown curls had disappeared. A fluorescent-green mop of hair sat on my scalp in stiff spikes. It was the sort of hair that stopped traffic.

I poked at my head to make sure. Yep, I definitely had several inches of stiff green hair attached to my scalp.

WHAT. THE. HECK?

Where was my actual hair?!

I felt sick with anger. There was no way I was setting foot out of this room, let alone starting a new school, until my hair was back to normal.

"Daaaaaaaad!" I screamed at the top of my voice. He was in my room in an instant.

"Helen, please use your indoor voice. You're not in the playground now," he said. Then he looked up at my hair, and his eyebrows nearly shot off his face. "I don't think that's, um, suitable for school, Helen." If my hair shocked Dad, then it must have looked bad. I mean, he's seen it all. Literally.

"Then get her," I yelled, pointing upstairs to where Aphrodite had disappeared, "to change it back!"

"I may be able to help, darling," Dad said. His hand reached tentatively to stroke the top of my head. "Right. It really is rather spiky—"

"Dad! Not helping!" I said through gritted teeth.

"Sorry! I'll try to bring it back. Helen, remind me. You had curly brown hair that sort of did … this," he said, waving his hands in an imaginary halo around my head.

He was absolutely useless. "Just get HER to fix it!"

"Aphrodite, come down here, please. You know the rules about using your powers outside of Mount Olympus," he said. Like she had taken the last chip off my plate, and not given me the hair of a tropical bird.

"Helen was curious about my powers, so I gave her a little taste. It was a bit of fun, Father," she said. Aphrodite clicked her fingers once again.

I rushed to the mirror and patted my head. Finally! My hair was back to normal. I breathed a deep sigh of relief. I'd never been so happy to see my ordinary frizzy curls. I even ran my fingers through it, just to make sure it was all there.

I slammed my bedroom door shut. "How is this my life?" I muttered under my breath.

Would I have to deal with this all the time? Having a super gorgeous, self-absorbed big sister was bad enough. But Aphrodite could turn me into a neon-green toilet brush with a click of her fingers!

This whole immortal-family-with-powers thing?

It wasn't going to be an easy ride.

# TWO

I came out of the shower as a delicious smell wafted up the stairs from the kitchen. I wandered towards the stairs in my dressing gown and heard Dad's voice downstairs. And the voice of a woman I didn't recognize. Please tell me I don't have any other surprise half-sisters moving in? Aphrodite is enough for a lifetime.

Dad opened the kitchen door. "Come down for dinner, Helen. There's someone I'd like you to meet," he said.

I walked down the stairs and into the warm kitchen, rich with the smell of onion and herbs. It was the first time I'd seen anyone using the kitchen since we moved in, apart from boiling the kettle and Aphrodite blitzing her green smoothies.

A small woman with silver-streaked brown hair stood at the kitchen sink, draining cooked spaghetti in a colander. When she turned around, I noticed she looked older than Dad. Unlikely to be one of his children, then, but you could never tell with the gods. They can do what they like with their appearance, after all.

"You must be Helen! I've heard so much about you," the woman said, and bundled me into her arms for a hug. Even though her head only reached my neck, she had quite the grip on me. Her warmth and smile reminded me of Grandma Thomas.

"Helen, this is Maria. She's going to be our housekeeper, taking care of things while I'm at work," Dad said.

"That means you," Maria said, letting me go finally. "It's vital that you have another half-mortal in the house. Someone you can talk to."

"Um, are you my sister too?" I asked.

Maria laughed. "Not quite. I'm a child of your Aunty Demeter, so I suppose that makes us cousins. I'll take you through my family tree over a cup of tea, one day. But now it's time to eat."

I began to lay the table for three, but Dad stopped me. "I won't be eating tonight, Helen. I rarely do," he said. "But I'll stay with you over dinner. We need to have a chat."

I sat down at the table while Maria plated up the food and cleared the kitchen.

"I see that Aphrodite introduced herself," Dad began.

"Yeah." The less said about that, the better. "What's a half-lifer?" I asked.

Maria gasped like I'd said a terrible word. Dad clenched his jaw, and I swear that his eyes flashed yellow for a split second.

I broke the silence. "It's something that Aphrodite mentioned a couple of times. Is it bad?"

Dad sighed. "It's a term that ignorant immortals sometimes use to describe half-mortals. I'll have a word with Aphrodite about that."

Even my half-sister needed a separate word to describe what I was – that's how big of a gulf there was between us. We were already knocking this whole sister thing out of the park.

"Anyway. I imagine you have many questions. But before you ask them, I want to—"

"Let me guess. Lay down some ground rules?" I said.

"Well, yes, Helen. I'm afraid I do have some rules.

But they are less to do with your curfew, and more to do with the somewhat, ahem, unique issues our family face," he said. "You've already been told this, but I can't stress it enough – it is absolutely vital to keep our true identity hidden from all mortals."

Boy, I didn't realize how good I had it with Grandma Thomas. Her only rules were not to wear shoes in the house or leave an empty plate.

"I'm obvs not going to tell anyone that you're a god and I'm half-mortal, Dad, it sounds totally ridiculous," I said between mouthfuls of spaghetti. "Everyone in this new school would think I'm a compulsive liar."

"That's good to know. But you need to understand this rule isn't in place to prevent embarrassment. It's a binding contract, one that all immortal beings enter into when they leave Mount Olympus. It's a condition of living here on earth."

Dad propped both his elbows on the table. "As you know, I am the head of the gods. But there are beings more powerful than me in Mount Olympus, and we must abide by their rules. It's for the good of all involved . . . though not everyone in this family agrees."

Hmm, I wonder who that could be? Something told me that Aphrodite and rules don't mix.

"More powerful than gods?" I asked.

Dad nodded. "That's correct, Helen. We are under the jurisdiction of the Mount Olympus Council. The Council is composed of twelve Mount Olympus residents. They're not gods, but they are immortal. Sort of like an impartial panel. They're the ones who decide which gods can live on earth and enforce the rules about living here."

A council? That's something my childhood books about Greek mythology left out. I guess it's way less exciting than one-eyed giants and winged horses.

"What sort of rules?" I asked. And did destroying my hair count as breaking them, I wanted to add.

"Quite simply, if we immortal beings want to live amongst mortals, then we must ensure they don't ever find out about our powers or our heritage. And we are never to use our powers to meddle in their lives," Dad continued.

"But Mum knew that you were a god, right?" I asked, confused.

Dad nodded. "As you know, darling, Sharon didn't want you to know until you were older."

I put down my fork. The spaghetti and sauce had congealed on my plate. Talking about Mum always ruined my appetite, no matter how hungry I was.

"But Mum was a mortal. How come you were

allowed to tell her about your powers and stuff?" I asked.

"The Council will sometimes make exceptions, usually when there's a child involved," Dad said. "But they don't make it easy. You wouldn't believe the paperwork I had to fill out, tribunals I had to attend. . . And even then, it's at the Council's discretion. The most powerful member of the Council, Cranus—"

Maria's snort interrupted him. "Don't mention that man's name in front of me!"

"Cranus," Dad continued, ignoring Maria's outburst, "is not exactly a friend of our family. But, unfortunately, he does hold a great deal of influence within the Council. If he caught so much as a whiff of rule-breaking, he could make life on earth very complicated for us. He's somewhat difficult."

"Difficult? If he had his way, Helen's mother would never have known the truth!" Maria said.

Something wasn't adding up. "Dad, I don't get it. You're the head of the gods. Can't you do what you like?" I asked.

Dad laughed, being all irritating and patronizing. "History has proven that giving the gods unlimited power doesn't always work out too well. The Council aren't perfect, but they're necessary to keep us gods in check. Can you imagine if Aphrodite got her way all the time?"

So she could conduct more traumatizing experiments on my hair? Hours later, I was still touching my scalp every two seconds.

"Anyhow," Dad continued, "provided we abide by the rules, we have nothing to worry about. Not from Cranus or anyone else on the Council."

"What would happen if you did break the rules? Like, by turning someone's hair green, for example."

"You mean if *we* break the rules, Helen? I must stress that you're also bound by this law. Anyway, it would take more than a botched hairstyle to attract the Council's attention," Dad said. "But if we did use our powers to set off World War Three, for example, there would be a trial at Mount Olympus."

My eyes widened. World War Three? Did the gods have that sort of power?

"And?"

"And if we were found guilty ... well, that would depend on the seriousness of the crime. It could range from a short banishment in Mount Olympus to being stripped of our immortality status. Frankly, that would be fatal."

Whoa. The Council weren't messing around.

"Then why not live in Mount Olympus and use your powers there?" I was asking a lot of questions, but I didn't get it. Living on earth seemed like such a huge risk.

Dad smiled. "Because when you've spent an eternity in paradise, even that becomes dull. Some of the gods are content with their life there, but I craved new challenges. Mortals are fascinating, and I'd much rather be here than having my every whim catered to in a cloud palace."

Cloud palace! Mount Olympus was sounding way cooler than drizzly North London.

Dad noticed the look of wonder on my face. "It's truly not as exciting as it sounds, Helen. Perhaps you will get to see it one day and you'll understand."

"Oh, they will adore you there," Maria said as she loaded up the dishwasher. "A new child of Zeus is practically a celebrity."

As awesome as a cloud palace would be, imagine being completely surrounded by immortals who look like Aphrodite? I'd feel like a toad.

"It's a lot to take in, Helen. And I'm sorry to tell you this before your first day at a new school. But it's important that you understand what's at stake," Dad said.

"I get it, Dad. Seriously, I'm not about to start telling my new friends that you and Aphrodite are gods."

*If* I made any new friends.

"I'm glad you grasp the importance of keeping our heritage secret," Dad said. "But to be doubly sure, I'm afraid that any friends you make are forbidden from entering the house. This must be a mortal-free zone."

"Um, what? Isn't that a bit extreme?" Did this family want me to stay a friendless loser? First Aphrodite transformed me into a troll doll, and now Dad was banning me from having anyone over. EVER.

That meant no friends over for sleepovers or tanning in the garden or exam revision sessions (by which I mean Netflix binges). How was I going to explain that to any new friends without sounding like a complete weirdo? Telling the truth wouldn't be an option. I ran through potential excuses in my head. *Sorry, friends-to-be, you can't come over this weekend. My house has a leaky roof/rare spider infestation/visiting poltergeist. Maybe another time?*

They were making it impossible for me to be normal.

"Helen, I know it isn't ideal. But we can't risk a mortal discovering the truth."

I nodded. Deep down, I knew he was right. The

only thing worse than not inviting friends over? Them coming round and seeing Aphrodite stroll through the house completely naked.

"Now, you'd better get ready for bed," Dad said. "You've had a long day, and I want to make sure you're refreshed for your first day at school."

Bed before eight p.m.? Had he ever met a teenager? "Dad, I'm not ten years old any more. I won't go to sleep for hours yet."

"I know you won't, especially not with all the distractions you have on your phone. So much time wasted. That's why I've confiscated it for the evening," he said.

He did WHAT?

"That's impossible. My phone's been in my pocket this whole time." I patted my jeans pocket. It was empty.

I leapt off my chair and checked under the table, but Dad was right. At some point during our conversation, he had nicked my phone. SERIOUSLY?

"Why would you do that? Are you punishing me for something?" I asked, trying to stay calm.

"Punishing?" Dad looked confused and it was infuriating. "I'm not punishing you, Helen. This is for your own good. Many studies have shown that overnight exposure to mobile devices result in a poor night's sleep, and—"

"Dad, this is unbelievably unfair," I interrupted. "I need my phone alarm to wake me up, for a start." More importantly, I wanted to chat with my friends back home. I needed to stay in touch, otherwise they'd forget me.

"Don't worry, Helen; you will have your phone by seven a.m. tomorrow morning. I'm sure you can manage a mere twelve hours without it," he said, getting up from the table. "Now if you'll excuse me, I have a lecture to prepare."

"But we need to discuss this, Dad. It isn't fair!"

I bit my tongue, holding back the sort of language that he would be shocked I knew.

Dad turned around. This time he didn't look so calm. Oh god. What if he could hear my thoughts? If he heard the names I wanted to call him, a confiscated phone was the least of my problems.

"Helen. I have seen many fair and unfair things in my time: miscarriages of justice, grinding poverty, millions of deaths caused by thousands of wars. Believe me when I say that this isn't one of them."

I stomped my way upstairs, slamming my bedroom door behind me. I didn't care what he said, Dad had no right to take my stuff. And this wasn't even a punishment. Imagine what he'd do if I broke curfew or failed an exam?

To think that just a few hours earlier, my biggest problem was making sure I had someone to sit with at lunch on Monday. Now I had to make sure I stayed on the right side of Dad and Aphrodite. Otherwise, I'd end up a socially isolated loser. With green hair.

Could my life just end now, please?

# THREE

I always thought it was strange when people described their palms as sweaty. But here I was, about to take a step into my new classroom, and my palms were sticky and gross. I caught my reflection in the glass doors. My cheeks looked as burning red as they felt.

The last time I felt this nervous was the morning of my drama summer school play (we did *Bugsy Malone*, and I nearly threw up over my sequinned costume). But this time, I didn't have to dance the Charleston on stage. All I had to do was walk into the class and take a seat.

I took a deep breath and pushed open the door. Two dozen pairs of eyes stared back at me in silence. Including the teacher.

"Miss Bloom?" I asked.

"Yes. Can I help?"

"Umm. It's my first day. And I'm meant to be in Double English?"

Miss Bloom pulled a face. The same one that Grandma Thomas makes when she realizes she's forgotten the milk. "Ah, yes."

She motioned for me to come in, her wooden bangles rattling, and said the dreaded words: "Introduce yourself!"

My tummy flipped into somersaults. Severing my little toe sounded more appealing. I willed my mouth into action, but my tongue seemed glued down.

"Now is not the time to be shy. Can you tell the class a bit about you?" Miss Bloom prompted. I swear someone sniggered at the back of the classroom.

What could I say? Say something, Helen!

*Hi, everyone, my name is Helen Thomas and I'm half-immortal. I've just moved back to London with my dad, who happens to be the ruler of the gods, and my big sis Aphrodite, who is so flawlessly beautiful she would make Kendall Jenner sick with jealousy.*

That certainly wasn't an option, even if it was the truth.

I took a deep breath.

"So I just moved to London with my dad," I said quickly. Public speaking was never my strong point. "From Derby? Where I lived? With my gran?"

Miss Bloom blinked. "Marvellous. And your name?"

"It's Helen," I mumbled.

"Thank you, Helen. Sit where there's room and I'll bring you up to speed in two ticks."

Miss Bloom carried on taking the register while I scanned the room. I clapped my eyes on a spare seat near the back, on a table with three other girls. I walked towards it and sat down at the table while everyone in the room stared.

"Your eyeshadow is fierce!" the girl with black hair and light brown skin whispered to me. "I'm Noor, by the way."

I smiled back, happy that I took the time to put on the blue eyeshadow Aphrodite left me last night. Still, I wasn't about to tell her that when I got home. I wasn't through being mad at her.

"I'm Daphne," said the blonde girl with the polka-dot pencil case and round-cheeked face. "And this is Yasmin," she said, nodding to the black girl with long braids skimming her back. She was scribbling furiously in her notebook.

Noor, Daphne, Yasmin. I memorized their names to myself.

"Yas doesn't like to talk during lessons because it distracts from her plan for world domination," Daphne said, smirking.

Yasmin looked up from her notes, and pushed her black-rimmed glasses up her nose. "There's nothing wrong with having high expectations, Daphs."

"So what's the set text here?" I asked.

Yasmin closed her notebook, the cover of which said *You Have as Many Hours in a Day as Beyoncé* (Dad would never buy me stationery that cool). "*Frankenstein*, but you don't need to worry about that in this class," she said. "Miss likes to think she's more therapist than English teacher."

Noor piped up. "Yas is right. Miss is such a hippy. Get this – our next essay is about our hopes and dreams for the future. She wants us to 'show her the person behind the uniform'."

"This is such a weird topic. Who thinks about the future beyond next week? I don't even know what lippy I'll wear tomorrow," said Daphne. She examined her blonde fringe in a compact mirror before tucking it in her blazer.

By the time Double English finished, I'd forgotten

about my awkward introduction and relaxed a bit. The girls had actually been nice. Maybe this wouldn't be so bad after all.

I took a peek at the timetable handed to me that morning. I still had the rest of the day to survive. "Does anyone have French after this? With Mr Parsons in 4C?" I asked.

"*Oui, mon petit pois*," said Noor. "I should warn you that his class is drier than the Sahara. And that's before he starts talking about perfect infinitives."

Miss Bloom dismissed us and we filed out of the classroom, a few of the boys scuffling and honking out unimaginative nicknames. Just like in my old school. The behaviour of the average teenage boy was universal.

"I'd kill to swap my advanced science with your French. Can you believe I'm the only girl in my class?" said Yasmin.

"Serves you right for being such a nerd," Daphne said with a wink.

Yasmin smirked. "Carry on like that, and you'll have to find someone else to help you with your English essay."

Daphne pretended to shoot herself in the head. Essay writing wasn't her strong point, clearly.

"Relax! It's going to be the easiest essay you've ever written. You must have some idea about what you want to do with your life, Daphs?" asked Yasmin.

Before Daphne had a chance to answer, a distractingly gorgeous guy bounced out of his class. Her eyes went dreamy as he walked right through the middle of our group.

"Um, Daphs, Yasmin asked what you want to do. Not *who* you want to do," said Noor. We collapsed into giggles. I felt like I'd known these girls for years, not hours.

"That's Jayden Taylor," Noor said to me. "Ever since he tried to grow a beard he went from being kinda cute to this unbelievably hot Drake/Zayn Malik hybrid."

"Oh crap. You don't think Jayden heard that, do you?" asked Yasmin.

"Why do you care, Yasmin?" I asked.

She pursed her lips, ignoring the question, and we all burst out laughing again. The answer was obvious.

"By the way," said Noor. "He's the only guy in this school who looks like that. So don't get your hopes up."

"Anyway, back to the question," said Yasmin. "What do you want to do when you grow up? You must have given it some thought, Daphne."

"Yas, chill," said Noor. "Not everyone has planned

out their career on a whiteboard in their room. Anyway, Daphs, you know what Miss Bloom is like. Knock out a page about wanting to save the dolphins or start an organic lavender farm. She'll lap it up."

It was hard to believe just how nervous I'd been that morning. Now, I was chatting with my new mates about boys and homework. Joking around with them felt so . . . normal. And a single god didn't interfere all day.

After my weekend, it was exactly what I needed.

# FOUR

My first week at school had gone far better than I expected. Even though I had nightmares of eating lunch alone or having to introduce myself at assembly, I managed to avoid both. To top it off, I even got a sleepover invite from Daphne. Success!

Dad may be immortal, but he has one thing in common with every other father in history: he hates to part with cash. Especially if it's for something fun. I had to fight tooth and nail with him to get some money for Friday night's sleepover.

I think Dad is making up for lost parenting time by being stricter than ever. From what I've read, I don't recall him caring this much about his offspring two thousand years ago. Just my luck.

I mean, did Hercules have to ask permission to hang out with his friends after completing his quests? Doubt it.

I caught Dad before he went to spend the evening pottering around in the shed with his antiques. Immortals don't have to sleep, and this helped him fill the time overnight. Last time I made the mistake of visiting him there, he subjected me to a twenty-five-minute lecture on Edwardian silverware.

He can be soooo dull, even by dad standards. That, and the fact that he wears Crocs outside of the house, makes it hard for me to see Dad as the head of the gods.

So I was on red alert. Get in and get out before he bored me to death – that was the mission.

"Come in, Helen," said Dad as I was about to knock on his office door. That always creeped me out. I know he has incredible hearing and could tell it was me from a mile off, but I wish he'd at least pretend to be normal.

"Hey, Dad." I climbed over a couple of unpacked cardboard boxes to sit in the worn leather chair opposite his desk.

He was marking essays with his reading glasses perched on his nose. I know for a fact these are a prop, as all the gods have perfect vision. It's one of the little things Dad does to prove to the world that he's normal.

"Yes?" he asked. Dad looked up at me impatiently, like I was one of his students dropping by to ask for a deadline extension.

"My first week at school went well. I even made some new friends," I said. Thanks for asking.

Dad raised one eyebrow. "Glad to hear it. I hope the curriculum isn't too different from your previous school?"

"Um, yep. All good on the old curriculum front." And honestly, who cared? "Anyway, Dad. Daphne, one of my new friends, is having a sleepover tomorrow night."

He stared blankly at me. "Remind me, Helen. What happens at a sleepover exactly?"

"You know. A sleepover?" I said. The clue was in the name. Wasn't he meant to be a professor? "We're going to stay the night at Daphne's, watch a few films, and order a pizza. I'll be back in the morning."

"I see." He didn't look or sound convinced. "But surely you can do all of that here, Helen? Minus the hassle of taking your overnight things, disrupting your bedtime routine. . ."

"Yes, Dad. But it's more fun with friends." It was like talking to a Martian.

"I suppose it's one of those teenage pastimes I'll never understand, like theme parks and discotheques," he muttered.

"And I'll need some spending money," I said.

"Why on earth do you need spending money? Is your friend charging admission?" Dad asked, chuckling at his pointless joke.

"The takeaway pizza won't pay for itself!"

"Doesn't your friend have any food at home? In my time, Helen, hosts provided meals for their guests."

"In your time, they threw people to the lions and called it a wholesome day out. Times have changed!"

Dad reached for his wallet. "This is all I have. And by the way, that was Ancient Rome, not Greece."

He gave me a measly fiver – a quid for every minute listening to Dad bang on. *So* not worth it.

"Thanks, I guess. I'd better get on with my homework," I said, getting up to leave.

"That reminds me, Helen, please keep Sunday afternoon free," he said.

"Cool. I don't have any plans this Sunday."

"And all Sunday afternoons, going forward. I want us to use that time to make sure you're on top of your studies. A little extra tutoring won't do you any harm."

I groaned. "Is that really absolutely completely necessary, Dad?"

"Why, yes. Your exams are over a year away, and I know that seems a long time, but. . ."

I tuned out as Dad twittered on about coursework and my last school reports being "less than satisfactory".

"Fine," I said through gritted teeth. "Sunday afternoons. Got it."

I bounced out of the room, and Dad turned back to marking his essays.

I spent Friday afternoon counting down the minutes until biology ended. Time seemed to stand still. I was too nervous and excited to concentrate on the life cycle of a plant cell.

Tonight was more than a sleepover. It had to go well with the girls. If I was going to settle into this new home, I needed to have friends. I didn't want to spend my weekends dodging Aphrodite's sharp tongue or getting roped into Dad's latest torture regime (aka Sunday afternoon tutoring).

As soon as biology ended (I swear the clock was going *backwards* at one point), I met everyone at the school gates and we walked to Daphne's house.

"Mum, we're here!" Daphne yelled as she unlocked

her front door, but the house was cold and dark. "She must still be at work."

We padded up the stairs and dumped our bags in Daphne's room.

"Daphs, I'm gonna get changed in your bathroom," said Noor before leaving the room with her bag. Were we getting into our pyjamas already?

Daphne pulled out a powder-blue dress with a white collar from her wardrobe. It was seriously cute – Aphrodite would have approved.

"Is that for tonight?" I asked.

"Yeah, Mum found it for me at a second-hand shop near her office," she said, holding it up against her curvy figure. "Isn't it adorbs? I'm obsessed with *everything* vintage. What are you changing into?"

I pictured the contents of my rucksack: toiletries, hairbrush and pyjamas. And that was it. No top or jeans. What idiot goes to a sleepover and doesn't pack a spare pair of clothes? I had no choice but to stay in my uniform until bedtime. Now the girls would think that I'd never been to a sleepover before, and never ask me over again. I saw rain-sodden car boot sales in my future.

"Oh gosh. I remembered everything but my clothes," I said.

"You have your pyjamas though, right?" asked Yasmin, clutching the jeans and top she was about to change into.

"Yeah, I have those." I'd spent ages deciding which pair to pack.

"Then you have clothes! Put them on. It's not like anyone but Daphne's mum will see us," Yasmin said. "I'm going to wear mine too."

"Yeah! It'll be like a real pyjama party," said Daphne. She hung her dress back inside the wardrobe.

Soon we were all wearing pyjamas and debating which movie to watch while we waited for our takeaway to arrive. Already, Daphne's house was a million times more fun than mine. Dad would never abandon his shed for a movie night. Because, apparently, nothing beats the thrill of adding to one's antique spoon collection.

"Helen, you need me to save your eyebrows," said Noor, unpacking her make-up bag. "I won't take no for an answer."

I didn't like the idea of Noor fiddling with my face. But she looked so excited! If it was going to make me friends, I'd be willing to sacrifice a few eyebrow hairs.

Plus, she had the thick, perfectly arched brows of an Instagram model. If there was anyone I could trust with the two furry caterpillars on my face, it was Noor. She pulled her long black hair away from her face and into a high bun, and selected her tweezers. This girl meant business.

"You're so like my half-sister," I said, while Noor examined my eyebrows between her thumbs.

"Oh yeah? Is she also buff, with the best brow game this side of the river?"

"Very funny," I said, trying to keep still under her grip. "She's desperate to sort out my face. Always giving me make-up and telling me what to wear, just because she's a make-up artist. It's so annoying."

Noor pulled back. "Shut the front door. Your big sis is a make-up artist. For real?"

Uh-oh. Here came the questions. I had to deflect big time.

"*Half*-sister. And she works on some breakfast TV show with Z-list celebs. It's nothing special."

"Babe, it doesn't matter if she's your third cousin twice removed. Getting paid to do make-up is, like, my life's ambition. And now I finally know a real make-up artist!"

Just. My. Luck. I should have known that Noor, who has more lip gloss than stationery in her pencil case, would be all over Aphrodite's job.

"Do you think she'd give me some advice?" she asked.

I thought about Aphrodite's mood swings. If she was this terrible to me, her half-sister, imagine how rude she could be to my friends? "Um, maybe, but I'm not so sure that—"

"I know! The next sleepover should totally be at your house."

My heart sank. There's no way Dad would let me have a sleepover. Noor was welcoming me into their gang, and I was forced to lie my way out of it.

"I'd love to, but my dad's not too keen on me having friends over. He works late in his office and doesn't like the house to be too noisy," I said, hoping they'd buy it.

Noor's smile dropped. "Oh. No worries." Now I'd upset Noor, who had been kind to me from day one. Great.

"What's the point of putting on a film if no one's watching it?" interrupted Yasmin. "You two are chatting, and Daphne's taken about a million selfies since the movie started."

"OK, Daphne, who are you texting that's more important than pizza?" I asked. She had barely touched her slice of pepperoni.

"Huh? It's Adam from Spanish. He was asking me

for . . . homework help," said Daphne, her pale cheeks flushing pink.

Yasmin paused the film and side-eyed Daphne. "Homework help? On a Friday night? I don't buy it."

"What did he say?" Yasmin asked, now peering over Daphne's shoulder. "Spill!"

"He said 'What you up to now, señorita?'" said Daphne.

"That's not all! He left two kisses and a red heart emoji," said Yasmin. "That almost makes up for the fact that he spelt 'señorita' with the letter 'y'."

"The red heart emoji is no jokes, babe," said Noor. "He must be into you."

Daphne broke into a shy smile and the tips of her ears went pink.

"Not gonna lie, I'm kind of jealous. It's been ages since I messaged a guy. And even longer since I last kissed someone," said Yasmin, fiddling with her box braids.

"I know the feeling," sighed Noor. "Can you forget how to kiss? Because it's been months."

Luckily they didn't ask me when my last kiss was. Because the answer would be "never". Unless you count the time some boy ran up to me in the playground, gave me a peck on the lips and ran away. I was five, and Mum always joked it was my first ever kiss.

All of the girls seem to have kissed someone before, and I've only ever kissed a five-year-old in a playground. With my mum watching. Was I stamped "LOSER" at birth? Was there an invisible force field around my gob only detectable by cute boys?

I was probably the only girl in my year dealing with No First Snog Syndrome. The average age of first kisses is fourteen, and I don't turn fifteen until the summer, so there's still time. But it'll take even longer if I insist on holding out for true love. Or at the least, a boy that doesn't overdo it with eye-watering amounts of Lynx body spray.

At least I wasn't the only one without a boyfriend. Maybe they were all as fussy as me?

"It's not just you, Noor. The ratio of eligible guys to girls in our school is seriously off," Yasmin said. "I've done the maths."

"That's hella depressing," Noor said. "You did maths out of *choice*?" Yasmin playfully smacked her with the nearest pillow.

"You know what we need to do, gang?" I asked. "Make a list!"

They were all quiet for a second.

"Um, do you need to go to the shops or something, Helen?" Daphne asked.

"Let me explain. My mum always said that saying things out loud is the first step to making it happen," I said. "You know: speaking it into existence. We could do the same for our future boyfriends?"

After a few minutes, we each read out our Ideal Guy lists:

Daphne: mustn't be embarrassed by nipping to the shops for tampons and chocolate once a month. Or at any other time, for that matter.

Yasmin: must not be intimidated by a girl who is smarter and more ambitious than him.

Noor: must think of romantic dates. I'm not spending hours on these eyebrows for a Friday night at the cinema.

Me: must be able to handle an eccentric family.

"Eccentric family, eh," said Noor "will he be dating you or your dad?"

"He can be a bit overprotective sometimes, that's all," I said.

"Ugh, story of my life," Yasmin said. "The only reason I'm not being forced to tag along on my parents' trip to Ghana this Christmas is because my big bro is seventeen now. Apparently he can finally 'babysit'."

"Isaac can babysit me any time," Noor said, raising one perfectly groomed eyebrow.

Yasmin pulled a face. "Please! You'd end up looking after him. He can't even microwave popcorn without smoking out the kitchen. He's seriously annoying. And my parents let him get away with murder."

Daphne looked thoughtful. "How long are your parents away?" she asked.

"Pretty much all of the Christmas holiday. They go every year. Why?"

"Isn't it obvious?" asked Noor. "You're meant to be the clever one," she said, squeezing Yasmin playfully.

"Yas! Your parents will be in another continent on the biggest party night of the year. You should have a house party," Daphne said.

Yasmin's eyes widened behind her glasses. "Are you mad, bruv?! If Dad found out, he'd put me under house arrest until uni."

I dreaded to think what would happen if I broke any of Dad's rules. I wouldn't see my phone for weeks. Maybe this thunderbolt temper I'd heard so much about would make an appearance, too.

"*If* he found out. And they won't, if you get their golden boy Isaac to help cover it up," Noor said.

"Plus, if Isaac and his mates are there then the party won't get out of hand," Daphne chipped in. "It would be so much fun! I'd much rather spend New

Year's Eve with my besties than here at home. Mum and her friends will just drink too much, sing 'Auld Lang Syne' and ask me if I'm 'courting'."

"I don't know. . ." Yasmin said. "There are so many risks to factor in."

"You know what, babe? We could invite Jayden Taylor, get you both some one-on-one time," Noor said, scrunching her lips into a smooch. Just in case anyone wasn't clear by what "one-on-one time" meant.

"You reckon he'd come?" Yasmin asked.

"He'd be mad to miss it," Daphne said.

"Fine. I'll speak to Isaac tomorrow and see what he says. But I'm not making any promises!" Yasmin added with a smile.

Noor and Daphne squealed.

"Helen, you've been quiet. Are you in?" Yasmin asked.

There was no way I could miss out on this party. Especially if they've all already had their first kiss and I hadn't. From the sounds of it, I had some serious catching up to do.

"Yeah, I'll be there."

"You should invite your sister!" Noor said. "I'd seriously love to meet her."

"*Half*-sister," I corrected her. "And I'll ask, but she

might be too busy. She's always out partying or on a date."

No way was I inviting Aphrodite to Yasmin's house party. If my lips were going to get any action, then I had to keep potential boyfriends away from Aphrodite. Next to the goddess of beauty, I wouldn't stand a chance.

# FIVE

I came home from the sleepover to find Aphrodite in the kitchen. She was hunched over half a dozen packages, unwrapping layers of bubble wrap. I breathed a sigh of relief when I saw she was wearing a dressing gown. This time.

Aphrodite turned around when she heard me come in. "Helen! Just the girl I need."

I nearly jumped out of my skin. A piece of ivory paper clung to her skin like a mask, with slits cut out for eyes and mouth. It looked like she'd papier-mâché'd her face.

"You do realize Halloween was six weeks ago?" I said.

Even through the mask, I could tell Aphrodite was

giving me a dirty look. "This is not a costume. It's the miracle ingredient of the year. My placenta extract sheet masks finally arrived! It's quite extraordinary how far mortal cosmetics have come in the last fifty years."

Gross! I suppressed the urge to gag.

"I'll take your word for it. What's all this?" I asked, looking at the packages on the kitchen table.

"My latest online purchases. The other MUA at work – that stands for 'make-up artist' – raved about this underground cosmetics brand. Said I had to try it, apparently. This reminds me, Helen. Can I ask a favour?"

One thing I learned soon after moving in with my family: it's good to know what the favour is before you agree to it. I still wasn't over having to help Dad prep his latest batch of sauerkraut. I could still smell the vinegary cabbage.

I narrowed my eyes. "Depends. What do you want?"

"Are you free tonight? I need to test my new make-up out before I use it at work."

"A makeover?" I pulled a this-is-so-tiring face.

"Come on, what else are you going to do on a Saturday night? Unless you've got a hot date I don't know about," she said, cackling a little too hard at her own unfunny joke. Was my single status so hilarious? "I'll buy you whatever takeaway you want."

Then I had a brilliant idea.

"You can use me as a guinea pig whenever you want. If you'll do me a favour," I said.

"Well?"

"My friend Noor wants to be a make-up artist when she's older. Is there anything you can do to help her out?"

"Is that it?"

I thought for a few seconds longer. "And I want a delivery of salt and pepper chicken wings."

Aphrodite smirked. "Aren't you going to ask me for a real favour? Something that befits my status."

"Like?"

"Oh, the possibilities are endless. I could grant you everlasting clear skin or make sure you never have a bad hair day for the rest of your little life."

A life without split ends and spots (especially the whoppers lurking under the skin, right at the tip of your nose) did sound tempting. And if anyone could do it, it's Aphrodite. But I didn't trust her sly smile. Or the fact that she was probably only being nice to me because she needed something.

"If you could help out Noor, I know she'd appreciate it."

"Suit yourself. I have a stack of old kit taking up

space in my attic. I'll leave them in your room, and she can have what she likes," Aphrodite said.

Yes! I couldn't wait to surprise Noor on Monday.

"I'll take off my mask and be back down in five minutes," Aphrodite said.

Once Aphrodite peeled off her sheet mask (revealing radiant skin – nothing new there), I sat down at the kitchen table while she did her thing. She was so quick and light with her hands. I barely noticed her apply a metric tonne of her foundation, which she mixed to the perfect shade of light brown for me. It turns out she took her job seriously and wanted to be good at it. She could have left out the commentary, though.

"An organic kelp smoothie every morning would clear up those spots in no time."

"You're not using *wipes* to clean your face at night, are you?"

"It's never too early to think about an anti-wrinkle regime."

Finally, she finished.

"That'll do, I suppose," Aphrodite said.

I hopped over to the mirror to see what she'd done to my face. The reflection of a girl with my big, curly hair stared back. But the similarity ended there. My face was now an expanse of smooth skin that appeared to glow from within. Cheekbones I'd never seen before were carved out of my round face, my eyebrows extended dramatically, and my eyes took on Disney princess dimensions.

I wanted to gasp. Maybe having Aphrodite play around with my face wouldn't be such a bad thing? Especially if I get invited to more parties (thinking positive thoughts here).

"I'll admit it's not an everyday look. It's the sort of face that works best in front of the camera. Speaking of. . ." Aphrodite pulled her phone out of her handbag. "I'll need a photo for my records."

Usually I was shy taking photos (I never knew what to do with my face), but the vain side of me wanted this look recorded for ever.

"It'll take moments, Helen. Then I'll order your greasy fried food."

Aphrodite was true to her word. After she took the photos, my chicken wings arrived and I ate them at the kitchen counter while she fiddled with her phone.

"Don't you dare sleep in that make-up, Helen," I heard her say as I went upstairs.

My scalp and I had survived an encounter with Aphrodite. Even weirder, she was kind of nice to me as well.

# SIX

Dear Mum,

I'm sorry that this letter is later than usual, but I've had a bizarre few weeks.

I'll start with the good stuff. School began, and I made new friends pretty much straight away. You'd like Daphne, Yasmin and Noor. They've invited me to sleepovers, and even a house party. On New Year's Eve!

It started out small but word is spreading fast. Yasmin and her big brother Isaac (well, mainly Isaac) seem to know loads of people between them. Boys from at least three other schools near ours are coming. Most of the girls are going because of Isaac. He and his mates on the school football team must know half of North London, and it doesn't hurt that they're 100% boy candy. Like me, Yasmin knows what it's like to have vastly superior older siblings.

They must think I'm a bit strange, though. I haven't invited them over to my house once. Can you believe that Dad's banned me from having any friends over? Must be because of the weirdo gods about. If anyone got the slightest whiff of weirdness, the family could be in serious trouble.

Sometimes my new friends ask too many questions about my family (but never about you. There's no easy way to ask about your friend's dead mum, I guess). I'm sorry to say it, but I'm turning into a great liar. I know you hated lies, but in this case, I think they're allowed. Our family just can't have anyone knowing the truth about our heritage.

Are all siblings as petty as Aphrodite? I can't even risk asking her to hurry up in the bathroom, or she might play some awful trick on me. And I'm not talking whoopee cushions or rubber snakes, either. She would fully mess me up if I got on her wrong side.

Dad's not interested in being a peacemaker, anyway. He's too busy marking essays or cataloguing his Edwardian postcard collection. As long as she doesn't use her powers on mortals, it seems like Aphrodite can do what she wants. But I have to be on perfect behaviour at all times.

At least I have Maria to confide in. It feels so good to speak to someone else who gets it. She's like the half-mortal aunt I never had. She says Aphrodite is annoying because she's bored. She can't torment mortals, so she's doing it to me instead. How can someone be around for millennia and still act like such a child?

Maybe Dad's bored too, which is why he's so fixated on my schooling. He's dedicated Sunday afternoons to homework time. Honestly? He sucks at being a tutor. He tried to help with my history essay on the Tudors this afternoon. All he did was bring up useless facts ("Queen Elizabeth the First had quite the potty mouth, let me tell you!") and insisted on trawling through his dusty books for research. Even when I told him that Wikipedia existed!

Christmas back at Gran's can't come soon

enough. I'll have two weeks without school, Dad confiscating my phone for no reason, or Aphrodite judging my outfits.

Grandma Thomas can't wait to see me. She spends every phone call asking me what I want to eat over the holiday. I've told her that I'm well fed, but she doesn't believe me.

I'm even looking forward to seeing Shara and Chantelle. After living in this house, a few days with my hyperactive cousins sounds like bliss.

Love for ever,

Helen xxx

# SEVEN

When I finished writing my letter to Mum, I put it in the shoebox under the bed. Along with all the others. Maybe one day I'll read them again.

It was a Sunday afternoon, and that usually meant a car boot sale somewhere off the North Circular for Dad. But for once he was home, along with Aphrodite.

Today was a special day. The best early Christmas present ever, besides a new pair of Air Max. My cousin Eros (technically my nephew as he's Aphrodite's son, but that sounds weird) was coming back from travelling in India!

Eros and I have always been close. Unlike most of my family, he stayed in touch with me long after Dad introduced us. During my few visits to see Dad in Edinburgh over the summer holidays, Eros always made sure to spend a couple of days with me. And he came to Mum's funeral, too. He's like the Beyoncé of my immortal family.

I heard the front door creak open and slam, followed by loud voices talking happily in the living room. He was here! Voices aside, I could feel he was back too. It sounds like hippy nonsense, but trust me on this. Eros has an aura of wholesome love that follows him like fragrance. When he's near, I'm more at ease and relaxed. Maybe that's why we get on so well.

"And where have you been, young lady?" Eros asked when he saw me walk through the door.

I skipped into the living room and gave him the biggest squeeze.

Other than the smell of patchouli that hung around him like a halo, Eros still looked the same as he did when I first met him. It's a strange quality that all the gods seem to have. They don't look young, but you can tell they're not spring chickens. He has the same tight black curls framing a brown-skinned face that could be fifteen or thirty-five, and a lopsided smile framed by dimples.

Even Aphrodite was smiling, and for once it wasn't because she caught sight of her reflection. She was pleased to have her eldest son back. It's easy to forget that Aphrodite is a mum and Eros is her son, not a sibling. He's certainly more mature than she is.

Maybe dealing with matters of the heart made him more emotionally mature. Being the god of love has armed him with an uncanny understanding of relationships. He's the best agony aunt a girl could want. His bow and arrow days are long behind him (could he make someone fall in love with me if I asked? I have wondered. . .) but he's awesome at giving advice.

We all sat around the kitchen table while Eros told us about his adventures in India. I ate the dinner that Maria left for me while Dad, Aphrodite and Eros had a glass of the special Greek spirit that Dad keeps under his desk. I was allowed a sniff, and the stench wafting from the bottle was enough to put me off ever trying it. I hoped this didn't mean they'd be up half the night singing. They may be immortal, but that doesn't stop them from getting drunk.

With Eros back, the house started to feel livelier. He's Mr Popular in our family and everyone wanted to catch up with him. Maybe that's because he's one of the few gods who isn't totally self-obsessed? Just try asking Aphrodite for relationship advice. Her eyes glaze over the second she realizes she isn't the centre of the conversation.

It wasn't a surprise when Dad told me to keep Sunday evening free for a family gathering. When I told him it would interrupt my hair-washing routine, he was predictably dismissive.

"How long could it possibly take to wash one's hair, Helen?" Before I could explain my detangling and conditioning routine, he walked away muttering something about humans finding endless ways to fill their short lives with nonsense.

That's rich, coming from the man who has a filing system for every back issue of *Railway Digest*.

But my coconut hair mask wasn't the only reason I wanted to skip this family gathering. It was bound to be annoying as hell. All the gods seemed to do is moan about their lives, or how much better things were in ancient times. Even Eros couldn't make me want to sit through that. The modern times couldn't be all that bad, could they? We have Wi-Fi now. And soap.

Honestly, some people have no idea how lucky they are. The gods have everlasting life! Beauty! The freedom to do what they like! If I, an un-kissed loser with no romantic prospects, could stay positive about life, then they could too.

It had been a while since I'd last seen any of the other gods from my extended family. How long would it be until they brought up the fact that I had no powers? Or call me a "half-lifer"? Maybe they wouldn't dare say that word in front of Dad. He did say it was a slur.

I lay down on my bed, closed my eyes and took a deep breath. "Mum," I said to myself. "I know it sounds ridiculous to be nervous about this. But I am. I wish I had your don't-give-a-damn attitude. Wherever you are, can you lend me some?"

I opened my eyes, wriggling my fingers and toes. The churning in my tummy had slowed down. I was still dreading an evening with no one but immortal beings but reminded myself that my bedroom was just upstairs. I could always pretend that I had French homework due for Monday and make a dash for it (I mean, I do, but I'm sure Mr Parsons won't mind if it's a day late. Hair washing is clearly more important than Pierre's trip to the zoo).

# EIGHT

"Helen! Come and say hello," Dad called from the kitchen. I went to the living room, where my half-brother Apollo was subjecting Eros and Aphrodite to a song on his guitar.

I'll never forget the time I went to hug Apollo and he fist-bumped me instead. I haven't tried again since. That was a few years ago, but he looked pretty much the same as I remembered. His dirty-blond hair was tied up in a messy man bun, and his skin was tanned to a deep bronze. He looked as though the phrase "sun-kissed" was invented for him. I guess an everlasting tan is a major perk of being the sun god. That, and the fact that he spends his summers DJing in Ibiza.

Oh gosh. I hoped he wasn't going to hold our arms

together, compare skin tones and say he was nearly as brown as me. Firstly, it wasn't true because I will always beat Apollo on the melanin front. And secondly, it was a truly corny thing to say.

He was deep in concentration, singing along to a tune he strummed on his guitar. Eros and Aphrodite were indifferent, but I found myself sitting on the sofa and tapping my feet. The beat was infectious. When the song finished, I was the only one who clapped.

A smile lit up his face when he noticed me clapping. "How's it going, Helen? Long time no see," said Apollo. He looked pleased to see me, but Apollo looked pleased to see everyone. Kind of like a golden retriever.

"I'm fine, thanks. I just started at a new school, and—"

"You're still at school? What a drag," Apollo interrupted. "I'm up to the usual: DJing private parties, recording my next album and some private music tutoring. It's easy money, but every one of these kids is dying to be the next Ed Sheeran. Like, show some originality."

"God, that sounds dreary. Hanging around with children all day. Just awful," said Aphrodite, shuddering.

Apollo shrugged, pretending that her comment didn't bother him. "I'd take private school brats over D-list celebs any day."

Shots. Fired. We all knew that Aphrodite was far

from satisfied working on a breakfast TV show, even if it was the most viewed show before ten a.m. I pursed my lips to keep from giggling (I didn't want a repeat of the crazy-green-hair incident).

Just as Aphrodite looked ready to explode, Dad called us in from the kitchen for dinner. That was strange. Maria's the only one who cooks around here, and she didn't work on Sundays. Was Dad going to make something other than coffee? Impossible.

We took our seats at the kitchen table, but there wasn't a hint of food anywhere. Not on the stove, or in the oven.

"Is the takeaway on its way, then?" I asked Dad.

"Takeaway? Of course not! This is our first family meal in your presence. As you've all made an effort to keep this evening free, you will be served a very special meal indeed," he said. Some of us had been given no choice but to come, I thought.

"I found one of my most beloved objects while unpacking. All you need to do is think about the most splendid meal you've ever eaten and it will create it for you. That is what you'll have for supper," Dad said. He looked very pleased with himself.

"Let me get this straight. You can conjure up any meal I choose out of thin air?" I asked. Why was I only hearing about this now? It seemed too good to be true.

"Not quite out of thin air," he said. He went to a cardboard box on the counter and pulled out what looked like a huge ... horn? "Remember this, gang? I found my old cornucopia!"

"Now, Pops," Apollo said. "Won't those cranks in the Council have something to say about you using the horn of plenty?"

Dad peered over his fake spectacles. "I won't tell if you won't."

"What does this giant horn have to do with dinner?" I asked.

"Like Apollo said, it's the horn of plenty. It'll produce any food that you like," Dad said. "But I thought it would be fun if we conjured up the best meals we've ever eaten. Now, who wants to go first?"

Aphrodite looked deep in concentration. "The best meal by far was a feast in Tuscany around the 1470s. Florence, I think. I was the artist's muse, and all the guests were utterly besotted with the portrait he painted of me. I wore the most fabulous emerald silk gown, and—"

"The food, Mother? I'd like to eat this century," said Eros, winking at me.

Aphrodite cut her eyes at Eros, annoyed at having her reverie interrupted. "I hardly touch refined sugar, but I'd make an exception for the marzipan cake they served during the dessert course. It was the height of luxury, in those days."

"As you wish, Aphrodite," Dad said. "Your turn, Apollo. What will you dine on?"

"I once ate a particularly good roasted pigeon dish. Back when I played for an audience in the Ottoman Palace. In the thirteenth century, few people knew their way around the zither as I did," Apollo said wistfully.

Wow. Had Apollo gone from playing in the presence of emperors to tutoring ten-year-olds? What a comedown. No wonder he was obsessed with the past.

Dad nodded. "Your turn, Eros. What delights can I summon for your dining pleasure?"

"Easy! It has to be the vegan noodle soup with fermented tofu I tried while hitch-hiking my way across Vietnam in the 1970s. I haven't found it anywhere else since."

"That's for a good reason, mate," Apollo muttered.

"My wish is your command," said Dad. He was practically bursting with excitement. "Last but not least. Helen, what will you have?"

I was at a slight disadvantage, seeing as I hadn't been to any palaces, feasts or far-off continents. But I wouldn't swap their exotic meals for my choice. "I'll have curry goat, please," I said. "Mum's version."

When I was eight, I had a three-day tummy bug and couldn't keep a thing down. When my appetite returned, the only thing I wanted was Jamaican curry goat. Even though it meant going against her vegetarian principles, Mum called Grandma Thomas for the recipe and made a whole pot for me. After three days of plain crackers and water, it was the best thing I'd ever tasted.

"Very well," said Dad. "Let's hope this works!" He rolled up his sleeve and stuck his arm through the hole in the horn. Not for the first time since moving here, I wondered if they were all in on a practical joke at my expense.

But then the smells appeared. The unmistakable scent of roast meat and almond biscuits mingled with the spiced fragrance of the goat curry. My stomach rumbled and I realized how hungry I was.

Dad pulled out several mismatched plates and bowls (yes, from the horn), directing them with a swish of his finger to the kitchen table. Aphrodite had introduced me to levitating objects, but I'd never bore of that trick.

The plate landed in front of me with a gentle thud. I inspected the food. It was uncanny – it looked, smelled and tasted exactly like my favourite ever meal. Even the plate (blue with a white floral border) looked exactly like the plates Mum used to have.

Tears pricked my eyes and I jerked my head down to hide it. Luckily, everyone was too impressed with their meals to notice me getting emotional over crockery.

"Oh, this brings back memories," Apollo said, nibbling on a pigeon bone. He looked ecstatic.

We ate in silence, punctuated only by the sound of soup slurps and cutlery clanging against bowls and plates.

"Oh, I nearly forgot," Dad said, getting up from the table. "My organic fermented broccoli is nearly ready!"

He opened the heavy glass jar of green mush and placed it on the table. "Dig in, folks."

The rankest smell *ever* invaded our nostrils, forcing us to cover our noses. "Dad, it smells like bin juice!" I said while Aphrodite fled the room and Eros opened every kitchen window.

"Oh mate, this is going to put me right off my food," Apollo groaned.

"So melodramatic," Dad muttered. "I'm putting it back in the fridge. But you're all missing out on an excellent source of probiotic bacteria."

Aphrodite returned with a huge canister of air freshener, spraying it liberally around the fridge. Once it was safe to sniff, we returned to our meals.

I looked over to see what Dad was eating. He was working his way through a large round flatbread topped with different meat and vegetable stews.

"What's that, Dad?" I asked in between spoonfuls of curry-soaked rice.

"Why, you've never had injera? I'm surprised your mother didn't feed you Ethiopian food," Dad said, smiling. "One of our first dates was at this Ethiopian place next door to her flat. She wanted to surprise me with a cuisine I'd never tasted before."

I smiled, remembering the jars full of unfamiliar grains and pulses Mum was fond of cooking. "Sounds like the sort of thing Mum would love."

"I didn't have the heart to tell her that I was familiar with Ethiopian food," Dad continued. "In fact, I've been eating it for centuries. Anyway, this meal always reminds me of that night. We talked and talked until the manager was ready to shut the place down."

The lump in my throat grew heavier. I realized that Dad must have loads of stories about Mum that I'd never heard before. Even though they split up when I was a toddler, they still had a few years together before I was even born. What was Mum like back then?

"Ah, Athena is here finally," Dad said, interrupting my thoughts.

It took me a few seconds before I heard the front door open and close, followed by Athena appearing in the kitchen.

"Sorry I'm late, Father. The law firm is keeping me busy at the moment," she said while unravelling the woollen scarf she didn't need to wear.

Why, oh why, couldn't Athena live here instead of Aphrodite? Athena wouldn't judge me for wearing hoodies or point out my split ends like Aphrodite does.

I always feel brighter after I've talked to Athena, like her intelligence is a substance that rubs off. And no matter what the myths say, she is every bit as beautiful as Aphrodite. She'd scraped her black curls into a bun and wore her usual uniform of khaki trousers and a plain white shirt under her winter coat.

"It's wonderful to see you all," Athena said. Dad, Apollo and Eros rose to kiss her on the cheek. Aphrodite did not.

Athena pulled up a chair next to me and gave my shoulder an affectionate squeeze. I realized this was the most of my immortal family that I'd seen in one room. No wonder Dad looked so pleased, being surrounded by his daughters, son and grandson. In fact, they all looked good. Their skin glowed with an amber hue that deepened as the evening went on. It was like they had an energy boost just by sharing the same room.

"Darling, you must tell me everything about your new job. It sounds fascinating," Dad told Athena. She'd channelled her intellect and passion for justice into taking on pro bono cases at a local law firm. She helped people sue dodgy landlords, that sort of thing.

Aphrodite snorted. "Yes, please do tell us everything, Athena. I want nothing more than to hear about your contact with the great unwashed," she said.

"Some of us like to put our skills to good use, Aphrodite," she replied. "I must say, it provides the most invigorating challenge. I could use my powers to give us a head start in our cases, but where's the fun in that?"

"Oh, I always put my skills to good use," Aphrodite purred. "Just ask Paris."

Apollo guffawed like they were on the playground slinging "your mum" jokes. What was the big deal about Paris?

"Enough," bellowed Dad. "I told you both after the Trojan War that I never wanted to hear about that blasted apple again."

That was it! I remembered why Athena and Aphrodite had beef. In one of my Greek mythology books, there's a story about the Golden Apple of Discord. There was a beauty contest (um, patriarchal much?) between Hera, Athena and Aphrodite. Somehow, this kid called Paris of

Troy ended up being the judge. The winner's prize would be the golden apple. Aphrodite used her so-called charms to dazzle Paris and won the golden apple, much to Hera and Athena's anger. One thing led to another, and soon enough it ended in a colossal war won by a wooden horse.

All that over a sparkly bit of fruit? No, I don't get it either.

"I mean it when I say I'm fascinated by your career path, Athena," Dad said. "It must take tremendous self-control not to use your powers against the opposition."

"Completely. Take my current case. This slimy landlord went years without doing repairs and now—"

"Ugh, this is depressing," Aphrodite said not so quietly under her breath. "Look at how pathetic we've become. Sitting here, discussing mortals."

Eros sighed, reaching over to squeeze his mum's arm. "I'd much rather be here than there. Don't you remember how dull Mount Olympus was when we left? I'd have given my bow and arrow to escape," he said.

"I want to avoid Mount Olympus for as long as I live," Aphrodite snapped. "But living on earth amongst mortals used to be fun. I could be myself, and everyone adored me for it."

"Aphrodite has a point," Apollo said. "Don't get me

wrong. I love making music, whether one person listens to it or one million. But an audience helps, you know?"

"I thought you did have an audience?" I asked. It seemed to me that Apollo was always DJing in clubs or playing at parties.

Apollo shook his head. "It's nothing like the crowds I could command in the old days," he said. "I've enchanted hundreds of thousands of people with one note. I've charmed audiences in Roman auditoriums, Viennese opera houses, and New Orleans jazz clubs. With one instrument, I could set up on any street corner, and hundreds would flock to see me in a matter of minutes, just by following the sound of my voice on the wind."

Wow. I knew so little about Apollo's past. I wondered if the rest of my family had such a cool history too.

"Stop feeling sorry for yourself, Apollo," Athena said. "You can still make music without applauding, adoring fans."

For the first time that evening, Apollo stopped smiling. "It's more than not having a decent-sized audience. You know very well that I can't make music like I used to. If I unleash the full extent of my skill around mortals, it will bring global attention and the

Council would be on my back. You know Cranus is looking for any excuse he can get to take us down."

"Ugh, don't remind me," Aphrodite said.

"I can't perform to more than one hundred people, otherwise it risks exposure. Honestly, Helen, you've never heard me truly play. If the world saw my talents, I would have every human in the palm of my hand."

Apollo looked so down in the dumps, it was hard for me not to feel sorry for him. But as someone with chronic stage fright, being upset about not performing in front of millions wasn't something I could relate to.

"We've had this conversation before, my son," Dad said. "You can practise all you like in Mount Olympus, a place where you can legally use your powers. But on earth, we must be more careful."

Dad gestured to the fridge door, where he'd printed out a copy of the rules and stuck them on with magnets. Another reason why I can't invite my friends over without a thorough tidying.

He cleared his throat. Aphrodite muttered "here we go" under her breath.

"Rule One: gods must not reveal their immortal identity for any reason."

That made sense to me. Who would believe them anyway?

Dad continued. "Rule Two: gods must not use their powers to interfere with the fate of mortals for any reason. We must not grant mortals beauty, love, wealth, long life and/or happiness. We must not agitate wars, create natural disasters, and take sides in matters of international diplomacy..."

"Yes, Father, I know," said Aphrodite. "We must keep our powers under wraps so we're allowed to leave that toy town Mount Olympus. A terrible bargain, if you ask me."

"Need I remind you, Aphrodite, that the rules are twofold? They prevent mortals from discovering our existence, and keep them safe from harm."

"Ever since these rules got put in place, I constantly have to keep my talent dimmed," Apollo said, pouting.

"So the rules weren't always in place?" I asked.

Dad shook his head. "Sadly, Helen, the rules were established because they became necessary," Dad said, looking at Aphrodite. "The Council at Mount Olympus felt we were intervening too often in human affairs."

Aphrodite shrugged. "Honestly, it was just one little war! We all know what mortals are like with wars. They always blow over, whether we push them along or not," she said. "And I, for one, was sick to death of that clothing ration. It was impossible to find stockings!

Everyone was pleased when that world war finally came to an end."

Dad pushed his spectacles up, brushing past his greying temples. "That's not the point, Aphrodite. Humans must make their own mistakes, and there is little we can do to stop them."

"Even if we watch them slowly destroy themselves and the planet?" asked Eros. "I'd love to help with more than litter-picking by the canal every other Sunday."

Dad nodded. "It's out of our hands. But there's plenty we can do without resorting to our powers and exposing our immortal identity. Athena never takes on high-profile cases, for example. Aphrodite has turned down modelling contracts but her career as a make-up artist is thriving. And Apollo's music must never reach a large audience. We all make sacrifices."

Looking at the sullen faces around the table, it seemed like no one was thrilled with these decisions.

"And I suppose having dozens of half-mortal infants over the centuries doesn't count, hmm?" Aphrodite said.

I rolled my eyes. I didn't appreciate the thinly veiled reference to Dad's (many) relationships with mortals. It made me uncomfortable to think about all the half-siblings I had that I'll never meet.

Eros reached across the table to hold my hand. "And we're so glad you're here. Helen is my favourite child of yours by far."

I smiled weakly. I appreciated Eros's kind words (no one in this family has my back like him) but I still felt like an outcast. My family had these incredible gifts and talents. Gifts that made the world a better, more interesting place. They've lived for centuries and travelled to every continent. I've never even been on a plane.

I mumbled something about having school in the morning and excused myself for bed.

"Lights out by ten p.m., please," Athena said. "It's vital that your brain gets a full night's sleep if you're to perform at your best for school." Ugh. Why are the gods in my family either indifferent to me or *way* into how I spend every waking hour? Maybe it was best if Athena didn't live here. It would be like having a round-the-clock private tutor.

As I was leaving, Dad said, "Helen, don't forget that I'm out on Tuesday night. It's my department's Christmas party."

"Well, don't expect me to babysit," said Aphrodite. "I might have a date."

"I'm not five. I can take care of myself for one

evening," I said. Besides, Aphrodite would be a rubbish babysitter. She'd have to think of someone other than herself for once. Not possible.

I woke up to a quiet house on Wednesday morning. Usually Dad is around before his lectures, making coffee, nagging, that sort of thing. But he wasn't reminding me that I had to leave in four minutes while I brushed my teeth. Where was he?

Then I remembered. Last night was his work Christmas party! Maybe he didn't even come home. He must have had a good night, then. Still, it wasn't like him and I wondered where he was.

I told Daphne about it at morning break.

"He probably met someone in a bar, got too drunk to drive and went home with her," she said.

The gods get drunk but not *that* drunk. But going home with someone he met at a bar? That could be possible. I honestly didn't know Dad well enough to be sure.

I sent him a text later that day to see where he was up to, but I didn't get a reply.

What. A. Hypocrite. If I went out all night and didn't leave so much as a courtesy text, I wouldn't see the light of day until after A levels.

I knew that there was no way Dad was in trouble, but that didn't stop the nagging sense of worry. Even if he often forgets to lock the back door, he can take care of himself. He's a god, after all! Plus all the gods have this weird psychic bond. If something went wrong, Aphrodite or Eros would have felt it right away.

But the thought bothered me all afternoon. I kept checking my phone between classes for a reply to my texts, but nada.

By the time school was over, Dad saw fit to reply to my texts:

*Apologies for the radio silence. Battery died and I forgot my charger. Will you be home after school?*

There wasn't even a kiss at the end! And how dare he demand to know what I'm doing? He didn't even give me a proper excuse. He could have lied and said there was a work emergency. Maybe there was a major breakthrough in the study of dusty bits of junk, I don't know.

I was too annoyed to reply. It didn't matter anyway because the answer was waiting for me at home.

# NINE

Daphne was right. Well, half right.

The reason why Dad was out all night was because of (drum roll, please!) a lady friend. And not just any lady friend. A special lady friend. Why am I saying lady friend so much? Because Dad referred to Lisa as his lady friend about seventeen times over the course of the evening. Even weirder, she didn't run screaming from the dinner table when he did.

I was in the kitchen finishing off my French homework (and watching DIY hair mask videos) when I heard Dad come in, along with the voice of a woman I didn't recognize.

"Helen, you're here!" Dad said brightly. I was low-key annoyed at Dad for his silence all day.

I grunted in response. "Where else would I be on a Wednesday night?"

Dad ignored my sarcasm, turning to someone in the corridor. "Lisa, meet my youngest daughter, Helen. Helen, this is my . . . lady friend." Yes, it was as awkward as it sounded.

A petite dark-haired woman walked in. "Hey, Helen, it's lovely to meet you. George told me a lot about you," Lisa said.

It took me a second to realize that she was talking about Dad. George was the name he used at work. And when he was hooking up with women, it seemed.

"Will you join us for dinner?" Dad asked. So he's allowed friends over and I'm not? Such a double standard!

I wanted to give him the cold shoulder for ghosting on me. But curiosity got the better of me. Who was this woman who kept Dad so busy that he couldn't reply to a text?

"Depends. Are you cooking?" I asked.

Dad laughed too loud. "Of course I'm cooking, darling. Who else?"

I narrowed my eyes at him. It was my subtle way of telling Dad "we both know that the closest you get to cooking is switching on the espresso machine, but I'll stay quiet this once".

While Dad rummaged through the drawers trying to find the can opener, I got to know Lisa a little bit more. Even in her baggy jeans and crumpled blouse she was attractive. Her black hair was streaked with silver and scraped back into a ponytail. I couldn't quite place her accent at first, which had a slight American twang to it.

Dad didn't leave me wondering for long. By the time he'd finished heating tinned tomato soup and grilling cheese on toast, the only thing I didn't know about Lisa Chen (aged forty-three, born in Queens, New York City, to two Chinese immigrant parents) was her blood type.

"So, how did you both meet?" I asked once we sat down to eat at the table. I had to ask something, otherwise they were in serious danger of gazing lovingly into each other's eyes for the entire meal. They might even have kissed. And then there was no chance of me finishing my meal. Gag.

They looked at each other and giggled. My dad, the head of the Olympian gods, *giggled*. He must really be into her.

"Oh, it's the strangest thing, Helen. I happened to be at George's university for a conference on medieval Korean pottery," Lisa said.

Conference? Pottery? I already regretted asking.

"I was in the campus cafe looking at pastries. Super strange, because I don't have a sweet tooth in the least. But I suddenly felt like I needed a sugar hit." Lisa paused to take a bite of her cheese on toast. Dad gazed at her like he wished he was the toast.

"I spotted the pastry display and noticed that they had one single, glorious cinnamon bun left. George was in front of me, but I never imagined this sophisticated James Bond type would want it too. I thought he'd order, like, a black coffee or something."

Dad blushed when Lisa called him a "James Bond type". I tried not to roll my eyes.

"But I also had my eyes on that cinnamon bun. When I ordered it, I heard this voice behind me say 'No!' I turned around, and there you were," Dad said.

Since when did Dad crave pastry? The only time I've seen him eat anything was at our family gathering last Sunday.

They were holding hands now. Lisa ate her soup with one hand, and Dad held the other under the dinner table. Like they were in Year 5.

I crunched my cheese on toast, quietly seething. How come Dad could bring home someone he literally just met, but I was banned from having friends over EVER? It was ridiculously unfair.

I finished my dinner in record time, and went back to my room to finish my French homework/watching my YouTube videos. At least Dad would be too distracted with Lisa to triple-check my verbs.

As the sound of their conversation snaked its way upstairs, I realized it was the first time I'd heard Dad laugh since I moved in. Not the chuckle he made at his crap jokes or when I mispronounced a Greek word (who cares how you say "Odysseus", anyway?). But a proper belly laugh.

I guess I should be happy that Dad met someone as boring as him. The woman made a career out of pottery shards, which told me everything I needed to know about her.

Maybe Dad is lonely. Maybe he does love a cinnamon bun from time to time.

Dad still felt like a stranger to me. But this woman that he'd known for less than two days seemed to know him better than I did.

Before I knew it, the Christmas holidays rolled around. As we weren't going to get to see each other until Yasmin's New Year's Eve party, my friends and I decided to spend our last day together at Winter Wonderland, a Christmas-themed funfair in Central

London. Even though I hadn't known the three of them for long, I knew I'd miss not seeing them every day.

"The playlist for the party is looking sick," said Yasmin as we queued up at the hot chocolate stand. "Don't forget to send me your song ideas."

"Deffo," said Daphne. "I have a few slow dance numbers in mind."

"Oooooh!" said the rest of us in unison.

"Who are you going to slow dance with, Daphne?" I asked.

"Let's just say that Adam from Spanish asked me if I was going. I didn't even invite him! He already knew about it," she said.

"*Everyone* knows about this party," said Noor. "You know what this means, right? Our outfits have to slay."

"I've narrowed my outfit choices down to eight," said Daphne. "And I've asked Mum to get me these gorge platform heels for Christmas."

I asked Dad for a new pair of trainers. Should I have asked for party clothes instead? It sounded like everyone was going all out, and I didn't want to be left behind.

Just as we reached the front of the queue, we heard someone calling Yas. We turned to see Jayden Taylor, walking towards us. No one looked more surprised than

Yasmin. Even more so when he reached down to give her a hug.

"How's it going, Yas? I didn't know you were Isaac Mensah's little sis," he said. Yasmin managed to nod in reply.

"Isaac is killing it this term. I swear our football team would be nothing without him." Again, Yasmin managed little more than a nod.

It was clear that Yasmin wasn't going to invite Jayden to the party. She could barely form a syllable. One of us had to step in.

"You around on New Year's Eve?" I asked.

"Yeah!" Yasmin suddenly remembered how to use her mouth. "We're having a house party. Come?"

"I'm *there*," said Jayden. "Just tell me where and when. You've got me on Snap, right?" After checking his phone to make sure he was following Yas, he gave her shoulder a little squeeze before walking away. Most of the girls in the queue watched him leave, too.

"Did . . . did that just happen?" asked Yasmin.

"Yep. Looks like the hottest guy in our school is gonna be at your party, babe!" said Noor.

I had mixed feelings about this. On the one hand, the hottest guy in school and his mates were coming to our party. YASSSS!

On the other hand, the hottest guy in school and his mates were coming to our party. Oh god oh god oh god.

What if someone tries to kiss me? What if someone *doesn't* try to kiss me?

This party was the perfect chance for me to lose my snog virginity. So why did I feel so nervous?

# TEN

Dear Mum,

Merry Christmas! I know you weren't a big fan
of the festive season, but this time of year still
reminds me of you.

Dad offered to drive me up to Grandma
Thomas's, which was a surprise. Did that mean
he wasn't surgically attached to Lisa (who'd
become a permanent fixture in our lives) after
all? Maybe it was motivated by guilt. He hasn't
tormented me about my homework recently
because he's hardly ever in.

Whatever the reason, I said no to his offer.
Grandma Thomas has always despised Dad.

Seeing them together is so awkward, Dad standing around in the living room while Gran pretends he isn't there. I'm old enough to take the train on my own, so I'd much rather do that. At least this way I can choose my own music rather than being subjected to Golden Oldies FM, Dad's radio station of choice.

Remember the Christmas with the blizzard, when all the trains were cancelled? We had to stay in London instead of going to see Grandma Thomas in Derby. I was devastated at not spending Christmas Day with the whole family (missing out on the presents didn't have anything to do with it, of course).

You tried to recreate a Christmas dinner that was just like Gran's. You even skipped being vegetarian for the day and roasted a turkey crown. But we fell asleep in front of the sofa watching The Wizard of Oz, woken up by the smoke alarm. Dinner was ruined. So you made it up to me by letting me choose what we ate. Everyone at school was so jealous when I told them that I had a never-ending stack of pancakes and ice cream on Christmas Day. Loads better than sprouts.

*This year, I have my fingers crossed for snow. Most of all, I can't wait to see my nice, normal, slightly boring family.*

*Your side of the family is worlds apart from Dad's. At Grandma Thomas's house, there's no danger of century-old feuds being brought up over dinner. We just eat too much food, argue about which classic film to watch and talk all the way through it anyway. Nothing weird ever happens there and I love it. (I mean, Great Aunt Rita may overdo it on the rum punch, take out her false teeth and pretend to be a witch. But that's standard.)*

*This year's Christmas dinner was much like all the others: busy and loud. It made me realize how quiet my house in London is – I can go days without seeing Dad or Aphrodite. With all the chaos, it wasn't until this morning that I got to spend some time alone with Grandma Thomas. Just like it used to be.*

*I woke up way earlier than usual. Gran was still in her quilted dressing gown and undertaking her main chore of the morning – making Boxing Day soup from the Christmas turkey leftovers.*

"Madam is awake, is she? I'll get the breakfast on," Gran said disapprovingly. Like sleeping past eight a.m. on a school holiday made me lazy. Maybe she has more in common with Dad than I thought?

I put the kettle on and hoped no one would see the two and a half sugars I was sneaking in. Then I remembered that you weren't here to chide me on my sugar intake, and I felt that intense pang in my stomach I sometimes get when I think about you. I suppressed a sniffle while Gran prepared breakfast.

"I remembered to pick up your favourite," Gran said, motioning to the bread bin on the counter. I discreetly wiped my eyes and opened the bread bin.

Hard dough bread! The white stodgy loaf spread with salted butter was literally all I ate when I came to stay with Grandma Thomas as a kid. You were never a fan, but Gran and I could eat it all day. Sometimes with strawberry jam or with tomato soup. I never really had it in London. It would be weird to eat it anywhere but Grandma Thomas's kitchen table, spread with soft butter from the crystal dish.

I squealed and immediately carved myself a doorstep slice of bread.

"Why you looking so marga, child? I don't know what that father of yours is feeding you in London, but you are as bony as a bird. I bet it's beans on toast every night."

Gran never missed the chance to critique every element of Dad's parenting, from how much sleep I was getting to how much I was (or wasn't) eating. Can you believe Gran still hates Dad?

No matter what I said or how I said it, Grandma Thomas would paint him as an immature man-baby who ruined your chances of marrying someone decent, like a doctor or pastor. All I have to say is: Grandma Thomas ain't ever told a lie. But he isn't as bad as she makes him out to be. I think you knew that too, Mum.

"Don't worry, Gran, I'm eating loads," I said, through a mouth full of bread and butter.

"That reminds me. I've got some ackee and saltfish in the freezer with your name on it. You mustn't let that greedy father of yours eat it either. He always was fond of my cooking," Gran said with more than a hint of smugness.

*I used to find it hard to believe that you were related to Grandma Thomas, let alone raised by her. You loved nothing more than a spicy tofu stir fry and only let me have sweets on Saturdays. Gran, on the other hand, doesn't think a meal is complete without meat and always makes sure the biscuit tin is fully stocked.*

*You look completely different, too. You were tall and reed-like, while Grandma Thomas barely pushes five feet. Gran's accent carries a faint Jamaican lilt, while you sounded like a born and bred Londoner. Gran's hair was relaxed, cropped and dyed the same shade of nut brown as long as I'd known her. You changed your hair whenever you felt like it, braids, wigs, your natural Afro – whatever suited your mood.*

*But after being away from Gran for a month, I can see your similarities. When I arrived at Gran's house, the first thing she said was "are you hungry?" just like you used to say when I came back from a friend's house or visiting Dad over the school holidays. You both love to feed me, even if you did so in different ways.*

*Now Grandma Thomas is stirring up a pot of cornmeal porridge, grating in fresh nutmeg*

*and sweetening it with condensed milk. Like*
*you, she never weighs or measures anything, but*
*it still turns out just right. Did you know that*
*you and Gran cook with the same radio channel*
*on, Mum? It's humming in the background and*
*the heady scent of nutmeg is in the air. It's the*
*most at home I've felt in ages.*

*Love for ever,*

*Helen xxx*

# ELEVEN

I was back home from Grandma Thomas's for about thirty seconds before everything kicked off. The unexpected bit? This time, it had nothing to do with my bonkers family.

Dad picked me up from the train station, but I don't know why he bothered. Did he ask me a single question about my Christmas break? Of course not. He spent the whole drive chatting about what he had planned with the Lady Friend. Salsa-dancing lessons, a romantic New Year's Eve getaway in the countryside, blah blah blah. I couldn't decide if Dad raving about her was better or worse than hearing a concise breakdown of the latest *Antiques Roadshow* episode.

Dad was halfway through repeating one of Lisa's

*hilarious* anecdotes when my phone began to bleep like crazy. The group chat was on fire! I started to unlock my phone, but guess who had a problem with that?

"Helen, it would be wonderful if you could resist the siren call of your device for twenty minutes," Dad muttered.

"But I just need to check something!" I bet it had something to do with the party. Outfit choices, song playlist suggestions, that sort of thing. All essential discussions that I HAD to be a part of.

"If you can't go twenty minutes without checking your phone, then I have half a mind to confiscate it. It's far from healthy, Helen."

I put my phone back in my pocket, if only to shut Dad up before he launched into a lecture on dopamine and shortened attention spans. I had the urge to put in my earphones and block out his droning with Rihanna. But it wasn't worth the risk of having my phone nicked. Again.

Several minutes later and my phone was still vibrating with new notifications. This had to be more serious than which Little Mix bangers were going on the party playlist. What was going on?

Once I got home, I ran up to my room and checked the group chat. I scrolled quickly through the conversation that started an hour before. By the time I'd caught up, I felt terrible for Yasmin. Her party was ruined.

We needed to have an emergency meeting (and milkshake because Yasmin was going to need the sugar boost). I wrote a quick message in the group chat:

*So sorry Yas :( Let's meet in the milkshake place near school and figure something out x*

Half an hour later, we slurped choco-caramel shakes with extra fudge sauce while Yasmin explained what happened.

"We thought Mum and Dad would be in Ghana until January third," Yasmin said while holding back tears. "But Dad strolled in this morning! Isaac and I couldn't believe our eyes."

"Why did he end up coming home early?" I asked.

"Because of his dumb job," Yasmin said. "Apparently he spent the entire trip stressing about the building works on his latest property development. Mum said if he was going to spend all of Christmas on the phone to the site manager then he may as well come home and sort it from here."

"So he's definitely going to be around on New Year's Eve?" Noor asked.

Yasmin nodded her head. "Sorry, guys, but there's no way I can throw a party."

"Gosh. You're lucky they didn't come home a few hours later. Can you imagine your mum and dad bursting in on your house party? I would actually die," said Daphne.

"I feel like dying anyway," said Yasmin, pushing away her barely touched milkshake. "I have to message every single person I invited and tell them the party's off because my dad is home. It's so humiliating!"

By "every single person", she meant Jayden of course.

"I had the perfect dress sorted, too," Noor said wistfully.

There goes the best chance at having my first real kiss, I thought.

No one wanted to say it and make Yasmin feel worse, but we were all gutted.

"You're all welcome to come round to mine, girls," said Daphne, trying to sound cheerful. "I'm sure if we play music loud enough, it'll drown out Mum singing with her friends."

"Sounds better than being at my house," Noor said, slumped in her chair. "My little brother won't stop talking about poo. It's a phase, apparently."

I felt so bad. What could I do to make Yasmin feel better?

Suddenly, everything clicked into place. Dad was out on New Year's Eve. Aphrodite was sure to have plans on the biggest party night of the year, too. Could we have the party at my house?

The group chatted about alternative plans for New Year's Eve while I stayed quiet and ran through the risks in my head. What if Dad came home early for no reason? Then I remembered – didn't he say he was going on a romantic trip with Lisa in the car? Judging by how gooey-eyed he was talking about her this morning, there's no way he'd leave that trip early.

Sure, he'd officially banned mortals from the house. But Lady Friend was a mortal and she was at the house every other weekend, I reasoned. Why was it one rule for him and another for me? Didn't the ancient Greeks, like, invent the meaning of democracy? It was my house, too. Being able to invite my friends (and a few of their friends too) over was only fair.

I looked around the table. My friends looked so deflated, especially Yasmin. They'd done so much for me since I'd moved back. If it wasn't for them, I'd probably still be spending lunch breaks and Friday nights alone.

Throwing this party had its risks, but it was the least I could do for my friends.

I sat up. "Guys, I have an idea."

# TWELVE

I had the biggest task ahead of me. All I had to do was make the house a mortal-friendly zone and erase every trace of immortal beings ever existing in our home. No biggie.

The minute the house was empty, I sprang into action. Armed with a cardboard box, I tucked away anything that was a dead giveaway. Basically, if it looked more like it belonged in a museum than a home, in the box it went.

Dad's ancient marble figurines could stay (there was nothing weird about those, after all – unless an actual historian came and worked out that they were thousands of years old). However, the printed copy of "The Rules" on the fridge door had to go. There would be no easy way to explain that.

I also found a few pairs of winged sandals lurking in the shoe rack. Yes, I tried them on and no, the wings didn't even flicker. They probably had to be activated by a god with powers. Still, I popped them in the box to be on the safe side. They were to stay with the tubs of Aphrodite's mysterious ointment jars in the bathroom cupboard (they could be harmless, but why risk it?) and the metal-tipped arrows hiding in the airing cupboard (almost certainly not harmless).

Finally, I blocked the attic stairway with a couple of cardboard boxes full of junk from Dad's office. I was sure Aphrodite would know instantly if a mortal was in her room. That wasn't a scenario I wanted to see play out in front of half of my school.

As I rolled up the living room rug to make room for dancing (I saw that in a film once), someone came through the front door.

Uh-oh. Had Dad forgotten something for his trip? Had Aphrodite decided she was going to have a cosy night in front of the mirror instead of going out?

"Why are you rolling up the rug? Ooh, are you going to do that mermaid yoga pose I told you about?"

It was Eros. I'd forgotten about him! And now he was in the living room. The party flashed before my eyes. Was it ruined?

I didn't like the idea of lying to my favourite family member, but needs must. "Oh, I'm just having a few friends over for New Year's Eve. You've got big plans too, right?" I asked, not at all subtly.

"I think I've celebrated New Year's Eve in every way possible, Helen," he said. "This year I'll be burning sage and playing my cleansing meditative music playlist. You know, start the year right."

NO. NO NO NOOOOO.

Eros was going to be in all night. Why, oh why, did I assume that Eros would be partying it up? He loves nothing more than a night in of burning incense and chanting.

If this party had any chance of going ahead, I had to come clean. But could I trust him?

"The thing is, Eros, it's going to be more than a few friends," I said.

I told Eros everything: about this party being the party everyone's talking about, and how we could never show our faces at school again if it got cancelled. Plus, Yasmin's big chance with Jayden would be ruined and that would almost certainly result in heartbreak. That was bound to grab Eros's attention.

"So let me get this straight. Father doesn't know about the party?" he asked. I shook my head.

"I did think it was unusually lenient of him to have a bunch of unsupervised mortals in the house."

"It will be fine though, right? Aphrodite and Dad aren't here, I've hidden all the weird immortal things around the house, and—"

"It's not that, Helen," Eros said. "Believe it or not, we gods are more than capable of hiding our identity in front of mortals for a few hours. We've been doing it for centuries."

They may not reveal their identities, but they could be hella embarrassing. I pictured Dad boring my friends to sleep with his collection of Edwardian postcards (some of which are rude for all the wrong reasons), and shuddered.

"If Father isn't aware of the party, then chances are that he hasn't deactivated the intruder lock," Eros said.

"What, like an alarm system?" I asked. Whatever it was, it didn't sound like it'd be good for my party.

Eros smiled indulgently at me, like I was a small child. I hated it when the gods did that.

"Not quite. Allow me to demonstrate," he said, and we walked to the hallway.

That was one more immortals-only secret they were all in on. Couldn't they keep me in the loop? You know, at least pretend we're part of the same family.

"When we moved in, Father created an intruder lock. No one outside of our family can come into our house unless expressly welcomed by an immortal."

He opened the front door. "Stand outside," he said. I obeyed. "Obviously you can come in and out as you please. But this is what your mortal friends will feel if they try and come in. Give me one sec."

Eros muttered something under his breath. "I'm changing the intruder lock settings so only full gods are allowed through."

"This is getting silly now. I'm coming back in." I tried to walk back in the house, but my feet couldn't get past the entrance. The door was wide open. I could see that with my own eyes. But I couldn't get through it, like there was a wall of invisible brick.

Eros held his hand out and pulled me into the house. The invisible brick wall didn't hold me back this time.

"Do you see what I mean, Helen? Unless Father deactivates the intruder lock or another god is here to override it, no mortal is getting into this house."

"Can you override it? Please, Eros, I'd owe you big time."

Eros sighed. "Thing is, I really had my heart on trying out my new sage incense at midnight. . ."

"I wouldn't ask if it wasn't important. My new

friends are the only ones keeping me sane – I can't let them down, Eros."

"Fine, I'll help just this once. But you should know that my powers are weaker than Father's. The easiest way to override the charm is for another god to welcome them in," Eros said. "I'd have to greet every single party guest."

Eros looked too old to pass for a friend. But with his brown skin and curly hair, we actually bore a resemblance to one another.

"I'll just have to introduce you as my cousin, then," I said. That wasn't even a lie.

"I could make it work for a few hours at least," he said. I gave Eros a massive hug. What would I do without him? If I'd tried to have this party alone, how would I have explained an invisible FORCE FIELD that literally wouldn't let my friends in? I pictured a queue forming round the block while I stood at the front door, trying not to have a meltdown.

It was entirely too weird. What other secret booby traps was I oblivious to in this house?

Now that I had Eros on board, the house looked nearly normal and the small matter of how people were going to get into the house was solved, I had a much more important crisis on my hands.

WHAT THE HECK WAS I GOING TO WEAR?

I emptied the measly contents of my wardrobe on to my bed, but there was nothing suitable for a New Year's Eve party.

As I looked at the only four dresses I had in my wardrobe (a floral number I wore for church with Grandma Thomas, two sundresses and what appeared to be a dress but was actually a really big T-shirt), I realized there was no other way. I was going to have to jailbreak an outfit from Aphrodite's wardrobe.

I crept upstairs to find the bedroom empty. The first thing I noticed was the sheer size of the room. I got shafted on the bedroom choice, that's for sure. Aphrodite's room was three times the size of mine at least. She had space for a four-poster bed, for goodness' sake! Why was I living like a second-class citizen in my single bed?

The second thing I noticed was Aphrodite. Not Aphrodite in the flesh, thank goodness. But she had images of herself everywhere. A huge Andy Warhol-style portrait dominated the room, and it didn't stop there. Photos of herself throughout the years hung on the walls and in frames on the dressing tables (yes, she had more than one). I took a closer look at a small black-and-white framed photo that looked like it came from a 1940s murder mystery film. It was Aphrodite, all right.

Maybe it was the huge vases of white orchids dotting the room or the soft lighting, but even though it was a miserably grey day, the room felt bright and airy. This room felt like it belonged in another house altogether.

I made a mental note to ask Aphrodite for interior design tips, then remembered I was explicitly told never to come up here. Back to business!

I turned on the light in her walk-in wardrobe (which was bigger than my entire room – ridiculously unfair). The rows of clothes were organized by colour, with dozens of shoeboxes neatly arranged on the floor and top shelf. It was like a fashion wonderland, if you were into that kind of thing. It would have made Daphne weep.

There was no time to flick through the rails and have a proper look. Honestly? I was more scared of Aphrodite catching me in her wardrobe than Dad walking in on my house party. There was no knowing how she'd react.

A flash of peach peeked out at me from underneath a dust jacket. I pulled out a dress that looked to be around my size. When I went to try it on, the dress slipped over my head and stopped just above my knees. Sorted.

The matching shoes – a pair of fabric-covered T-bar heels with a diamante flower on each – were labelled in a box beneath the dress. Thank goodness for Aphrodite's militant streak when it came to fashion. I grabbed my ill-gotten gains and rushed back downstairs to my room, convinced that she'd come back any minute, murder of a dress thief on her mind.

I had every reason to be nervous. If the myths about Aphrodite are true, her vengeance knows no bounds.

# THIRTEEN

The doorbell buzzed, and I rushed downstairs to meet Eros by the front door. I looked through the glass peephole to see Yasmin and a tall guy I didn't recognize – it must've been her big brother, Isaac.

I leaned in to Eros. "Are you ready?" He nodded, but he looked nervous. I didn't blame him. Neither of us wanted to be on the wrong side of Dad's lightning-bolt temper.

I opened the front door. "Hey, Yas. Come in!"

"I'm Helen's cousin. So great to meet you!" Eros shook both of their hands, and they walked through the door without a hitch. We'd cheated Dad's intruder lock!

I could see why half of the girls in our year were coming to the party because of Isaac. He was seriously hot. He stood head and shoulders above Yasmin (which isn't hard, she's quite petite) and his beard made him look way older than seventeen. When he thanked me for letting them use the house, I felt my face turn beetroot.

"Didn't I tell you Helen was the coolest?" Yas said. "And don't worry. We won't leave you to clean it all up tomorrow morning."

"Tomorrow morning?" I said.

"Yeah! I assumed we could sleep over seeing as your dad is away. That cool with you?"

I nodded even though I felt like rolling up into a ball, armadillo style. What if Aphrodite came back in the morning? What if Dad arrived before we cleaned up the party debris? What if— I stopped myself right there. I couldn't spend the entire night worrying about if/when Dad would come back.

The party was happening now. It was too late to turn back, so I may as well enjoy it.

Over the afternoon, a steady stream of Isaac's friends turned up with drinks, snacks and music equipment. Including a massive sound system. It was shaping up to be *that* type of party.

I was trying to squeeze the cans of soft drinks into the fridge, Tetris-style, when Yas tapped me on the shoulder.

"Helen, what's your postcode?" Yasmin asked.

"It's N7 9—wait. Why do you need that?"

"Isaac's barber's cousin's girlfriend and her mates are stopping by at some point. You OK with that, hun?"

I nodded weakly (this was the fourth time I'd given my postcode out in the last hour).

"Listen, Yas. Do you think we maybe, possibly, have enough people already? I just don't want the neighbours to—"

"There she is!" Isaac said. He was with a couple of equally gorgeous guys. "This party would be nothing without you, Helen, yeah?"

I blushed crimson and shrugged. "It's nothing, I had a free house so. . ." I mumbled.

"Don't worry, Helen," Yasmin said when Isaac and his ASOS-model friends went next door to set up the speakers. "The boys won't let anything get out of hand. Neither will I."

Still, I couldn't help but feel uneasy. I had complete strangers messaging me for my address! The scale of the party was finally sinking in. Was I going to regret this?

Daphne and Noor soon arrived, armed with enough make-up and hairspray to kit out a fashion show. Even though we spent a lot of time on make-up (well, Noor did) at our sleepovers, doing it for a party felt way more exciting. The thought that I could have my first kiss tonight crossed my mind. It gave me butterflies, but not the giving-a-monologue-in-drama-class kind. The good kind.

After Noor did my make-up, I had to sort out my hair. What was I going to do with it? I didn't have the time or energy to blow-dry and straighten it.

"You should totally wear your hair down!" Daphne said.

"Do it, babe," chipped in Noor. "Set your curls free!"

The last time I wore my hair down to a party was in Year 7. Boys compared me to a garden hedge, and most of the girls plunged their hands into my hair like I was a fairground attraction. It was rude, and all the touching made my hair frizz out even *more*. I'd avoided wearing my hair down ever since.

But I couldn't go to a party with my hair in the same style I wear to school every day, so I took a deep breath, teased my hair out of the elastic and worked product into my curls.

After all, I was throwing a forbidden house party and wearing a stolen outfit – letting my hair down (literally) was the least wild thing I could do that night.

I changed into the dress and took a look in the full-length mirror. The rosy coral of the dress was the perfect colour match for the pink gloss on my lips. Mini beads covered every surface of the dress, making it shimmer from rosy pink to gold whenever it caught the light. The top half was sleeveless with a simple V neckline (it was a little lower than I would have liked, but it's not like I have much to show off), but the skirt was an explosion of sequins in a unique floral pattern. I'd never felt more glamorous. Goddess-like, even.

Maybe Aphrodite's powers of beauty extended to her clothes? Because I couldn't believe that fabric and sequins and thread could have such an effect.

Yasmin interrupted my moment of vanity. "Rah, Helen! This look is flames."

"You look increds!" Daphne examined the hem of my dress. "Is it vintage? I'd say 1930s, but that's impossible. The condition is too good."

"Wow! You're giving me strong Zendaya vibes," Noor said.

I finally understood why women spend hours looking for that perfect dress, deliberating over lipstick shades. Because, for the first time in a while, I felt like I could take on the world.

I'm not stupid. I know having perfect hair and a

perfect dress doesn't make me smarter or nicer or more fun to be around. But it gave me a superhero surge of confidence that I don't have in my usual jeans and trainers.

I looked so good that I didn't feel a shred of guilt for breaking into Aphrodite's closet and stealing a priceless vintage dress. And I'm sure it doesn't count as breaking in if a) the door was unlocked and b) the room is in your own house. Right? Right.

"Selfie time!" said Noor, brandishing her phone.

Usually, I protested when Noor wanted to take selfies – which was every waking hour – but what the heck? It's not very often you're glammed up to the nines and hosting a party with half of North London talking about it. This was a milestone for sure, and I wanted to remember every second of it.

# FOURTEEN

Over a dozen people arrived at the door, one after the other. Eros had to welcome them all in one by one, but because he's so warm and charming no one seemed to think it was odd. In fact, it seemed to put them in an even better mood. Eros has that effect on people.

The party had officially started. Isaac and his mates (I had boys in my living room!) switched on the sound system. It all seemed to be going . . . well. Better than well. If the sound of laughter was anything to go by, people were having a good time.

I couldn't quite believe that I was pulling this off. Me, the girl who blushes when she's asked to read aloud in lessons, was throwing a banging house party without her parent's knowledge. Who'd have thought?

I didn't want to rest on my laurels, though. I did a periodic sweep of the upstairs rooms, just to make sure Dad's office and Aphrodite's room were safe from prying eyes. Something told me the gods would definitely know if their private rooms were invaded by mortals.

I checked the kitchen and found Eros surrounded by several girls I didn't recognize, hooked on his every word.

"It's like I always say," Eros said, "if the feelings are mutual, the effort will be equal. It's as simple as that."

"You're so right," said one of the girls in the group, nodding like Grandma Thomas at church. "I'm the one doing all the work with this boy."

Eros was playing agony aunt, and loving every minute of it. If there was one god I could trust around mortals, it was Eros. I left him to it.

Yasmin made a beeline for Jayden (she wasn't the only one feeling more confident in a new dress), and Adam found Daphne. It left Noor and me chatting. She gave me the dirt on all the people I didn't know. She was like a human Wikipedia, but for gossip instead of homework facts.

"That girl in the black jumpsuit? That's Jessica Chambers. She works in her dad's funeral parlour, which is why she smells a bit like embalming fluid," Noor said.

"And those two giving Yas the evil eye?" I discreetly turned to see a pair of girls who looked around twenty-five. "That's Tanya and Georgia. They're in our year. Georgia is Jayden's ex-girlfriend," Noor said. The venom in Georgia's expression was Medusa levels. Yikes. I was definitely going to steer clear of her.

The party swelled and the living room got hotter and hotter. The last thing I wanted to do was sweat to death in this dress (plus Aphrodite would definitely make me pay for the dry-cleaning bill) so Daphne, Noor and I grabbed our coats and stepped out in the garden for a few minutes.

It was a cloudless night and music seemed to come from every direction. We sat on the swing bench as more of the party flowed outside, lured by the fresh air and the prospect of fireworks at midnight.

That's when I saw him.

I told Daphne and Noor not to turn around. Immediately they turned around. Argh! Like me, they were looking at the fittie leaning against the garden fence. He was too busy scribbling in a notebook to notice the three pairs of eyes staring at him. Thankfully.

"Ooh, mysterious," Daphne said. "There's no way he's here alone."

"You don't recognize him?" I said. "I thought he might be someone in a different year at school."

"I seriously doubt that he goes to our school, Helen. I bet he's at college," Noor said.

It was dark, but I could make out a mass of black curls, wide lips and a mole on his chin. He didn't look that much older than us, sixteen at the most, but he had an aura of maturity. Like taking notes in my back garden, at a party, was normal. When he stopped writing, he tucked his notebook away into the pocket of his black wool coat and we locked eyes. Uh-oh.

"A super babe has landed in your lap! Maybe this is good karma for saving Yasmin's party?" Daphne said.

Even though it was cold I felt my cheeks flush red. I glanced up. He was still staring.

Noor nudged me. "You should talk to him, Hels."

For the first time ever, the thought of talking to a guy with a face like *that* didn't fill me with fear. Maybe it was the glamazon dress, or the fact that I was pulling off a house party, but I didn't feel like the normal Helen Thomas. I could do this.

Next step: approach the hottie. Could I compliment his notebook? His coat? His mole that I had the urge to nibble?

No, Helen! Do not nibble the mole. Or anything else on his face.

"What the heck do I say?" I had never been in this situation before and was going to need some guidance.

"Relax. Just ask him how he knows Yasmin, and it'll flow from there," Noor said.

"I need the loo. Noor, do you want to come with me?" Daphne asked.

Noor giggled. "Yep. Good luck, Helen!" Then they both went back in the house, leaving me alone to talk to this mega-babe.

With my traitorous friends inside, I had nothing to keep me busy. Even my phone battery had betrayed me, so I took an intense interest in Dad's ornamental holly bush. As I reached over to see if the berries were fake or not, I became aware of someone next to me.

I turned around. My tummy flipped 180 degrees. Because it was mystery notebook guy, sitting on the bench next to me, and he looked so gorgeous I didn't think he could be human.

Close up, he was mesmerizing. He had smooth, tanned skin, jet-black curls and deep brown eyes framed by eyelashes so lusciously thick they'd make Aphrodite weep. It was like the universe had worked out the algorithm for Helen's Ideal Boyfriend.

He was, quite simply, perfect.

And he was sitting next to me.

"Guuuh." What was that sound? Oh yes, it came from MY MOUTH. Good job, brain. I thought we were in this together?

Luckily, he ignored (or just didn't hear) my mouth fart.

"I'm Marco," he said, and shook my hand. This, much like my mouth, didn't do anything in response. It just hung limply. "Is there space for me?"

"Sure, don't mind me and my bush!"

Oh. My. God. Why did my brain/mouth filter go into meltdown, tonight of all nights?

"*The* bush. Not *my* bush. And there's space for all of us," I stammered.

Did he think I was a complete freak? If so, he was doing the gentlemanly thing of not showing it.

"Thank you. I didn't catch your name?" he asked with an accented voice. Uh-oh. This guy sounded as delicious as he looked. This could be dangerous.

"Helen," I said. Thankfully I didn't muck up saying my own name.

"Helen? I like that name," he said. "Are you having a good time?"

"Yeah. I'm having fun," I said, trying to give off an air of calm and nonchalance (even though I wanted to eat his face).

He smiled slowly. "I'm glad you're enjoying your own party. It would be a great shame if the hostess was tired of it."

All I could do was smile and nod in response. Why, oh why, couldn't I will my brain to spit out complete sentences? It didn't seem to bother Marco, though.

"And what do you do with the rest of your time? When you're not looking gorgeous at house parties, of course."

He was flirting. With *me*. I'd read about stuff like this in novels but never experienced it. How was this my life? Last New Year's Eve, I was eating cake frosting and watching *Clueless* for the gazillionth time. Now I was throwing a house party in London, and making small talk with someone who could be a model or work in Abercrombie & Fitch. He really was *that* hot.

I kept my answer simple. "I'm studying," I said. He probably thought I was one step up from a goldfish in the IQ stakes. But at least it wasn't a lie. I am studying. So what if it's for my GCSEs and not, say, at college?

Thankfully he did most of the talking from then on. Marco was taking a gap year to improve his language skills before going back to start his A levels in September. He'd been travelling all over Europe, and he planned to spend a bit of time in London during the winter with his uncle's family. I didn't catch where his accent was from, or why it seemed so familiar.

"I would love for a native Londoner to show me the sights sometime. Can I have your email address?" he asked, getting his notebook out.

Oh god oh god oh god. In my defence, I signed up for my email address years ago and barely use it. I obviously couldn't give him my school email address – so saddo teachers can read my messages in the staffroom? No thanks.

"Sure," I said in the most nonchalant voice I could muster.

I reached over to take the pen and notebook from him. And he flinched away from me! Did he think I was going in for a kiss and was completely revolted by the idea?

Just my luck. I'd probably misread the whole situation. Maybe Marco wanted to make friends (and only friends) with people in a new city?

"Would you mind reading it out? My notebook

absolutely must not fall into the wrong hands," Marco said with a wink.

Ahhh. He didn't want me to see his notes. I wasn't revolting, after all! But I still had my email address to read out...

I was going to have to say it. Why couldn't he have asked for my phone number or Instagram handle, like any other normal guy?

"It's curlygirlypants05@hotmail.com," I said as fast as I could. He raised an eyebrow but didn't say anything.

I looked up and noticed that the garden was a lot busier. It was nearly midnight, and everyone wanted to get a good view of the fireworks. Suddenly, I heard people shouting.

"Ten, nine, eight..."

Marco put the notebook into his coat pocket.

"...seven, six, five..."

He put his hand on my waist.

"...four, three, two..."

He leaned in.

"...one..."

He kissed me gently on the lips. And I couldn't tell if the sound of fireworks exploding was coming from the sky or inside my own head.

I don't know why I was so nervous about my first kiss. All those hours reading about techniques online and debating their various merits with my friends were pointless. Marco kissed me, I kissed back, and that was all it took to set my whole body alight. It didn't feel like a sea monster on my face. I couldn't taste what he'd had for dinner. My nose stayed in the right place. For a first kiss, I think we knocked it out of the park.

By the time we stopped kissing, the fireworks display was in full swing, and my insides gently fizzed.

Then I noticed something that made my stomach plunge in a very different way.

There were people on my roof! Dad's office window had a large window leading out on to a flat roof. It was the perfect spot for getting a better view of the fireworks.

I pulled away from Marco and gasped.

Strangers in Dad's office! Climbing through windows! Fiddling with ancient junk! I had to get them out.

"What's wrong?" he asked.

"I've got to go!" I yelled "And thank you!" I said over my shoulder as I bolted inside (why did I thank him for kissing me?!).

"Dad's office. Now!" I barked at Eros while I ran up

the stairs two steps at a time (not easy in such a fitted dress, let me tell you).

I burst into the room. Several people sat on the roof, some taking videos of the fireworks.

But that wasn't what made my heart stop in my throat.

A few people I didn't recognize were rooting through the cardboard boxes left over from the house move. Why were they wearing white sheets as dresses? And vines on their heads? Then I realized. They were wearing togas and laurel wreaths. *Dad's* togas and laurel wreaths. Something told me these outfits were not to be touched.

"What do you think you're doing?" I screamed as one girl jammed her foot into a winged sandal.

"Oh, we found this fancy-dress box," said the girl. "Want to try some on?" She said, holding out a bundled-up toga.

"Do you reckon this fur is real?" said another guy, hauling up a heavy cloak complete with the head of a lion.

I gulped. Dad had kept this stuff secret for a reason. It wasn't meant to be touched.

"OUT!" I shouted, still breathless from my jog up the stairs.

"Babe, chill," said a girl taking selfies with her shiny new laurel wreath. "It's just charity shop junk. Who else would want it?"

Eros appeared in the room, a picture of calm. "Hey, guys, this room is kinda off limits, I'm afraid. Would you mind going back downstairs?"

The effect was instant. The girl broke into a wide smile before Eros finished talking.

"No, no, we totally get it," she said. "Sorry if we messed up the room."

"And you'll have to leave behind everything," he added.

They obediently put the winged sandals, togas and lion head cloak (the thought of which made my stomach turn – I couldn't look the poor thing in the eye) back in the boxes.

They filed out of the room with dazed smiles on their faces. The last guy to leave even hugged Eros, who had clearly inherited Aphrodite's power to charm.

We stopped at the top of the stairs. Why was it so quiet? "Is the party over already?" I asked.

Then we heard something else. Guitar chords, maybe? Followed by a man singing along.

"There's always some jerk who brings out the guitar

at a house party and kills the vibe," Eros said. "If the party isn't over already, it will be in about ten minutes."

Then I remembered where I had heard that voice before and my stomach sank. What the heck was Apollo doing here? The more gods that knew about the house party, the more likely Dad was going to find out about it.

We burst into the living room to see him standing by the window with his guitar. We couldn't get much further than the front door – the room was rammed. Dozens of people stood and sat on every available surface, entranced by Apollo's music. As in, they looked literally entranced. I'd seen that dizzy smile before.

Some swayed, some closed their eyes, but everyone looked peaceful and happy. A few recorded Apollo with their phones. It was so weird. Just fifteen minutes before, the thump of music and laughter rolled through the house. Now it was like naptime at nursery.

Apollo wrapped up his last song. "That was 'Your Golden Love' by me, DJ Sunny. And now for my next track, called—"

I caught his eye by waving frantically. "Give me one sec, guys," he said, and left his guitar behind while he waded through the people on the floor to see me and Eros.

"Hey, fam. How's it hanging?" he asked, blue eyes wide and shining. Apollo was in his element when he performed, even if it was only our living room.

"What on *earth* have you done to my party?" I hissed.

"Relax, little one. I'm doing you a favour. A fight was this close to kicking off, but my music calmed everyone down." Apollo leaned in closer and hushed his voice. "Forget Father, how do you think the Council would react if they heard about that?"

Eros chimed in. "Helen, he has a point. Cranus despises us as it is. If a mortal got hurt in our home and the Council found out, it'd be game over."

"You see, Helen, as well as being a musical virtuoso, I'm a skilled clairvoyant," Apollo said, folding his arms. "And those two –" he pointed to a couple of Isaac's friends, who were now sitting cross-legged on the floor "– were minutes away from getting into a punch-up."

"Fine," I muttered. Apollo may have saved us from certain punishment, but he'd killed my party. Not only that, but my chance to find Marco slipped further away by the minute. I don't know much about boys, but surely he wouldn't stick around after I ran away mid-kiss?

"You're welcome. Now if you'll excuse me, my fans

await," Apollo said, walking back to the living room. He picked up his guitar. "My next tune is called 'Sound of the Sirens'. Peep my mixtape on SoundCloud: I'm DJ_Sunny."

I hated to admit it, but Apollo did the right thing. By the time he'd finished his guitar set, the crowd was so chilled that they practically floated out of the house. No noise, and hardly any mess. It was a miracle.

As I washed my face and brushed my teeth, my head swam with the thought of Marco (well, his face, hands and lips). The kiss couldn't have lasted longer than 7.5 seconds, but I'd relived the memory millions of times. My last "kiss" was in Year 2 and, much like this one, came out of nowhere. But the similarity starts and ends there, let me tell you. Duncan Prior's whelk-like kiss in the playground couldn't compare to Marco's.

I gargled mouthwash, spat it out and stared at myself in the bathroom mirror. I wasn't sure what I was looking for. Some sort of transformation that would show the world that I, Helen Thomas, had lost my snog-virginity, maybe? But I didn't look any different.

While the memory was fresh in my mind (it might have faded by the morning!), I needed to tell Mum.

I went to my room and got out the shoebox tucked away in my wardrobe. I was too tired to write a full letter, but I had to scribble something down before bed:

Dear Mum,

Guess what?! I had my first kiss tonight!!!

His name is Marco, I think he's from somewhere in Europe and his face is so pretty it makes me drool a little.

Wherever you are, please cross your fingers that I'll see him again.

Love for ever,

Helen xxx

# FIFTEEN

"Rise and shine!" Someone was whispering in my ear and shaking me awake. I looked up to find Eros's face staring down at me.

I groaned and rolled over on the sofa. I wasn't in the mood for Eros's chirpiness. Not at this hour.

"If I were you, I'd get up now and sort the house out before Father returns. And I come with treats," he said with a wink (unlike 99% of men, Eros can wink without looking creepy or corny).

*Now* I was awake. I woke up my friends with the promise of milky coffee and glazed doughnuts.

"Your cousin's so thoughtful, Hels," Daphne said.

"And fit too," Noor whispered.

"What's his name again?" Yasmin asked whilst reaching for her second doughnut.

"It's Eros. Strange, right?" I said in response to the expression on their faces. "My family has this thing for old-school Greek names. I got off lightly with Helen!"

"Hels, I meant to ask!" Daphne shrieked. "How did it go with Garden Hottie last night?"

Noor's eyes widened. "Oh yeah! Did you speak to him?"

I smiled and felt a blush creeping over my face. "I did more than speak to him."

"Shut. The. Front. Door. Tell us *everything*," Yasmin said.

I told my friends about last night's encounter with Marco. They wanted every tiny detail, and telling them all about it was nearly as fun as the real thing.

"Helen, this is ridiculously exciting," said Yasmin. "Most people have their first kiss behind the bike shed at school. But yours? With a mystery guy under fireworks at the stroke of midnight."

Noor clutched her chest. "I know, right? It almost makes my cold, icy heart believe in the power of love."

I talked about Marco while we cleaned up the last of the party debris – paper plates, cups, that sort of thing.

"So what I don't understand is, why didn't he ask for your number?" Daphne asked, wiping the kitchen table.

"Maybe his phone isn't registered in this country yet. He's been travelling all around Europe, remember?" I said.

Daphne didn't stop there with the questions. Where was he from? How long was he in London? How did he find out about the party?

I didn't even know the answers to these basic questions. In the space of our conversation, Marco had turned from sexy and mysterious to shady and secretive. My brain was such a bag of mush last night that I didn't think to ask any useful questions. I put all my energy into not saying anything stupid.

My romantic high slowly slipped away. What's the point of meeting a gorgeous stranger at a New Year's Eve party if you don't have so much as an Instagram page to show your squad?

"It sounds like I made him up, doesn't it?" I said.

"I know you didn't make him up," said Daphne, rolling her eyes. "I saw him looking at you! It's just a shame that—"

The front door clicked and slammed. We froze.

Busted.

# SIXTEEN

As soon as I heard the click of high heels against the hallway floor I knew it wasn't Dad in his leather loafers. I never thought I'd be so relieved to see Aphrodite. She strolled into the kitchen, a fur coat hanging from her shoulders and diamonds dangling from her ears. She looked like a movie star. My friends were dazzled into silence.

Aphrodite took a bottle of water from the fridge. "I see you have company, Helen. Does Father know about this?"

I folded my arms. "He knows I had a few friends over last night, yes," I said. I hoped that detecting lies wasn't one of her powers.

Aphrodite's lips curled into a cruel smile. She didn't believe a word of it.

Noor cleared her throat and stepped over the bin bags. "Um, I just wanted to say thanks for the make-up. I really want to be a make-up artist when I grow up," she said. "It's dead exciting to meet a real one like you!"

Aphrodite kicked a plastic cup at her feet. "You missed something." I glared at her, and hoped Noor wasn't too upset at her rude dismissal.

As she walked out of the kitchen, dress trailing behind her, she turned around and looked me dead in the eye.

"My room had better be untouched, or else," she hissed.

Once she was out of sight, I turned around. "She's the worst," I mouthed to the girls.

"I guess when you look like that, you don't have to have manners," Yasmin said.

"At least it wasn't your dad," Daphne said.

"I know, right?" Noor said. "I was ready to backflip out the kitchen window."

A few hours later, my friends had left, and Dad still wasn't home. Eros helped me to remove any traces of illicit activity in his office, and make sure Dad's bookshelf of precious junk was in order. I put the immortal junk back where I found it, apart from the arrows – Eros was more than happy to be reunited with those ("My babies! I wondered where they went").

"Tell me everything I missed last night," Eros said. "I spent most of the night solving romantic woes. God, I forgot how messed up teenagers can be. It was glorious!"

"Talking of romantic woes..." I began. "I might need your help sooner rather than later."

I told Eros everything in detail, from the moment I first saw Marco to the kiss at midnight. He was hooked on every word.

Eros held his hands to his chest and sighed deeply, like he'd just finished watching *Titanic*. "Helen, this is one of the most romantic things I've ever heard."

"I guess. It's just annoying that he still hasn't emailed me."

"Um, Helen? It's been less than twenty-four hours," he said. "And even if you never hear from him again, just think about the moments you'll treasure for ever. You've probably had the best first kiss that any teenager in history will ever have. And I should know!"

Eros had a point: gorgeous masked stranger, fireworks at midnight and a kiss that made me fizz like a bottle of pop. This story was almost too romantic to be true.

A full day had passed since the party, and Dad was none the wiser. If Aphrodite was going to terrorize me for borrowing her dress, she would have done it by now.

But, as I went downstairs for breakfast, guess who called me up to her room?

"Helen? Upstairs, please."

I gulped and made my way to the attic.

Aphrodite sat at her marble dressing table brushing her hair (for the hundredth time that morning, probably). "You are a fool to think I wouldn't detect the scent of mortals the minute I stepped in the house," she said. "Or notice that you stole a priceless dress. The audacity!"

I fidgeted uncomfortably, because she was right. I did think I could get away with it.

"I hope you don't have any plans today," she said. "Because you and I are going to be very busy."

Oh gosh. Whatever she had planned would be a lot worse than the mountain of French homework I'd left until the last minute.

"Well, tomorrow I'm back at school, so I need to finish my—"

Aphrodite lifted her palm to silence me. "Helen, please. I'm asking nicely but you do not have any say in the matter," she said. "Unless you want me to tell Father about your . . . misdemeanours?"

I shook my head. She was blackmailing me! Furious as I was, there was nothing I could do about it. Not unless I wanted to deal with traffic-light hair again.

"Wise choice. I've seen Father's temper reduce grown men to quivering wrecks. Now, sit."

My heart raced while I imagined the terrible punishments she had lined up for me. After all, that cockatoo thing she did with my hair? That was for *fun*.

"Let me fetch my tools," she muttered before leaving the room.

TOOLS?! Even Aphrodite must know that you can't go around torturing people for stealing dresses (priceless vintage or not).

She came back in the room with several boxes full of tubs, creams and cloths. Aphrodite was not planning on harming me. But honestly? What I spent all day doing should be reviewed by the UN Convention of Torture.

Aphrodite needed me to test out a skincare line she's been working on for the past few months. That explained why she was always out of the house, then.

As she's not allowed to test it on rabbits and puppies, I had to be the guinea pig.

"I have centuries of beauty expertise, Helen. And it's going to waste!" she said, rubbing gloopy white lotion on my face.

While Aphrodite droned on about the ingredients, I checked my email inbox for the fiftieth time that day. Still no word from Marco.

"This product will blitz blackheads, zap zits and make your skin glow like you've spent a week in a Swiss spa," she said. "That's if I've cracked the formula."

"If?!"

"Honestly, the world has never seen a product like this. And once the formula is perfect, every man, woman and child on the globe will kill to get their hands on this stuff. Imagine it! One product that will cure any skin ailment. It'll make me fabulously wealthy of course, but I'm not in it for the money. Everyone will have no choice but to recognize my beautifying powers. Once again, I'll be the world's most famous beautician."

"Isn't that getting a bit close to breaking the rules?"

Aphrodite waved her hands dismissively. "Don't you see, Helen? The rules are there to protect mortals from harm," she said. "But I'll be using my powers to *help* them."

She stood back. "The lotion appears to be taking well to your skin. But do let me know if you experience any itching, burning, redness, flakiness, scales, that sort of thing."

Crap. There was a very real chance I'd start my first school day of the new year with an allergic reaction.

That wasn't all Aphrodite had in store for me. She planned on going global with this wonder cream and needed my help to do it.

I spent the rest of the day downloading video-editing software, setting up a webcam and creating a YouTube channel. Which she totally could have done by herself if she wasn't giving herself a manicure.

Aphrodite clapped with delight once the page was all set up. "I'm going to call it Aphrodite's Beauty Parlour. I simply can't wait to get started."

"I simply don't care. Can I go now?"

"You may. Oh, and Helen?" she added as I got up to escape. "This is our little secret. I'd like to keep this project quiet until it's ready to dazzle."

Whatever. Like I'd be promoting her silly videos for her anyway.

I groaned as the alarm clock beeped on my phone. I'd gotten used to lie-ins over the last couple of weeks.

Getting up early again was going to be a struggle. I pulled the duvet over my head (so warm! So cocoon-like!) and allowed myself a little extra time in bed.

So much had changed since pre-Christmas. I'd thrown my first house party, had my first kiss and was waiting for my first potential boyfriend to email me back – although with every minute that went by that seemed less and less likely.

Would my new air of maturity be obvious to everyone else at school? Dad hadn't noticed, but I'd have to turn into a scarecrow before he'd notice anything different about me.

I wandered bleary-eyed into the bathroom and hopped into the shower. Then I remembered. The lotion on my face! My skin wasn't burning and it appeared to be flake-free. I wiped the condensation off the bathroom mirror and looked back at my reflection.

My skin was fine. More than fine, actually. It looked great. Maybe Aphrodite was on to something with her wonder lotion? Or maybe kissing was good for my complexion?

My friends at school noticed it, too.

"Seriously, Helen, what have you used on your face?" Noor said in the lunch queue. "Foundation? Powder? What?!"

"Nothing new. Just a good night's sleep, I guess?"

There was no point in telling them about Aphrodite's lotion. They'd only want to try it, and Aphrodite had sworn me into secrecy.

"Must be the glow of luuurve," Yasmin said.

It had been three days since the party and Marco still hadn't emailed me back. Like I needed to be reminded.

"Have you heard back from Mystery Marco?" Daphne asked.

"Believe me, you would all be the first to know if I did," I said.

"Hey!" said Noor. "Positive vibes only. I'm sure he's planning the perfect response. Probably composing a poem and all sorts."

We spent lunch discussing the reasons why Marco hadn't emailed back (did he lose his notebook with my email address? No Wi-Fi? Or maybe it's customary to leave several days between messages where he's from?).

"Aww, Hels," Daphne said. "I didn't realize you were sick on the first day back!"

Sick, me? That hadn't happened before.

"Your nose is all red around the nostrils. Do you have a cold, hun?" Yasmin asked.

Then it clicked. Didn't Aphrodite say that redness was a potential side effect of her wonder cream?

"Oh, yeah! You know, I was feeling a bit bunged up this morning. Let me get some tissues," I said, before leaving the canteen to run to the loo.

This was no ordinary sore nose. By the time I made it to the girls' toilets, the redness had intensified and spread. My nose was strawberry red! And not the sort of red you get when you have a cold. I mean the sort of red that hurts to look at, it's so bright and intense. With this schnozz, I could give Rudolph a run for his money. I stared in horror at my reflection. How the heck was I going to fix this?!

I could tell the school nurse I felt sick and go home early. But then they would call Dad to pick me up. He'd find out I was Aphrodite's guinea pig and she'd tell him about the party. So skiving was out.

In the end, I grabbed a handful of tissue and pretended I had a runny nose for the rest of the afternoon. I kept my hand clamped over my nose until home time, then legged it home straight after school. Not only was it incredibly embarrassing, but I needed to keep a lid on any immortal weirdness coming from my family. It seemed like I cared more about that than Aphrodite did.

I stayed in my room until she came home, getting angrier by the minute. Maria knocked on my door to check up on me, but I lied and said I had a headache.

The minute I heard Aphrodite walk up to the attic, I burst out of my room and into the corridor.

"Look what you've done to my face!"

Aphrodite recoiled. "Goodness, Helen. Your nose looks . . . jolly!"

"Yes! I have a clown nose now and it's entirely your fault!" I was shrieking now but I didn't care.

"This really throws a spanner in the works," Aphrodite muttered to herself. "It'll delay launch by at least a few days."

I couldn't believe it. All she cared about was her stupid cream, and not the fact she'd ruined my face.

"Forget about your launch! How are you going to fix this?"

Aphrodite pinched my nose playfully, like she was talking to a toddler. "Calm down. It's already fixed."

I looked in the bathroom mirror, and she was right. My nose was once again brown and freckly.

"You're welcome, Helen," she said sarcastically. If Aphrodite was waiting for me to thank her, she'd be waiting for a long time.

"Back to the drawing board I go," she muttered.

# SEVENTEEN

All week my body was in school, going through the motions from lesson to lesson. But my head? That was stuck in Marco Land. I'd been doing that a lot. I spent my lessons imagining, in intense detail, what Marco was up to right that moment. Maybe he was visiting an art gallery or heading to the gym (he had a great physique under that winter coat – or at least he did in my head).

Whatever he was up to, it wasn't emailing me.

But then, five days later, when I was daydreaming in an I.T. class about our fifth date together (this would be the one where he declared his passionate love for me), I noticed it.

An email from Marco! But it had the subject line "Sorry." Oh god. Was he about to tell me that this whole thing was a terrible mistake and he never wanted to see me again? Why else would his first email to me be so negative? How could he do this, we haven't even—

I stopped my thoughts from racing away like a freight train. *Just open the email, Helen.*

Somehow I managed to hold it together while Miss Anderson droned on about databases. Noor, who was sitting next to me, must have sensed my internal panic. She sent an email to my school address:

FROM: noor.yildiz@highburygreen.org.uk

TO: helen.thomas@highburygreen.org.uk

Everything OK? You've gone bright red! N x

FROM: helen.thomas@highburygreen.org.uk
TO: noor.yildiz@highburygreen.org.uk

Got an email from Marco!! Should I read it? X

FROM: noor.yildiz@highburygreen.org.uk
TO: helen.thomas@highburygreen.org.uk

!!!!! YES !!!!

I couldn't bring myself to open the email in the lesson. Who starts an email with "sorry" unless they have something dreadful to say? I'd burst into tears, and everyone would think I was upset about databases.

Seeing as I.T. was the last lesson of the day, I decided to wait twenty minutes and read it with Daphne and Yasmin there too. After school, we all met in the usual place by the gates, and I told them what happened.

"Let's go to Cafe Gio's and read it over hot chocolate with whipped cream," said Daphne with a decisive nod.

Uh-oh. Daphne only suggested hot chocolate with whipped cream when one of us was in serious need of comforting. The pit in my stomach became a little deeper. I almost didn't want to read the email.

"Crap! I promised Mum I'd be home to watch my little brother after school. She's gone to visit my aunty and won't be back until late," Noor said. "Come to mine instead?"

"Fine, but let's hurry up. I want to see what it says!" Yasmin said.

After what seemed like several years (and several flights of stairs), we made it to Noor's flat. The dark skies and cold seemed like the perfect setting for disappointment, which added to my nervousness. Was I about to read a humiliating email in front of my friends?

Noor let us into her flat and hustled us to her bedroom. Her little brother sat on the living room floor, glued to his video game. "Hasan, I'll be in my room with my mates. Stay where you are and try not to do anything dumb, yeah?" I heard Noor say.

She came back with armfuls of snacks and dumped them on the bed. "I thought we might need supplies."

With Daphne's arm around my shoulder and a packet of crisps on my lap, I read out the email.

*Dear Helen*, it started. My heart nearly beat out of its chest. *I'm so sorry for only contacting you now, several days after our night under the stars. I must admit I was in two minds about emailing you. You see, you left in such a hurry that I wasn't sure if you wanted to hear from me again.*

*The thing is, I haven't stopped thinking about you. I'd love nothing more than to get to know you. If you feel even slightly the same, please give me a call on the number below and we'll take it from there. Marco x*

"Awwwwwww," the girls said in unison.

Every cell in my body quivered and swooned. I felt like I could dissolve.

*I haven't stopped thinking about you.*

His words expanded in my head like a party balloon, pushing out thoughts of anything else.

"Wow, this boy knows his way around a keyboard," Yasmin said approvingly.

"I know, right? Who knew he'd be this poetic! It's so dreamy," Daphne said, sighing.

"Babes? Earth to Helen, can you read me?" Noor said, clicking her fingers in front of my face.

"Huh?"

"Oh god, we've lost her," Daphne said, giggling. "Yas just asked what you're going to say? In your reply?"

After agonizing and deleting at least twenty different attempts, I read out my reply:

"Hey, nice to hear from you. How have you been? I'll give you a call sometime this week. Helen x"

I was proud of the message. It struck a balance between being interested and nonchalant. The girls murmured their approval.

"I think it's cool that he gave you his number," Yasmin said.

"Same," Noor said. "It's like the ball is in your court."

"Honestly, this guy sounds too good to be true," Daphne said. "Gorgeous, and a feminist? Swoon."

We heard the front door open. "That must be my baba," Noor said. "Dad, we're in my room!" She shouted.

"It's gone six, ladies. I need to go home and get a head start on my religious studies essay," Yasmin said.

"Same, Mum will be back from work soon," Daphne said.

"Hels, you're welcome to stay for dinner if you want?" Noor asked. "Mum's made way too much stew."

Even though I knew Maria's prepared dinner would be waiting for me in the fridge, I didn't fancy the thought of going home to an empty house again. I joined Noor and her family for dinner instead. Eating with people, laughing and talking (even if Hasan and Noor argued the entire meal), made a nice change.

That evening I had a choice between finishing off my (late, thanks to Aphrodite) French homework or calling Marco. It seemed rude to leave him on tenterhooks. Like Daphne said, he did sort of pour his heart out in that email.

I took a few calming breaths but my fingers still trembled as I dialled his number. Seriously, Helen? He was just a boy (sure, a total hottie with an accent that made my knees wobbly, but no big deal).

The phone rang. Oh crap. What was I going to say? I should have rehearsed my opening line with the girls, maybe something like—

"Hello?" Marco answered the phone (I mean, who else was it going to be?). His voice was so swoony I may have dribbled a bit.

Miraculously, I managed to will my mouth into action. "Hey, Marco. It's Helen?"

"Ah, Helen. It's so good to hear from you," he said. I could hear the smile in his voice. He was happy I called! My nerves faded.

"Listen, I'm sorry for leaving like ... that," I said, cringing at the memory of me running into the house after our kiss. "But I saw some people messing up my dad's office. He didn't know about the party."

Marco laughed. "Wow, Helen. I didn't have you pinned as a rebel," he said. "So the party stayed secret?"

I lowered my voice. "Yeah, I think we got away with it. His new girlfriend is keeping him busy, anyway." Being a parent didn't seem to matter to Dad as much lately.

"If you ask me, Helen," he said. *Ungh!* My tummy flipped whenever he said my name. "I'd rather a laid-back dad to an overbearing one. I'm just saying it could be worse."

"Oh, you haven't met my big sis. She found out about the party and totally blackmailed me!" I said. "I think she might by pure evil. Or at least 99.9 per cent evil."

I ended up telling Marco about Aphrodite's stupid wonder cream, and me being the guinea pig. I even told him the embarrassing story about my skin "allergy" on the first day back at school. It felt good to make him laugh.

"Remind me to steer clear of anything your sister makes. What's she going to call this disaster product?"

"She wants to set up an online shop. Call it something like 'Aphrodite's Beauty Parlour'," I said. Oops. Had I given too much away? "She's obsessed with Greek myths," I added.

"No way! Your sister and my father have that in common. Maybe we could rant about them on the weekend? Are you free on Saturday?"

It took every bit of effort not to scream "YES YES YES" down the phone.

"I'm pretty sure I'm around on Saturday," I said. "But can I check and get back to you?" Playing it cool like Daphne said.

"Yeah, get back to me," he said. "Goodnight, Helen."

Once again I forgot to ask so many basic

questions – I still didn't even know where Marco was from! But if I had to guess, I'd say somewhere in Southern Europe. Everything about him seemed Mediterranean, from the tailored coat he wore at the party (even I can recognize quality fashion when I see it) to the tanned skin that had seen many long, hot summers. The kind you can only get here for about ten days in August.

I was making assumptions about Marco's heritage, which I knew was wrong. Goodness knows it's irritating enough when it happens to me ("So where are you *really* from?"). But I'd never do it to his face, obviously. I just couldn't stop thinking about him.

I also didn't know Marco's surname, what exactly he was up to in London or how he ended up at my party. Most importantly, I didn't have an Instagram page for me and my friends to inspect.

But that didn't seem to matter. I had my first ever Saturday night date to think about.

And I was bricking it.

# EIGHTEEN

When I came in from school, Aphrodite was showing Maria something on her laptop. Which was weird, because a) she's hardly been home lately and b) Aphrodite barely talks to Maria unless it's to complain that she didn't buy the right brand of granola.

"375,689 and counting," Aphrodite said triumphantly.

"Eh?"

"It's the total number of views my latest skincare video has on YouTube!"

"How?" I was struggling with complete sentences, clearly.

"Because I am brilliant, of course. And mortals, despite being dim, recognize greatness when they see it. No offence."

I was about to take offence and launch into what Aphrodite calls my "tiresome rants", but it wasn't the time. How had she managed to get so many hits on an ordinary beauty video? Aphrodite hadn't used her powers, had she?

That would be phenomenally stupid, even by her standards.

"It's a trending topic, apparently! I've been assured that you're *nothing* unless you've trended."

"If I were you, I'd keep that laptop away from Zeus," said Maria, interrupting Aphrodite's reverie. "He won't like it."

Aphrodite shot daggers at Maria while she served up a delicious-smelling plate of pasta for my dinner (Maria, not Aphrodite. She won't go within three feet of refined carbs).

"Well, unless I make it into *National Geographic*, I doubt Father will be finding out," Aphrodite snapped. "He still hasn't taken the smartphone I got him for Christmas out of the box."

"What would happen if Dad found out?" I asked, grating a small mountain of cheese on to my pasta.

Aphrodite shrugged. "Oh, he'd just get his beige chinos into a twist over nothing. It's just a bit of fun."

I wondered if she really believed that was true.

\*

At school the next day, I heard two Year 9s talking about Aphrodite's latest video. I caught the phrases "Foam of the Sea", "saw it on Instagram" and "old but gorgeous" (referring to Aphrodite I assume, hahahaha).

I guessed that Dad, working in a dusty university, wouldn't clock on. If he did find out about Aphrodite's fame, he'd have her packed off to Mount Olympus faster than you could say "tzatziki".

I came home to find Dad was out for the night again (with Lisa, probably). Lucky for Aphrodite. She'd been fielding press requests all afternoon – something she couldn't have done with Dad around.

She was in the kitchen with Eros, which seemed to have become her unofficial office (at least until Maria came back from the supermarket). I kicked off my boots and headed to the fridge for my usual snack of cereal.

"So that's a column in HuffPo plus an interview with BBC Radio One tomorrow, and we're just waiting for *Saturday Morning Breakfast* to confirm that you'll be sharing top beauty tips on this weekend," said Eros, scribbling notes.

Holy crap. Aphrodite was going to be on the telly?

"Perfect, darling. Thanks for being my little assistant!" Aphrodite said, kissing Eros on the cheek. She looked like the cat who got the cream.

"Wow. Was all this because of that one video?" I asked, crunching on my cereal.

"Well, that certainly kicked things off. I took advantage of the moment and spent all of last night creating new videos," Aphrodite said. "As an influencer, fresh content is key."

I forgot that, though they find the odd nap quite pleasant, the gods don't actually *need* to sleep. Another somewhat unfair advantage Aphrodite had over her competitors, but I guess all is fair in love and cleansing.

"The most popular by far is my 'Detox Your Skin in a Flash' video," she continued. I didn't recall asking about her videos, but whatever. "It shows how to hide the usual teen skin complaints with make-up so it looks like you've spent three weeks in an Alpine spa retreat. Although not eating sugary snacks would help, too," Aphrodite said, looking pointedly at my cereal. She'd never miss an opportunity to judge my diet choices.

If making her little videos (and not, say, making me her human guinea pig) kept Aphrodite busy then I was all for it. But I couldn't help but wonder what Dad would have to say about the whole thing. If he was ever here.

# NINETEEN

*Dear Mum,*

*It's official: my family have lost the plot.*

*Dad has one job, and that's to make sure his offspring don't reveal their immortal identity to the world. They keep a low profile, mind the rules and the Council lets them live their happy lives on earth. But that seems to be impossible.*

*Take Aphrodite. She seems hell-bent on making sure everyone knows how strong her powers are. Thanks to her hit YouTube channel, her Foam of the Sea wonder cream sold out in minutes and is set for global domination. Her make-up artist mates spread the word on*

Instagram, and now everyone with a face wants a tub.

I bet you're wondering why I don't tell Dad. It's a complicated situation. If I snitch, Aphrodite will definitely tell him about the secret New Year's Eve party I threw at the house when he wasn't there. I won't see the light of day until summer. So I have no choice but to put up with it and hope that Dad wakes up before things get out of control.

I don't get why he isn't paying the slightest bit of attention to this madness. He of all people should know how arrogant and self-obsessed the gods are. Why isn't he keeping an eye on them?

You'd think Dad would care about getting called back to Mount Olympus. He'd have to break up with Lisa and I don't know what would happen to me. Maybe he doesn't care about that last bit. I feel like I haven't seen him in months. I could have dropped out of school and run away to join the circus, for all he knows.

Dad definitely hasn't been himself since Lisa made her appearance. I haven't noticed him pottering about in his shed or fermenting any new vegetables lately. And he hasn't so much as glanced at my homework in weeks. Weirdly, I kind of miss our Sunday afternoon tutoring time together.

He should at least be around to keep Aphrodite in check. Especially at the rate her fame is growing. There's something off about this whole thing.

There is one tiny bonus to having an absent father. At least he won't be here to give me grief about my date this Saturday. That's right, Mum. I have a date! With the guy I met on New Year's Eve. I think he's sixteen, but you don't need to worry about him being older. I get the feeling he's a complete gentleman.

I'm sad you won't get to meet him. But I can't wait to tell you all about it.

Love for ever,

Helen xxx

# TWENTY

I spent Friday night (just one day to go until my date — eeeek!) at Daphne's sleepover. That night, Noor and Daphne wanted to watch this new reality TV show called *House of Stars*. It's like a cross between a musical talent show full of wannabes and *Big Brother*.

It was good fun, and the presenter was hot. They had the usual ratio of totally gorgeous, kooky and extremely fame-hungry people queuing up to join the show. I started to zone out, thinking about what I was going to wear on Saturday, when Daphne's voice broke into my thoughts.

"Helen, isn't that your brother?"

I froze. Because she was right. There, in skinny

jeans and a buttoned-up pale pink shirt, was my half-brother Apollo.

"Oh, I recognize him," Noor said. "He played that awesome set at your party. I didn't realize you were related!" Apollo, with his shock of floppy blond hair, didn't look a thing like me.

"Why didn't you tell us he was going to be on telly?!" shrieked Yasmin.

"I had no idea!" And it was totally true. Apollo must have kept this a secret from everyone. Aphrodite's endless publicity for Foam of the Sea was one thing, but playing in a prime-time TV talent contest? That *had* to be breaking the rules. No wonder Apollo wasn't blaring this news from the rooftops.

"Shhh, they're going to interview him!" Daphne said.

"So DJ Sunny," the presenter began, although you could barely hear him over the screams from the audience. "The ladies certainly love you. How are you feeling?"

Apollo smiled, and the applause went even wilder. If he had this effect on all female viewers, then he would be a shoo-in to win.

"I'm feeling good, Jamie." Another cocky smile and yet more applause.

"DJ Sunny, I see you've brought your guitar with you. What do you think will set you apart from the other contestants?"

"I'm one of those rare artists, right? Not only am I a producer and a DJ, but I also write my own songs from start to finish. Lyrics, melody, everything. Authenticity is, like, everything to me."

Ugh. Why wasn't everyone grossed out by his arrogance?

"Awesome. We can't wait to see you in action. Everyone, please give DJ Sunny a warm welcome as he enters the *House of Stars!*"

Apollo gave a barely-there nod to his new adoring fans before walking up the lit path and opening the door to a large stone-grey building. After he disappeared into a dark corridor, the camera cut to the presenter on stage outside.

"Will DJ Sunny light up the stage and win a recording contract worth a whopping £500,000? Come back next week for his first performance, where your vote decides if he walks away with a life-changing prize."

We watched the rest of the episode, but I wasn't paying attention. Instead, I was thinking about how much Dad was going to hit the roof when he found out.

And where I'd be hiding when it happened. What on earth was Apollo thinking?!

To be honest, it served Dad right. He shouldn't have been gallivanting around with a woman he'd only just met. It had been weeks since he'd been home for any decent length of time. He, of all people, knew that his offspring can't be trusted not to cause trouble.

"I wish I had cool siblings like you." Noor's voice interrupted my preoccupied state. "All I have is two little brothers who leave disgusting smells around the house. Don't ever live with pre-teen boys."

"Or teen boys. Having a big brother is the worst. I can't even use his ID!" Yasmin said.

"You're so lucky, Helen," Noor said, turning to me. "All your siblings are way older. You're practically an only child!"

"Yeah, and they treat me like a toddler. You saw how rude my big sis is," I said. And they didn't know the half of it. I could never tell them about the "makeover" Aphrodite gave me when I first moved in.

This conversation was starting to irritate me, and I couldn't work out why. Maybe I couldn't deal with my friends bickering about their perfectly normal families with perfectly normal siblings. I'd love to have the type of family where I could just invite my friends over at a moment's notice. The type of family my friends had.

"Helen, I completely forgot to ask!" Yasmin said. "Where are you going on your date with Marco tomorrow?"

I smiled and everyone went "oooooooooh" like the studio audience on *House of Stars*.

"He messaged me last night saying it was a surprise," I said. "All I know is that we're meeting at Holloway Road tube station at seven thirty p.m., and I should wrap up warm."

With this grim weather, it looked like I'd be smothered in a parka, scarf, boots and several layers anyway. January is definitely not the time for figure-hugging date outfits. Not that I have much of a figure to hug. But anyway.

"A surprise! That's hella romantic," Yas said. "What would you do if he took you to somewhere dead fancy? Ooh, like the Shard?"

"Nah, no one goes to the Shard on a first date," Noor said. "That's, like, marriage proposal levels."

"You're so lucky to have a boyfriend on the horizon, Helen. I turn fifteen this year and nothing!" Daphne said. "In the olden days, I would have had a husband and, like, five kids by now."

"Do you want a husband and five kids?" Yasmin said.

"Yeah, and it wouldn't stop there. You'd have to do all the cooking and wash their lice-infected clothes by hand," I said.

"Oh, forget it. I was just making a point," Daphne said.

"Anyway, what happened to Adam from Spanish?" I asked. The last I knew, things between them seemed promising.

Her ears went pink, but not in a good way. "He decided he wanted homework help from Sareeta Moore instead," she said. "But that was ages ago." Why didn't I hear about this?

"I'm still not talking to Adam," said Yasmin as she put her arms around Daphne. "He asked to borrow my protractor in maths yesterday, and I blanked him."

Daphne must have noticed my confusion. "It happened last week. The day after Marco emailed you," she said.

Waves of guilt washed over me (more like a splash than a tsunami – but still). I'd been so obsessed with Marco the last few days that I hadn't clocked Daphne's boy trouble. I wasn't going to be the type of person who dumps their mates the second they get attention from guys.

"Honestly, girls, I'm over it," said Daphne. "But Yas? Feel free not to lend him any stationery."

# TWENTY-ONE

I came home from Daphne's the next afternoon, welcomed by Buddhist chanting music and the smell of something delicious being cooked. But it was freezing — like the heating hadn't been on in days. I took off my ankle boots and went to the kitchen to switch it on.

Eros was there, frying onions and wearing nothing but khaki shorts and Maria's striped apron. Which would usually be weird in the middle of January, but the gods aren't bothered by the elements.

"It's so nice that you're home!" I went to give him a squeeze.

"Afternoon, lovely," Eros said, adding chopped red chillies to the pan.

Here Eros was, calmly cooking while his Uncle

Apollo was breaking nearly every rule in the gods' handbook. Did this mean that he didn't know? A part of me was excited to break the news to him like it was a juicy piece of gossip. Finally, I knew something the gods didn't.

"You won't believe who I saw on TV last night," I said.

"Spill!"

"Apollo, on that new reality TV show *House of Stars*! I was watching it at Daphne's last night, then suddenly there he was being introduced as a contestant."

Weirdly, Eros didn't look anywhere near as surprised as I expected him to be. He just carried on chopping.

"Typical Apollo, really. He never could resist the spotlight."

Maybe I wasn't explaining it properly?

"Eros, you don't get it. This is more than just a talent show. It's prime time, for one. And he will be watched by anyone who logs in online, twenty-four hours a day. Dad is going to hit the roof!" That got Eros's attention. He looked up from his chopping board.

"Maybe it's best that your father doesn't find out about this. It's not that big a deal, and he'll only overreact."

"How can he not find out about this? It'll be the

biggest thing on telly every Saturday night!"

We all tease Dad about his allergy to anything he considers "lowbrow", so he's unlikely to accidentally tune in. But he's the head of the gods. How could he not sense that something was off?

Also, and I didn't want to admit it, but a small part of me felt bad keeping a secret from Dad. Even if he was hardly home and seemed to forget about his parental responsibilities.

But I was not going to be the one to tell him about the TV show. And maybe Eros was right. If it was that big a deal, Dad would drag Apollo out of that house himself.

"I get it. So what's for dinner?"

"I'm making a batch of chana masala using the spices I brought back from India. It's a vegan chickpea curry."

"Oh."

"But don't worry, Maria left your dinner in the fridge as usual. Gods forbid you eat a plant-based meal," he muttered.

There were so many reasons why I was looking forward to my date with Marco, and not all of them were to do with his face, forearms or lips. The next episode of *House of Stars* aired that evening, and I didn't want to be anywhere near the house when it happened. My date would keep me out of the house for most of the evening.

The house was a strange (well, stranger) place to be. Aphrodite and Eros clearly weren't going to break the news to Dad about Apollo's big TV break. Aphrodite was in her room/studio all the time, handling Foam of the Sea orders and uploading new vlogs to her beauty channel, and Eros seemed to split his time between several different volunteering projects. It's almost like they were avoiding Dad.

Maybe I was overthinking it? When I told Eros about Apollo's bid for fame, he barely seemed to care. The gods have successfully lived in a mortal society for centuries, so what's the harm in them having a little fame now and then?

I was zipping up my parka in the hallway when the door opened, and in walked Dad with Lisa. Crap. I completely forgot to ask Dad if I could go out tonight.

"Hi, Dad. Hi, Lisa," I said, masking my internal panic.

"Ah, hello, Helen! On your way out? I thought we could have dinner together," Dad said, unravelling his scarf. Yeah, right. He probably only remembered

I existed because I was standing in front of him.

"I'm going to the cinema with Daphne, Noor and Yas, remember?" I asked.

Obviously I couldn't tell him the truth. How would he react if I told him about the date with Marco? Demand his full name (which I still didn't know), blood type and a reference check, probably.

"Sounds fun! What are you going to see?" Lisa asked. Uh-oh. What *was* I going to see?

"You know, that new romcom with that actor who's in everything these days," I said. "Anyway, I'm running late. See you both later!" I ran out of the door before Dad could object.

"Helen, wait!" Dad called out the front door. Please, please, please let me go!

"Get yourself some popcorn," he said, stuffing a tenner in my palm. Yes! The night was off to a good start.

I made my way to the tube station where we arranged to meet. The grubby, noisy main road wasn't the romantic reunion spot I had in mind, but whatever. Meeting at a station meant that wherever we were going wasn't in my neighbourhood. That made discovery by Dad even less likely.

I hoped that my outfit would fit in wherever we

ended up. I sent a picture of my final look (black ankle boots, skinny jeans and an off-shoulder purple jumper with my favourite hoop earrings) to the group chat. They all agreed that it struck the perfect balance between casual and dressy.

It didn't compare to the priceless vintage dress and inch-thick face of make-up I wore the first night we met. Would Marco be expecting a perfectly coiffed, ultra-confident glamazon? Would he even recognize me in my normal clothes?

Maybe it was for the best that I wore something more my style. If he truly wanted to date me, he'd have to date my windswept hair (seriously, it was smudging my lip gloss) and un-glam parka coat too.

I spotted him as I approached the station from across the road. He had his earphones in and was reading something on his phone, but I recognized his black coat. I waved to get his attention but it didn't work.

My tummy did somersaults as I crossed the road. I tapped him on the shoulder. "Hey, Marco," I said. He turned around and I nearly died.

It wasn't Marco. That was obvious the second he turned to face me. Just another guy with brown hair and black coat. Why why why.

Not-Marco pulled out his earphones. "Can I help

you?" he asked. I shook my head and willed for the earth to swallow me up. At least Marco wasn't there to see me embarrass myself.

Or so I thought.

"You were close, we do look alike," a voice behind me said. It was him.

Seriously?! Why did I have to embarrass myself every time I left the house?

I opened and closed my mouth, unsure of what to say. Marco ignored my goldfish impression and gave me a gentlemanly kiss on the cheek.

"I mean it, Helen. We have the same coat and everything. It's uncanny!"

Marco was kind enough not to laugh in my face. Not only that, but he insisted it was an easy mistake to make. We hopped on the tube and he soon forgot about it (at least, I hoped).

I fancied him so much it was hard to concentrate, but we managed to have a good conversation on the tube. We talked about everything on our way to the surprise date destination: family, school, our favourite toast toppings. Y'know, the essentials. But it seemed to be me doing a lot of the talking. I'm usually nervous about revealing too much about my immortal family, even when I'm with my friends. But it was unavoidable with Marco. He asked so many questions.

"So is the Greek side from your father or mother?" he asked, shouting over the sound of the tube rushing through the tunnel.

"Dad's the Greek one. My mum's family are Jamaican." I said. Then I blurted out, "She died when I was ten."

I just wanted to get it out of the way. Telling people your mum died always makes them awkward.

"My mother is alive, but I haven't seen her since I was twelve. She may as well be dead," he said.

That was not the reply I was expecting. It's not often someone replies to "my mum died" with something besides tuts, sad eyes or even an unwanted hug. It was kind of refreshing.

I wanted to know more, but the tube pulled into South Kensington station. "We're here!" Marco said, tugging at my coat sleeve.

We hopped out of the station, busy as ever on a Saturday night, and walked up the stairs leading out into the freezing night. "Glad I told you to wrap up warm?" Marco said, squeezing my arm. My skin tingled.

We were walking towards the Natural History Museum. I recognized the huge, churchlike building from days out with Dad. Thanks to his obsession with all things ancient (and cheap), I knew all the free museums in London.

Were we having a night at the museum? I guess that could be romantic, minus the fossils.

It was still decorated with fairy lights from Christmas. As we got closer, I heard the sounds of people laughing and yelling. Then I remembered. The ice rink!

I turned to Marco. "We're going ice skating?"

"Damn, you guessed it! Yes, we're going to skate. I hope that's not too clichéd?"

Ice skating! It was so romantic. I couldn't wait to tell my friends. The date hadn't properly begun but already Marco was racking up points. He was too adorable.

"It's completely unexpected," I said.

He looked pleased by that. "I must warn you, I am a terrible skater. There wasn't much ice in the Greek village I grew up in!"

"Which village was that?" I asked, but he'd already turned away to pay for our tickets.

Once we had our skates on, we edged towards the rink. Luckily, my after-school lessons came flooding back as soon as the skates hit the ice. I got my balance and jetted off, leaving Marco skating against the edge of the rink. After a few rounds of the rink, I decided to help Marco along, so I skated in front of him, holding his hands to keep his balance.

It took me exactly 0.2 milliseconds to clock that we were staring directly at each other while holding hands. It felt even more intimate than our kiss together, and I was tingling all the way to my toes (OK, maybe it was the too-tight skates).

Marco's relaxed facade slipped away. He looked kind of nervous. Ha! So there was at least one thing I could do better than him. I mentally patted myself on the back. Even though Marco wasn't much older, I felt like such a child around him. He seemed so mature and sophisticated. I, on the other hand, got confused for my little cousin on the phone. So it felt good to run rings around him, literally, in the ice rink.

After twenty minutes of that, he had decided that skating wasn't for him and left the rink to get hot chocolate. This date was getting better and better.

I stayed to do a few more rounds on the ice. I'd forgotten how fun it was, zooming past everyone else.

Marco approached the rink with two cups. "I got one with the whipped cream and one without. What would you prefer?"

"Whipped cream!"

"I'm glad you said that. I'm watching my weight after a few weeks at home," he said, winking.

He WINKED. Oh my gods. It was so sexy.

"Yeah, I know what you mean. I stayed with my gran on my mum's side over Christmas, and she was convinced I needed fattening up."

"I don't think you need to change a thing," he said.

Wow. Even my toes blushed. I took another gulp of hot chocolate.

"Don't tell Grandma Thomas I said that, though."

"You've done your research!" I joked, wondering how on earth he'd known I called Gran that.

He looked confused for a second. "Oh! No, it's nothing like that," Marco said. "Just simple deduction. See, your surname is Thomas – definitely not a Greek name. So, it must have been your mother's family name, right?" I nodded and smiled. He was sexy *and* smart.

A gust of icy wind forced me to pull up the hood of my parka. I could really feel the chill now that I wasn't ice skating.

"I think it's time we got dinner. How do you feel about American food?"

"I love it!" I said. Was he going to take me to Burger King?! That seemed quite unsophisticated by his standards. I couldn't imagine him eating a Whopper, burger sauce on his nose and fingers (at least, that's the way I ate it).

We hopped back on the tube and rode to Piccadilly Circus. I've never understood why this area is such an attraction for tourists, but it was rammed all the same. Ads on screens the size of double-decker buses glimmered and flashed, casting neon lights over our faces. A nearby busker began breakdancing to a Bruno Mars track, his audience swelling by the second, this song impossible to resist. The crowds, music, electricity in the air – it felt both incredibly exciting and way too much to handle at the same time.

Maybe it was the infectious fizz of the music, or the fact that I was out on a Saturday night (not watching everyone else have fun on Instagram, for once), but the night ahead felt magic and golden and full of wondrous possibilities. I wanted to bottle the feeling.

Marco looked around him, awe written on his face. "Is it ever possible to tire of London?" he said.

I guess, as a born-and-bred Londoner, I sometimes took the city for granted. But it was a pretty incredible place to call home.

"This way," Marco said, taking my hand.

We both wore gloves but I swear my skin shivered

when our fingers interlocked. I could hardly believe it. Here I was, in the middle of London, on a date with a guy so good-looking it made me stutter. And we were holding hands. Again!

In minutes, the garishness and frenzy of Piccadilly Circus transformed into quieter streets lined with cafes and quirky bookshops. We dodged people in pubs spilling out on to the street, despite the snap of ice in the night air.

"I think Soho is my favourite place in London," Marco said. "The Beatles, David Bowie, Jimi Hendrix ... they all walked these streets. I like to imagine it hasn't changed much since the 1960s, you know?"

"I love it, too!" I said. Yet another thing we had in common. "Mum used to take me here to go fabric shopping. And a couple of her friends owned second-hand clothes shops, too. We'd visit them, then buy a bag of nectarines from the market and eat them on the bus home."

"It's nice that you have such lovely memories of your mother."

I smiled, feeling warm all over.

At some point in the evening my butterflies had calmed down. I felt just as comfortable as I was with him on the phone, chattering away. I added "good listener" to the mental checklist I was keeping of Marco's best qualities.

We walked for a few more minutes until we got to a small restaurant with a neon sign and an amazing smell of barbecue.

"I hope you're not vegetarian," Marco said with a smile in his voice.

We were seated at a table in the basement. The menu looked amazing: chicken wings, pork ribs, burgers. Aphrodite would have a fit if she saw me consume this much salt, fat and sugar in one sitting. But I couldn't wait.

"I thought you were watching your weight!" I said with a cheeky grin, as our root beer floats arrived with a huge scoop of ice cream on top.

"I know, but I've missed this place. Funnily enough, this isn't the sort of food you can get back home," he said. "You're so lucky to have grown up in London, Helen."

I shrugged. "Yeah, I guess there are worse places to call home." But home was where my family was. And at the moment, it didn't feel like much of my family were around.

I got on with reading the menu. What could I

order that wouldn't make me look like a messy toddler? Barbecue sauce all over my mouth, hands and face is not a good first date look. I reasoned that anything I could eat with a knife and fork would work.

"What are you ordering? We should definitely start with the Buffalo chicken wings," Marco said.

"I think I'm going to have the mac and cheese," I said. His face dropped.

"Oh no. You really are vegetarian? You should have said!" He looked mortified. "I knew I should have checked first."

"No, it's not that. I just didn't want to make a mess," I said sheepishly.

He held his hands up, which made his fitted T-shirt stretch over his toned chest (YUMMMMM). "That's the fun of it! I hope you make a huge mess. Like, hot sauce in your hair and under your fingernails. Perhaps it'll make you less distractingly gorgeous."

I swear my heart skipped a beat or five. Luckily he mistook my quiet for hesitancy.

"Believe me, I won't judge. Will you at least try it?" he asked, his smoky brown eyes gazing earnestly at me.

Those eyes. If he carried on looking at me like that, I'd have serious trouble saying no. Honestly, he could ask me anything (run the London Marathon, rob a bank, sit through a month of double science) and refusing him wouldn't cross my mind.

"Fine," I said. "But you were warned!"

We went for a platter of pulled pork, ribs, beef brisket, Buffalo chicken wings, coleslaw and fries. You couldn't see the table for all the bowls and plates of food.

"Even if we don't eat it all, you must try a little bit of everything." Marco said this like it was a challenge.

And so we ate. As it turns out, the messy meal was a great icebreaker. Once we had Buffalo sauce all over our fingers and tore ribs apart with our teeth, the inhibitions fell away.

As we ate and chatted, my mind couldn't help but race ahead. When could we do this again? How much longer should I lie to Dad? And if we really hit it off, could I ever invite him home to meet the family?

And that's just the tip of the iceberg. When could I ever tell Marco who my family really were?

*Helen, stop!* I told myself. I pulled my mind away from family madness and back on to Marco. Who, apparently, could even make eating Buffalo chicken wings look hot. Here I was, focusing on the negatives, when the date was going ... well? We'd made each other laugh and I didn't get any sauce on my favourite jumper. Win.

Marco turned to flag down the waitress, and he looked so handsome from that particular angle (seriously, like he was carved from marble) that I spluttered on my final bite of mac and cheese. Ugh. I excused myself and nipped to the loo, grateful that I didn't choke. While I was there, I touched up my lip gloss.

I checked my phone, but there was no signal in the restaurant basement. I'd have to wait until I got home before updating the group chat.

When I came back to the table, Marco was taking care of the bill. It's not very feminist of me, but I was relieved that we didn't have to split. That would have been a whole week's allowance gone. On one meal! The tenner Dad had given me earlier was safe, for now.

"That's so kind of you," I said in my most gracious voice.

When we left the restaurant, I checked my phone to see how much longer we had together. It was just after ten thirty p.m. And I had seven missed calls from Dad. Oh crap.

Dad hadn't cared about my curfew in weeks, so why was he bothered now? Then I realized that the missed calls had been coming in since eight thirty p.m.

This was it. He'd found me out and I'd be grounded until the end of time.

"I'd better get home," I said, trying to hide the panic on my face.

What could be so urgent? And why couldn't he send a text message?

"Of course. Will you let me escort you?" Marco said.

Escort me? I kind of loved the formal way he spoke. But escorting me was out of the question. If Dad saw Marco, that would be the nail in my rapidly approaching coffin.

"No, I couldn't let you do that! But you can wait with me at the bus stop," I said.

I spent the tube ride home feeling queasy, and it wasn't just because of the Buffalo wings. If the myths are anything to go by, being grounded was the least of my worries. I've heard about some of the punishments that Zeus has doled out over the years (rolling a boulder up a hill for eternity, anyone?). Marco tried to make conversation, but my heart wasn't in it. I hoped he didn't notice.

When we finally got out of the tube station, my bus was just pulling into the stop. Marco wouldn't have to wait with me after all.

"That's my bus!" I yelled before giving Marco a quick hug (no time for a kiss) and jumping on. I waved from the top deck, and he waved back as the bus pulled away. Annoyingly, our time together was cut short. Again.

I had dozens of messages from the girls, but I couldn't think about those now. I messaged Dad saying that I should be home in ten minutes.

By the time I walked from the bus stop to my house, I'd imagined so many awful scenarios that I was nearly in tears, ready to confess everything and throw myself on to Dad's mercy. I followed the sound of voices into the living room, my heart in my throat, walked in and found Dad with his head in his hands.

The TV was paused on Apollo's face.

# TWENTY-TWO

Dad looked up when he heard me come through the door, his face hard as stone. I felt the rage radiating from him, like standing too close to a crackling bonfire.

"I suppose you knew about this?" He gestured towards the TV.

I nodded. There was no point in lying.

So that's why Dad was calling me all evening. It's not that he found out about Marco. He'd found out about Apollo's national fame.

Honestly? I'm not sure this was any better.

Dad's face turned a shade of red that could only be described as volcanic. "Helen. This. Is. Huge," he said in a low voice. "Why didn't you tell me? Do you have any idea of the ramifications?"

Hold on a second. Was he really going to lecture *me* about ramifications? I didn't break the rules.

He was the one who was never home. He was the one who didn't bother with his responsibilities. And he was the one who abandoned his family.

He abandoned *me*.

Lava rippled through my veins. If Dad wanted a fight, he was going to get it.

"How is this my fault?" I yelled. Dad froze but I was nowhere near done. "Maybe if you were actually home and not spending every waking moment with Lisa, then you would have noticed that Apollo is on national TV and Aphrodite is an internet superstar."

Dad looked confused when I mentioned Aphrodite. Like all of this was news to him.

"You didn't know that either?" I said. A part of me was stunned. He was even more clueless than I thought. "How could you have missed that? She's practically turned the attic into her studio!"

Dad sank back into the sofa, shocked. I hadn't imagined it. He really had no clue what was going on with his family.

"You're meant to look after us," I hissed, my fury boiling over. "It isn't my job to keep you updated. I could be doing goodness-knows-what every night once Maria goes home, and you'd never know!" I shouted.

Dad looked up. "Helen, I had no idea—"

"Save it!" I wasn't finished yet. "Do you have any clue how hard it is to be surrounded by a family of strangers? Strangers with superpowers?" I said. "We don't look the same, or even think the same. . . I have zero in common with any of you."

Tears pricked my eyes. I turned to leave, pausing at the door. "You've had literally thousands of years to practise being a parent," I said. "If you haven't figured it out by now? You never will."

I slammed the front door and ran up the stairs to my room before I burst into tears. Once I made it to my room, I let it all out. I cried until my pillow was sodden and covered in the mascara Noor had persuaded me to wear for my date. That seemed so long ago now.

I'd never spoken to Dad like that before. I don't think I'd spoken to anyone like that before. It wasn't like me to shout and slam doors, but it felt so *good* to finally show Dad how I felt.

If I was being honest, I hadn't realized how strongly I felt about Dad's absence. Mum always said that pushing down negative emotions would only do more harm than good, in the long run. Of course she was right, as always.

I lay on my bed, breathing in and out. I started to calm down and replayed the argument in my head. I *really* went for it. Wherever this inner rage came from, it wasn't from Mum's side of the family. My body practically vibrated with anger – it had to be an immortal thing. We had more in common than I'd thought.

# TWENTY-THREE

A few hours later, Dad came upstairs and told me he was calling an emergency family meeting. I didn't want to join, but I didn't want a bunch of useless gods deciding my fate for me either. I washed the mascara streaks off my face and went downstairs, feeling nervous about how this discussion would go.

When I walked into the living room and saw Apollo there without his usual relaxed grin, I knew that Dad wasn't messing around. Turned out he had called the *House of Stars* studio a few hours before and told them there was a family emergency. They'd bundled Apollo into a taxi and sent him straight home.

"You could have at least told me what was going on when I got into the cab, Father," said Apollo through gritted teeth. "I thought there was a real emergency! Like a break-in at my flat or something."

"ENOUGH," Dad shouted. I could have sworn that his eyes flashed lightning for a split second.

Apollo scowled, but he didn't say anything else.

"This IS a real emergency," said Dad, nursing a glass of wine. "We've had a written warning from the Council. They're aware that you've broken the rules. One more misdemeanour, and we'll be called back for a trial."

Aphrodite and Eros had the good sense to stay quiet. Apollo swore under his breath, muttering something about Cranus. I'd heard of this guy before. A powerful Council member, right?

"Don't blame this on our enemy, Apollo. Helen told me everything," Dad said.

They glared at me with eyes like hot coals. GREAT. Now I'd have to sleep with one eye open. Thanks for dropping me in it, Dad.

"Aphrodite earning worldwide fame on the YouTubes and Apollo on that TV show watched by millions: these are clear examples of rule-breaking," he continued. "You've made this so simple for Cranus. And for the rest of the Council."

"Whoa, whoa, *whoa*," Apollo said. "I don't know

what Helen told you, but Aphrodite and I totally earned our fame. Have you seen the losers on that TV show? There's a man who plays the ukulele with, like, his toes. I didn't need to use my powers to get a place!"

"Apollo is absolutely correct. Infants Helen's age can put together videos and get millions of hits. My success is entirely on my own merit," Aphrodite said.

"That is beside the point, and you know it," Dad said. "You're bringing global attention to the family."

And what would happen then? Why was no one else wondering what would happen to us? To me?

Apollo sighed. "It's so unfair that we can't have a little bit of fun. What's the use of being an accomplished musician without an audience?"

My selfish siblings were too wrapped up in their little bit of fun and fame being taken away to listen to me. I felt invisible. I stood up. "Can someone *please* tell me what happens to me if you all ruin your cover?" I said at the top of my voice.

"Your brother and sister have risked getting us all sent back to Mount Olympus, Helen," said Dad. "There would be a trial, and if found guilty, we'd be banished from the mortal realm. Or worse."

I fell back in my chair. "What do you mean by 'us'? I didn't break the rules."

Dad sighed. "The Council don't see it that way. We are a family, and we would be treated as such."

The thought floored me. I knew living with gods wouldn't always be easy. But apparently it could ruin my life, too. "So you're saying that I could be sent to Mount Olympus. *For ever*? Even though I'm not a god?"

Dad nodded. I felt like my BBQ dinner would make a reappearance at any moment.

Aphrodite shrugged. "But that won't happen, because we've done nothing wrong. It'll all blow over."

"Too right," said Apollo. "Since when did the Council get their knickers in a twist over a little love spell, anyway?"

Silence fell over the room. Dad froze.

Aphrodite glared at Apollo. "Now you've done it," she said.

I wasn't the only one who looked confused. Why was Apollo talking about a love spell? Dad and I watched Aphrodite, Apollo and Eros as they looked guiltily at each other.

Dad took off his spectacles and pinched the bridge of his nose. "Out with it, one of you."

Aphrodite smiled nervously. "Well, Eros and I noticed how antisocial you've been the last couple of decades. Hardly going on dates or out to parties like you used to. Just spending all that time in the garden, mucking about with antiques and smelly vegetables. We thought you might like to meet someone. A woman," she said.

It took me a minute to understand what was going on, but Dad grasped it instantly. He looked horrified. No, more than horrified. Crushed.

"Tell me *exactly* what you did and the precise order in which you did it. Don't leave anything out," Dad said, his voice low as thunder.

"Father, it really wasn't that bad. We simply arranged your meeting with Lisa at the university. Then when it appeared to go well, I had Eros accelerate Lisa's affection for you slightly."

"Slightly?" Apollo said. "I think she's one week away from proposing to Dad herself."

But Dad had been single for years. Why did they trick someone into being his girlfriend now?

Then it all clicked into place. Of course, Eros could never resist the chance to help with matters of the heart. Plus, if Dad was busy with Lisa, then Aphrodite and Apollo were free to do what they wanted. And it worked.

How could he not have realized?

I turned to look at Dad. His face was in his hands,

fingers trembling with rage. I didn't know whether to give him a hug, or back away before his temper exploded.

He lifted his head up. "I'm not sure when you, my own children, decided that this was an acceptable way to behave. But it isn't," Dad said. His voice boomed, echoing off the walls and filling the room.

"It's childish, manipulative and the sort of behaviour that will have the whole family banished to Mount Olympus for a century at least. Helen could lose the only life she's ever known!"

The three offending gods shifted uncomfortably. They had the good sense to look guilty.

"Eros, using your powers to cause a mortal to fall in love. . . This is huge."

I still couldn't believe what I was hearing. They could lose their powers. Because of these idiots, I could be banished to life on Mount Olympus.

No Marco. No friends. No Grandma Thomas. Just the thought made my head spin.

"It's vital that we keep a low profile," Dad continued. "I'm sentencing all three of you to house arrest for thirty days. During that time, you will be banned from making any contact with the outside world."

"But my views will plummet!" Aphrodite shrieked.

"This is ridiculous. I'm way too old to be grounded," said Apollo. He marched to the front door but it wouldn't open for him.

"Apollo, your house arrest is here. Not your own flat. I need to keep an eye on you," Dad said.

"But my record deal is on the line!" Apollo retorted.

Aphrodite stood up. "Father, this is grossly unfair. For the first time in centuries, my life has some purpose. I went viral, for god's sake. You can't take that away!"

Their selfishness was unreal. "So what?" I yelled. I was one more fight away from a sore throat. "You're going to RUIN my life because of a record deal and video views?!"

They looked at me like I'd appeared out of nowhere.

"Do I have to remind you that my life is here, on earth, and not in some fairy land in the clouds? Did that ever cross your minds?" Tears started to stream down my cheeks. I couldn't help it.

I was so disgusted with all of them. Even Eros, my favourite, didn't stop to think that his actions might ruin my life.

"Helen, I'm so—" Dad began.

"Oh, please, give it a rest," I interrupted. I pushed through the living room door and ran upstairs before anyone could stop me.

I checked my phone, which I had left upstairs (phones are forbidden in family meetings) and saw fifteen missed calls, eight Instagram messages and about a gazillion texts – all asking what the hell was going on with DJ Sunny. I guess the news had leaked that he was no longer a contestant on *House of Stars*.

It was nearly two a.m., only three hours since I'd come home from my date with Marco. Three hours ago, my body tingled with butterflies. Three hours ago, my biggest worry was having Buffalo sauce on my face when he kissed me.

Now, my biggest worry? Wondering if me and my family would be extradited to Mount Olympus. Tonight had turned from one of the best nights of my life to one of the worst. And it was all because of my stupid, childish, irresponsible family.

I sobbed myself to sleep.

# TWENTY-FOUR

On Monday morning I had one thing to look forward to. My plan was to float into school, tell my best friends about my dreamy date with Marco and enjoy the endless questions tinged with envy. Like that bit on the bleachers in *Grease*, where Sandy tells the girls about kissing Danny. Even better, it would help me forget about that disastrous family meeting on Saturday night.

But once again, my family were ruining my life. Instead of describing ice skating under the stars, I was dodging questions about stupid Apollo. His mysterious absence from *House of Stars* last night was all over Twitter. I don't know how the entire school found out that we were related, but I must have been asked the same question about fifty times in one morning: "What happened to DJ Sunny?"

And my answer? "There was a family emergency." I was under strict instructions from Dad to say this and nothing more. He even made me practise my poker face this morning like I haven't been forced to lie every day since I moved in with my ridiculous family.

To be fair, it technically wasn't a lie. Being put under house arrest to appease the Council so that my entire family isn't banished from the mortal world and stripped of their powers? Definitely an emergency situation.

Even teachers seemed to be treating me differently. Miss Bloom bumped into me in the corridor and gave me a sympathetic squeeze on the shoulder. It took me about twenty minutes of confusion before I realized why she'd done it. It's always hard to tell with her.

The same thing happened when I walked into double English. The first thing Noor said to me was "OH MY GOD! Helen! What happened to DJ Sunny?"

I clenched my jaw and said the same thing I'd been saying all day. "Family emergency."

Noor raised one perfectly groomed eyebrow. But if she didn't believe me, she didn't let on.

"You know you can talk to me about it any time, right, babe?" she said. I nodded and smiled weakly in response.

If only Noor knew how wrong she was. Because I couldn't talk about it to her. Not in double physics. Not after school. Not ever. My friends could never know about the epic trouble my family were in.

Just as I was considering making something up about Apollo's disappearance (a case of mega contagious adult chickenpox, maybe?), Daphne and Yasmin dropped their books on our table with a thud.

"Oh-em-gee!" Yasmin said. "I heard about your brother. Helen, you have to spill every—"

Noor made a cutting motion with her hand, instantly silencing Yasmin. "Actually, maybe we shouldn't talk about that right now," she said.

Daphne must've picked up the gloomy vibes I was radiating, and swiftly changed the subject.

"But you're gonna tell us about your date on Saturday, right?" she asked.

I smiled. The thought of Marco was an instant mood booster, like sunshine on a Saturday morning.

"Wowwwww," said Yasmin. "Where did that grin come from? You need to tell us *everything*."

The change in subject brought me out of my funk.

I told them about my date, from skating at the Natural History Museum to dinner in Soho.

"Did you get another kiss with bae, then?" asked Noor.

Sigh. I wished I could say yes. "I missed my curfew and had to rush home, so no time for a kiss," I said.

"No time for a kiss?!" said Noor. "But you were running late already!"

"Well, yeah, but I had like ten missed calls from Dad. Who thought I was at the cinema with you guys," I said. "I couldn't risk him driving to the cinema and picking me up himself. He'd implode."

The conversation stopped there as we went to lunch. I realized that it was the first time all day that I hadn't worried about what the Council had in store for my family.

I arrived home from school to utter chaos. Boxes of Apollo's music equipment littered the hallway, leading a trail to the kitchen where he was arguing with Maria.

"I don't care how much they're worth," she said. "That contraption is not taking up space on the table!" The contraption she was referring to? Apollo's DJ decks.

"They need to go somewhere! I can't swing a cat

in that pokey spare room, let alone find space for my decks."

"Aphrodite has loads of space in that attic of hers. Have you asked her?" Maria asked.

Apollo lowered his voice to a dramatic whisper. "Hell. No. I haven't seen her in this bad a mood since her favourite lipstick got discontinued."

My after-school snack of buttered toast could wait. The last thing I wanted to do was deal with their bickering. I usually did my homework in the kitchen when Maria was home, so she could tell me about her day. She talked and I pretended to listen whilst really I daydreamed about Marco, making sure I nodded and gasped in the right places.

But tonight I'd do my French homework in my bedroom, to be on the safe side. It was the only room in the house that my family hadn't ruined for me. Yet.

Just as I was about to write a paragraph on Pierre's favourite meal, my phone rang, Marco's name flashing on the screen. I answered the phone with all the casualness I could muster, praying that he couldn't somehow hear my pounding heartbeat through the line.

"Hey, Helen. How are things?" he asked.

I couldn't lie. And I didn't want to lie, either.

"Honestly? Not great. My family can't seem to stop arguing at the moment."

I gave Marco the censored version of recent events: a family emergency that caused Apollo to be yanked from his superstar debut on primetime TV. I thought Marco was too cultured to bother with TV, but he knew all about *House of Stars*.

"I've got to say, Helen," Marco said, and my insides exploded with glitter when he said my name. "I'm more concerned about this family emergency you mentioned."

Oh gosh. I forgot to think up a lie for this "family emergency". My mind whizzed through a carousel of untruths. A dead relative? No, too dramatic. Plus I'd have to fake going to a funeral, and that would be too far, even for me.

"Look," Marco said, interrupting my frantic search for a lie. "I don't need to know what's going on. But you know you can talk to me any time, right, Helen?"

"I know. Thanks, Marco."

The weird thing was, unlike when Noor said it earlier that day, I really believed it with Marco. Like, I could actually tell him every crazy thing about my family. He'd simply nod, and ask how I was coping.

He wouldn't ask me what it was like to have beautiful, talented, immortal gods as siblings. He wouldn't care about their powers. He'd want to know how they affected *me*.

"It's good to know I can talk to you," I added. "Literally all everyone wants to talk about is Apollo right now."

"So everyone wants to talk about your half-brother. How does that feel?"

"Lonely. I feel lonely." It was the first time I'd said the words out loud. My cheeks felt hot. It felt good to get it off my chest, but also strangely embarrassing.

The line was quiet for what felt like eternity, but was probably only a few seconds. "Helen," he murmured. "That must suck. Right?"

I snapped back to reality. I couldn't stand the thought of Marco feeling sorry for me. "I'm just being dramatic," I said. "It's too loud to be lonely in this house, especially with everyone arguing all the time."

Marco laughed, thank goodness. "I think our families have plenty in common, Helen."

After we said goodnight and ended the call, I couldn't stop thinking about what I'd said. Marco must think I'm pathetic.

What teenager ever gets lonely? I'm surrounded by friends and family, for goodness' sake. And I mean literally surrounded. With Apollo here, we had a full house.

I checked my phone and saw dozens of messages from the gang in our group chat. It wasn't anything important, just memes and GIFs and gossip. They wouldn't mind if I caught up with them the next day. And after opening up to Marco, I wasn't in the mood for jokes.

I felt like I couldn't actually talk to any of them about the stuff that weighed on my mind. The stuff that kept me awake at night. I couldn't talk to Marco, either. Not really. But being able to say the words "I feel lonely" to him? That felt like a big deal.

It seemed like he truly cared about me. Not my chaotic, talented, beautiful family. But me.

And the best thing about that whole conversation? He didn't press for answers when I mentioned the family emergency. Why couldn't everyone in my life be as sweet and understanding as Marco?

The one thing he hadn't mentioned was a second date. What if he misinterpreted me running to catch the bus? Did he think I was trying to worm my way out of a kiss? I really hoped that wasn't the case, seeing as I fancied him so much it affected my breathing.

My phone vibrated on my bed. I had a new message.

M: *Date number two is overdue. Free soon? x*

How could so few words cause my entire body to melt down? I hugged my phone to my chest and squealed.

# TWENTY-FIVE

*Dear Mum,*

*Things have taken a turn for the worse. We had
a written warning from the Council thanks
to Eros, Aphrodite and Apollo misusing their
powers. If they cross the line again, they will all
be called back for a trial at Mount Olympus.
And if they're found guilty? I can kiss goodbye
my life on earth.*

*To make matters even more complicated,
one of the leading Council members hates our
entire family. According to Eros, Cranus will be
looking for any opportunity to banish us all to
Mount Olympus. I'm not sure what happened*

for him to hate our family, but I'm not about to ask. I have a feeling that it's better to not know.

In any case, a trial won't happen. Dad took the major precaution of putting them under house arrest for thirty days with everyone banned from contacting the outside world (except for me, thank the gods . . . or not, as the case may be). By that time, Aphrodite's devotees will have moved on to the next big thing. And everyone will have forgotten about Apollo, too.

If there's one thing I've learned recently, it's to be careful what you wish for. For weeks I hated that Dad was always out and the house seemed quiet and empty. Now, the house is full to the brim and I can't get a moment of peace. If it isn't Apollo writing new songs at all hours, it's random crashes coming from Aphrodite's attic. I guess she's still angry about losing her internet privileges.

The only one who is quiet is Eros. He's taken his punishment quite badly. It's like he's taken on a vow of silence or something. Apollo seems more bothered about losing his new fans (#PrayForDJSunny trended on Twitter for about thirty seconds). And Aphrodite? I haven't seen her since our family meeting at the weekend. Knowing her bad moods, I'd like to keep it that way.

Dad's always home straight after work too. I guess he and Lisa broke up, and I do actually feel terrible for him. Sure, I didn't like that he always talked about her and whatever crap documentary they were watching. But she made him happy. Now he lives in his office, hardly making a sound. I haven't even seen him in his shed. If Dad has lost his interest in rusty antiques, I know things must be bad.

But at least everything in my life isn't terrible. I had a date, Mum! I think he might even be my boyfriend. Like, I think we're seeing each other exclusively. If I'm being honest, having Marco to distract me is the one thing getting me through this madness.

Since Apollo made his TV debut, I can't help but wonder if my friends care more about that than me. But Marco knew about Apollo being a celebrity and didn't care. He just wants to know how I'm feeling.

Mum, I think you'd love him. He's clever, kind, charming and sophisticated. And so beautiful, like a cartoon prince or spring sunshine. He has the type of face that people write music about. He's so perfect-looking it almost makes me mad. Like, what gives him the right to be so delicious?

He's a little older than me (don't freak out) but I think that's a good thing. He doesn't play annoying games like so many of the boys my age. I don't think he's the type to ditch me for someone bigger than an A-cup. There's something that feels solid and secure about Marco.

I'm not sure what it is. But I do know that I'm into him. Like, really into him.

And honestly? Amidst all of this madness, he's exactly what I need.

Love for ever,

Helen xxx

# TWENTY-SIX

"Hels, you haven't forgotten about the sleepover tonight, have you?" Daphne asked as we rushed out of our last lesson of the week. She did text me the night before, but I was on the phone to Marco and forgot to reply.

"Yeah, I'm there!" I said. It sounded FAR better than staying at home. Eros still wasn't talking to anyone, Aphrodite's foul mood put me on edge, and Apollo's speakers thumped non-stop. I leapt at the chance to have a break from my family.

I went to my locker and checked my phone for new messages (well, a message from Marco).

M: *Hey :) Free for coffee this afternoon? X*

I was about to text him back and say I wasn't free. But why couldn't I fit in coffee and the sleepover?

I was going to spend all night with my friends, after all. I could spare a bit of time for Marco.

*H: Deffo! Do you know Sprinkles? See you there in an hour x*

I met the girls by the school gates and told them I'd forgotten my overnight clothes. I said I'd go home, get changed and see them at Daphne's in a couple of hours.

"But you're definitely going to come, right?" Yasmin said. "Feels like it's been ages since our last sleepover."

I nodded. "Course!"

Noor looked like she was about to say something, but didn't. "See you later, then," she said.

I got home and checked the time. Fifteen minutes left to get ready before I had to leave for Sprinkles, the dessert parlour near my house. I wasn't going to stress about clothes or make-up today. Especially not for a coffee date. I pulled my hair back into a topknot and smoothed back my edges with hair gel. I was ready in five minutes, and out the door not long after that.

I took a slow walk to Holloway Road, glad that I'd sacrificed a cute dress for jeans with flat-heeled boots and my hooded parka. It was way too cold for fashion. Besides, if I can get away with looking like an Arctic explorer anywhere, it's North London on a freezing January night.

On the way, I took off one glove and checked my phone. I had half a dozen chat messages from the girls, telling me to hurry up, and that I was missing out on the pizza. I dismissed the notifications and stuck my phone back in my pocket.

Ten minutes later, I arrived at Sprinkles. The dessert parlour's purple imitation-leather booths and the shiny black floor were worlds away from the central London restaurant Marco took me to on our first date. But it was the only local place open until late that wasn't a bar or pub.

I walked in and eyed up the ice cream flavours. The flat-screen TV mounted on the wall displayed ads for waffles, pancakes and milkshakes in dozens of potential flavour combinations. That, and the warm smell of cookies baking, reminded me that I hadn't eaten since lunchtime. I queued up behind an older couple ordering strawberry milkshakes to go (boring) and settled on the chocolate waffles with mint chocolate-chip ice cream. Yum. When I ordered, I remembered to ask for two forks and spoons so that Marco could share. It looked polite, that way.

I paid, then turned around to find a booth. And there he was.

Were the butterflies ever going to stop? Marco was

sitting in a corner booth, deep in his book. That was enough to set off the fluttering feeling in my stomach. At this rate, he was going to ruin my appetite. I walked over. He didn't look up from his book until I plonked myself down into the seat opposite him. The cushy seat made a "pfft" sound, and I thanked my lucky stars that it didn't sound like something else. I would have *died*.

He looked up, put his book down and smiled. "Sorry, Helen, I didn't notice you. I was lost in my book," Marco said.

He reached over to take my hand. My skin fizzled and snapped like popping candy in the mouth. How was it possible to fancy someone this much?

"Hope I wasn't interrupting?" I said, lying.

"The book's great, but I'd much rather be looking at you," he said. Swoon central.

I looked down at his book. It was called *The Myth of Sisyphus* by Albert Camus, which sounded familiar. Maybe I'd seen it on Dad's shelf?

"Ah, Camus. I haven't read that one yet," I said.

Why was he smirking? "You mean Al-bear Camue?" he said.

Oops. So I'd completely mispronounced his name. I hoped that the dim lighting in our corner booth hid my blushes.

"'Seeking what is true is not seeking what is desirable.' Philosophy has a special place in my heart," he said.

"Let's not talk about the truth right now," I said. The guilt of lying to my friends weighed on my mind.

"Coffee?" A waiter in a purple baseball cap set down a steaming glass mug in front of Marco.

"I ordered before you got here. I hope you don't mind." Marco tore a sachet of brown sugar open and tumbled the crystals into his mug.

"I couldn't imagine you telling a lie, Helen," he said, smiling sweetly.

I gulped. If only he knew the half of it.

"How was your day?" I asked.

"Far from over, hence the strong coffee. I have an assignment keeping me up all night."

"Oh, philosophy?"

"I wish. This is just for pleasure," he said, nodding towards the book. "Anyway, seeing you is a much-needed break from my work."

"Chocolate waffles with mint choc-chip ice cream?" asked the waiter, placing a huge plate of waffles and two sets of cutlery on the table. I got stuck in, nibbling a corner of waffle drenched in thick melted chocolate. It smelled incredible.

"I assume your father doesn't know you're with me?" he asked.

That was unexpected. Was I talking about Dad too much to Marco? "He would *freak* if he knew I was here with you. Why, should he be worried?" I asked in my most flirtatious tone.

"I mean, I am two whole years older than you, Helen."

"But all we're doing is talking and eating!" I said, chewing my waffles. "It's not like I'm drinking, smoking or hot-wiring cars. I don't get why he doesn't trust me more."

"Perhaps it's because you'd give yourself diabetes if left to your own devices." Marco grinned, looking pointedly at my plate.

"Now I'm *definitely* not going to share," I said. "'Diabetes.' That's a Greek word, right?" I hoped my pathetic attempt to show Marco that I did have half a brain wasn't obvious.

He gave a small nod. "Many words in the English language have a Greek root. It made learning English a little easier for me."

Sometimes, I forgot that English wasn't Marco's first language. "How old were you when you started learning?"

"Young. About five years old. My father wanted me to have a head start on the other kids at school."

I got halfway through eating my waffle with ice cream before feeling queasy. I wasn't about to give up and prove to Marco that this dessert was a bad idea. I was just taking a small break, that's all.

"Dad's been trying to teach me Greek for years, with no luck. Still had to put up with his museum tours, though."

"I would have killed for a museum trip with my father," Marco said. "Between my boarding school and his demanding job, we didn't get to spend much time together."

Now seemed like the perfect chance to ask about his mum. I'd been curious since he mentioned her on our first date.

"So your mother left when you were young, and you don't have any siblings. Right?"

Marco nodded. "I'm sure you can relate."

Actually, I couldn't. There's no way Mum would have sent me to boarding school. And even though I only saw Dad once a month when I was little, he always gave me his undivided attention (even if he did drag me round museums I didn't care about). I thought that living with Dad would be more like that, but we haven't had a single day out together.

"That sounds like a lonely way to grow up," I said.

"Not at all. I had plenty of tutors to keep me busy: English, geography, and history. That sort of thing. One of them introduced me to philosophy, and I've loved it ever since."

I realized this was the most Marco had said about himself since we met. I wanted him to keep going, so I kept quiet. This was a tactic Mum used when she wanted to get something out of me. Most people will rush to fill silent gaps.

Except for Marco. He continued to sip his coffee, looking at me with that intense stare of his. I was forced to say something before my blushes took over.

"So are you going to study philosophy? When you start at college?" I asked. It was an innocent question, but it had an interesting effect on Marco. He broke my gaze, looking down at his coffee. Had I touched a nerve?

"No. Law," he said, with a weird false smile.

"Why, when you love philosophy?" I asked.

"Do you want the long answer or the short answer?"

I poked my spoon in the warm chocolate sauce puddling on my plate. "Both," I said.

"My father has an excellent legal mind." Marco stirred the dregs of his coffee with a long-handled spoon. "I thought that, maybe, we would spend more time together if I decide to take law as one of my A-level subjects. We'd at least have that in common."

"And have you?"

"Have I what, Helen?"

"Have you spent more time together now that you're planning to study a boring subject?" I asked. It was meant to be a joke, but Marco's face fell. There was no doubt about it now. I'd definitely hit a nerve.

He said nothing for five whole seconds. I counted. I wanted to gather up my words and stuff them back into my uncontrollable mouth.

"Yes, actually. We have. He's asked me to help out on a special assignment," Marco said quietly.

"Oh, awesome!" I said. Why didn't he sound more excited?

"Speaking of my assignment, I'd better get back to my work." I knew it. I'd prodded too hard, and now Marco was retreating.

"Do you have to?"

He smiled and gave me a funny look that had an even funnier effect on me. The butterflies destroyed my appetite once and for all.

"Don't do that," he said.

"Do what?"

"Smile like that. Pull that face. Ask me to stay. There's a very real risk that I'll do whatever you ask, Helen."

I smiled. "In that case, follow me."

Twenty minutes later, we were on the top deck of the 43 bus heading towards London Bridge.

"Are you going to tell me where we're going?" Marco asked once we sat down. We were lucky enough to get the best seats in the house: the row at the very front. It had the widest window, and sitting there felt like you were driving the bus.

"This is it!" I said.

"Helen Thomas, I know London is a lot bigger than my hometown. But I have been on a bus before."

"It's not the bus that's special, Marco. It's the journey. This is my favourite bus route."

"Oh. Why's that?" He looked genuinely interested.

"I'll show you. Think of it as a personalized tour of London, minus the tourists," I said.

The bus crawled up Holloway Road, stuck in Saturday night traffic. The closer we got to Highbury Corner, the less we moved. The more exciting tourist highlights were at least twenty minutes away. I had to improvise.

"See that building over there?" I said, pointing across the road. "That's my old library. I pretty much lived there on the Saturdays I wasn't with Dad. Sometimes Mum would take yoga classes in the Buddhist Centre next door."

"Free babysitting. Very clever," Marco said.

"I'd never thought of it that way," I said, laughing. "I was just so happy to be in the library."

Marco turned away from the window and put his arm around me. "A girl who's happiest in the library is one I think I'd get along with." The corny line didn't stop the heat from flooding my face. I unzipped my parka to let some cool air in.

The bus moved past the traffic jam at Highbury Corner and picked up the pace. We'd reached a stretch of high street jammed with pubs, bars, restaurants and boutiques. I knew a couple of these places, like Nando's and a Turkish restaurant Mum used to love. We didn't consider going anywhere else. The rest of the street was a little too fancy for our budget.

The bus wound its way past Exmouth Market. I pointed out the place where I took drama lessons one summer holiday. "Mum was friends with one of the tutors, so he got her a good deal," I said.

"I can't imagine you as a thespian," Marco said.

Sometimes, it was really obvious that English was his second language. He used the sort of words that belonged in a BBC period drama.

"I wasn't! I hated every minute of it, but Mum needed something to keep me busy over the summer break while she was at work."

I stuck out like a sore thumb at that place. Everything, from my skin to my hair to what I had in my packed lunch, set me apart from the posh kids who went there. I was almost grateful when September rolled around, and I started the new school year with familiar faces.

"I take it this is bringing back some unpleasant memories?" Marco asked. My emotions, including the bitterness of feeling like an outsider in my own city, must have danced across my face.

"Yeah. It's been a long time since I thought about how unhappy I was there," I said. "It's just weird, how certain places are linked to strong feelings. Do you know what I mean?"

Marco turned back to face the front of the bus. "Unfortunately, I do. After my mother left, I couldn't bring myself to set foot in her study. Neither could Father."

"That sounds awful," I said.

"Yes, it was. A part of me wonders if that's why Father had me start boarding school a year sooner than usual."

"Why? She didn't leave because of you," I said.

"Of course not. But it would have been a constant reminder."

"Well, now this bus route will remind me of something better," I said. "You."

Then I reached over and kissed him gently on the lips.

# TWENTY-SEVEN

Maria was at the end of her tether. The house arrest turned her into an unofficial prison guard/babysitter, and it wasn't fair. For example, apparently Apollo ate an astonishing amount for an immortal. You know, beings that have *no need to eat*.

"I've never seen anything like it. He demands three square meals per day, plus enough snacks to keep him going through the night," Maria said, exasperated.

"Maria, this isn't a hotel. Why can't he make his own food?" I asked while making my toast.

"I let him do that once and returned to find my kitchen turned upside down! You know what these fools are like. They haven't the faintest idea how to do anything for themselves."

Maria was right about that one. It took Aphrodite weeks to figure out that you have to *peel* bananas before they go into a smoothie.

As if on cue, Apollo came into the kitchen carrying a stack of dirty plates and mugs down from his room.

"Don't forget to load up the dishwasher," Maria called after him. Apollo turned and glared at us, but put his dirty plates into the dishwasher.

"Gossiping, are we?" Apollo said.

He finished loading the dishwasher and turned his attention to the fridge. "I'm having one of the most intense creative spurts I've had in decades, and I think better on a full stomach. You have no right to judge me."

Maria rolled her eyes. "Eat all you want, my darling, just clean up after yourself. That is all I ask. Goodness knows you have the time!"

"I don't recall anyone asking Michelangelo to wash his dishes in between painting the Sistine Chapel," Apollo muttered. "Anyway, Helen, how was school? Is the outside world coping without me?"

"Oh yeah, everyone seems to be doing fine. No one has bothered asking about you in days," I said, spreading some extra peanut butter on my toast corners. Apollo pretended not to care. It was in his DNA to adore being adored.

"Well, this house arrest is the best thing that's happened to me in years," he said. "I've had no distractions, so my creative output is off the charts. I just wished this place had a recording studio, like my flat in Hackney."

Apollo carried on talking about his "creative output" to no one in particular while he assembled a ginormous sandwich.

"I haven't spoken to Aphrodite in a few days. Have you?" I asked Maria once Apollo disappeared with his snack.

"No, and I'd rather keep it that way. That one is in a mood fouler than Medusa's face," she said.

It must have been tough for Aphrodite. Not only was she confined to the house, but she couldn't use the internet just in case she tried to go viral again.

Better her than me. How long could I go without Wi-Fi before smacking my head against the wall? Two or three days max, if I was honest.

# TWENTY-EIGHT

An almighty thud shook me out of my sleep. It came from Aphrodite's room above mine. What on earth was she doing *now*?

The time on my phone said it was just after midnight. I clamped my pillow over my head and tried to get back to sleep, but it was no use. I heard crash after crash, then Dad's voice. He and Aphrodite were arguing. At this hour? I had no choice but to march upstairs and remind them that some of us needed our beauty sleep.

"Guys, can you please argue another time! I have school in the—"

I cut off abruptly at the sight of Aphrodite's room. Every single item of furniture was upturned and the contents of her walk-in wardrobe littered the floor. In the centre of the chaos stood Aphrodite. But not like I'd ever seen her before.

She hovered a few feet above the floor. It was as though she was illuminated from the inside out. Her eyes shone white, and when she opened her mouth, white light poured out. Her dark hair stood on end, coiling towards the ceiling. She seemed to generate pure electricity, the air crackled with it.

*Whoa*. It was terrifying.

"It's no use, Aphrodite," Dad shouted. "You know I can't let you leave the house."

Aphrodite raised her hand, flinging a wooden chest of drawers across the room. It crashed against the wall, splintering into pieces.

"Silence!" Aphrodite shouted, and her voice boomed from every corner in the room. "You're weak and useless. A pathetic excuse for a god," she spat. "You thought you could imprison me in this house? I've kept my powers sharp by practising over the years. Your little spells can't stop me!"

Aphrodite lifted both arms, as though she was pushing a heavy weight above her head. Cracks appeared on the ceiling, followed by a whooshing sound as cold wind circulated around the room.

I looked up. "Dad!" I yelled. "She's taking off the roof!"

"Helen, get back downstairs!" he shouted. "It's not safe!"

Suddenly the room filled with a blinding white light. I closed my eyes and stumbled out of the room and down the attic stairs. Eros and Apollo were there, cowering behind me.

We heard a loud crack, then gusts of freezing cold night air flooded the house. I crept back into Aphrodite's room. An expanse of inky purple sky came into view, exposing us to the chilly night air. The roof of our house was nowhere to be seen. I looked up and saw clouds swirling in the sky above.

Where the heck was our roof?!

"Dad, what has she done?" I shrieked. He paced up and down the room, careful not to trip over the roof debris.

"Quiet, Helen," he snapped. "I need to think!"

Typical Dad. Our roof had been blown into oblivion but he needed to think? There was no way the neighbours didn't hear that. I expected to hear the sirens of a fire engine any minute. How on earth would we explain this?

And more importantly, where was Aphrodite?

I saw a blur of white from the corner of my eye. Aphrodite hovered in mid-air, right where our roof would have been. I crept over to her while Apollo and Eros stayed behind me.

"Helen," Eros said, grabbing my shoulder. "Let's give her some time alone. She might still be angry."

"We don't have time, Eros." I said. "What if the neighbours come outside and see Aphrodite floating over our house? The Council would find out and then we'll lose everything."

Dad was still muttering to himself in the corner. It was up to me to talk Aphrodite down from the roof.

I shivered in my dressing gown and walked closer to the glowing white apparition hovering several metres above me. "Aphrodite, what did you do with the roof?" I asked. "Do you reckon we could . . . y'know . . . get it back?"

But she wasn't paying attention to me. She swayed in the air, making a strange choking sound. Was she sobbing?

"I just want to be free," she said, in between convulsive sobs that shook her whole body. My fear of her softened a little.

"But it's only thirty days, Aphrodite. Then you can leave the house, and—"

"I'm not talking about the house arrest! I want true freedom," she said. "There was a time when entire nations worshipped me for my powers. I want the world to know what I can do. And all he wants to do is stop me," Aphrodite said, throwing Dad a filthy look. He was too deep in concentration to notice. "I just want to make the world a more beautiful place," she continued. "It's my reason for being."

"But you can make the world more beautiful, Aphrodite," I said. "You just can't be famous for it. That's the deal, right?" Aphrodite was silent, but I could tell she was listening.

"Do you know how lucky you are? I wish I had a fraction of your powers. You have everlasting life, for goodness' sake!" I said. "And you're willing to throw that away over a bit of fame?"

"You'll never understand what it's like," Aphrodite snapped. "Walk in my shoes for just one day, and you'll never want to take them off. The feeling of being adored . . . it's utterly intoxicating."

It was infuriating. Aphrodite had so much already. And if she insisted on pursuing global fame and adoration, it would tear what little family I had left apart.

Tears of rage filled my eyes. "Then go! You've

destroyed our home, so why won't you leave?" I was done with her.

Aphrodite's eyes met mine. The light glowing through her body had faded.

"You know my mum is dead, Aphrodite!" The words stuck in my throat as I spat them out. "Why would you want to take away my only other parent?" I cried. "You. This family. You're all I have left," I said, tears rolling down my cheeks.

Eros, Apollo and Dad put their arms around me. "Aphrodite, you can tear this house apart if you like," Dad shouted up at her. "But you still can't leave it. Not until your house arrest is up."

That explained why Aphrodite hovered in mid-air. It was the closest she could get to leaving the house.

"Eros and Apollo, I'm going to need your help," Dad whispered. "She's draining her powers. Together, we can bring her down."

"Don't bother," Aphrodite said. She had to have the final word, as always.

We watched as she floated back down to the floor of her room. "Helen's right," she said, once her feet were fully on the ground. "There's no point in giving the odious Council members an excuse to strip us of our powers."

Dad took a deep breath, as though he was calming himself down. Eros hugged Aphrodite while the rest of us stood back, still dazed. I shivered in my pyjamas.

"We have some cleaning up to do," Dad said.

We all pitched in. Aphrodite used what was left of her powers to mend the furniture. Eros and I hung her clothes back up in the wardrobe. Apollo and Dad transformed the rubble on the bedroom floor into the roof.

By the time we finished, the only traces of the night's activity were the cracks in the ceiling corners. It was quite a satisfying task, actually. And the first time we'd worked together as a family.

Dad turned to me. "Helen, you need to be in bed." The cold air and excitement meant I was far from sleepy, but I wasn't about to argue with him.

"I have a plan," Dad said, once we were outside my bedroom. "I'm going to conjure high winds and a thunderstorm just over the house. It's a highly improbable event to occur naturally, but it should explain the noise to our neighbours."

"Do you think it will get back to the Council?" I asked.

Dad sighed. "We will find out soon," he said, squeezing my shoulder. I walked into my bedroom.

"And Helen?" Dad said. "Thank you for tonight. It takes a rare skill to get through to Aphrodite. I'm so pleased you were here to help."

"No worries, Dad." Weirdly, tonight had made me feel closer to my family than ever. A small part of me finally understood why Aphrodite acted the way she did. I nearly felt sorry for her.

# TWENTY-NINE

Dad stuck to his word. Everyone at school was talking about the freak storm on my road. It was kind of exciting, being so close to the source of school gossip (at least when it's not about Apollo).

I rushed out of the school gates, eager to meet my friends. They'd been a bit frosty with me since my disappearing act on Friday night – I never did make it to the sleepover. I knew I had to make it up somehow, so I promised I'd treat them to salted caramel lattes.

As we dawdled home with our lattes in hand, I noticed a message from Marco.

M: *How are you, beautiful Helen? x*

It was the first time he'd called me beautiful!!! I reread the message several times, trying to absorb the full gravity of what he'd said. He was calling me, Helen Thomas, beautiful. Not pretty or cute or nice.

But beautiful.

*H: I'm all good :) Bit tired cos I was so close to that storm. Soooo loud, it kept me up all night ha! x*

"What's the matter, Hels? You giving us the silent treatment?" Noor asked. I'd been quiet for a few minutes, enjoying Marco's last message.

"Huh? Oh, no. I'm fine," I said. "Marco's in the area so I'm gonna head back and meet him at Cafe Gio's."

I looked up. Three pairs of eyes drilled into me. What did I say?

"Seriously, Helen?" Noor said.

"What's the matter? We're all going home anyway," I said.

Daphne sighed. "It seems like you skip any chance to hang with us!"

"And you don't say anything in the group chat any more. Even when I post awesome GIFs!" Yasmin said.

I rolled my eyes. Why were they giving me such a hard time? If only they knew how much I had to deal with at home. Then maybe they'd understand.

Daphne gave me a hard look. "Look, Helen. We're dead excited that you have a boyfriend and all. But we're still your mates. You can't abandon us for him."

"Plus you've been so secretive lately," Yasmin said. "It's like you're hardly here at all."

I had been distant, I guess.

"I get it. I do, honestly," I said. "But I can't talk right now. I need to go—"

"Let me guess. You're going to meet Marco?" Daphne asked.

I couldn't deal with them right now.

"I'd better get going," I said, ducking away from the main road. They shouted after me, but I didn't turn around.

The cafe seemed even busier than normal, full of people my age and young families with prams escaping the winter cold. I found a table in the middle, right by the counter.

Marco walked in and caught my eye. For the first time, seeing his face didn't make me want to collapse with lust. I was worried that I'd really annoyed the girls. I had been distant lately, but so what? Did I need to reply to every single message in the group chat?

He smiled and mouthed "coffee?" at me from across the cafe. I nodded. Not that I'd be drinking it. As much as I tried, coffee still left a gross feeling in my mouth.

Marco returned with an espresso for him and a milky latte for me. "I thought this might be more to your taste," he said, after giving me a kiss on the lips. If it was any other time, I would have appreciated the sweet gesture. But the sickly smell of hot milk made me queasy.

"Helen, I saw the weirdest thing last night," he said, eyes wide with excitement.

"I'm fine, thanks, how are you?" I said, smiling. It was unlike him to forget the pleasantries.

He laughed. "Honestly, once you see this video you'll totally forgive me for being rude."

"Show me, then! Unless it's something gross?" I asked. You could never tell with boys.

"Not gross, just . . . extremely weird." He handed me his phone and I pressed play.

The video was shot at night, and I couldn't see much at first because it was dark. Then I noticed a column of white light hovering in the sky. The video zoomed out to show a house on a street.

My street.

Marco had seen and filmed Aphrodite floating above the house.

When I realized what I was watching, I nearly dropped the phone.

The video zoomed back in again, close enough to see a face and long dark hair. It wasn't recognizable as Aphrodite unless you knew her face.

Which thousands of people now did, thanks to her aggressive self-promotion.

Marco watched my face for my reaction, as I desperately tried to hold it together.

"Strange, right? I saw that round the corner from here. I thought I was losing my mind!"

"Um, it certainly looks strange," I said. "But I'm sure there's a rational explanation for it."

"You think? It sort of looks like a UFO. I bet some newspaper will pay good money for it," he said.

I wanted to throw up. If this video made it to the national press, someone was bound to recognize Aphrodite. And how on earth could she explain floating in mid-air? The Council would be on my family like a ton of bricks.

I had to fix this.

I'd never been any good at drama class. But here I was, about to persuade Marco that the video wasn't worth sharing. "Any idea what it could be?" I asked. I tore open a sachet of brown sugar and stirred it into my latte, just so he wouldn't notice my trembling hands.

"I mean . . . who knows!" he said. "That's why it's so exciting. You know that I'm a rational person. But even I can't explain this one."

I stayed quiet. The sound of hissing coffee machines and children crying filled the silence.

"I'd love to hear your theories?" Marco asked as I stirred my latte. I still couldn't bring myself to drink it.

"Listen, I know it looks dead weird," I started. "But there must be an explanation for it. We just don't know it yet."

"Like what?" Marco challenged.

I leaned back and shrugged. "Oh, I dunno. Fireworks, police helicopters, a laser light display from a nearby concert. You know there's a stadium five minutes down the road, right?"

He nodded but didn't look convinced. "I don't know . . . it didn't look like any fireworks I've ever seen. Plus, it doesn't explain why the roof of this house was completely destroyed! I saw it explode but didn't have time to capture it on camera."

Oh *crap*. So Marco had seen Aphrodite slam our roof into oblivion. Persuading Marco that it was some trick of the light was going to be even harder.

"Isn't this really close to your house? Did you hear anything?"

I shrugged. "I heard the storm, but that's about it. Maybe that's what you heard?"

The only way I could keep this secret was if Marco realized how stupid he sounded. And I felt terrible, because I knew he wasn't making it up.

"I know how it sounds. But I'm telling you this because I trust you." Marco reached across the table and put his hand on my arm. "You don't think I'm lying, do you?"

I couldn't look him in the eye. "It's not that I think you're lying, Marco. But you've got to admit, it does look a bit like. . ."

"Like what, Helen?"

"It looks like the video could be made up, or something. Just a bunch of computer special effects that anyone could download."

It was so cruel of me to make out that Marco was crazy or a liar.

Desperate times called for desperate measures.

"If I saw this video from anyone else, I would think the same as you. Probably some prank." He leaned in closer to me. "But if *you* showed me this video, I wouldn't for a second think that you faked it. Because I trust you."

I hated myself. And I hated that the hurt look on his face was because of me.

"I'm not saying you made it up, Marco. But that is how it will look if you take it to a newspaper. I'm just being honest."

Marco stared deep into my eyes. "Thank you for your honesty," he spat out. "But it's a chance I'll take."

"What do you mean?"

"I mean that I'm going to get a second opinion. I'll share it with a few friends tomorrow."

Oh god oh god oh GOD. Despite my best efforts, Marco was going to share this video. No one else could see it. They'd persuade him to post it online or send it to a journalist for sure.

Marco stood up and put his coat on. "I wonder if they'll accuse me of being a fraud, too." Then he grabbed his rucksack and walked out of the cafe.

I wanted to punch the table but I held it together. This video getting out would mean a one-way ticket to Mount Olympus.

I couldn't let that happen.

"Marco, wait!" I yelled, squeezing through the chairs and people. He heard me and waited at the door.

"Let's go somewhere we can be alone," I said.

It was cold and dark, and the threat of drizzle hung in the air. The playground was empty. I sat on the swings, ran my feet across the tarmac and launched my legs in the air. It felt soothing to swing back and forth a little. I could almost pretend I was a kid again, with no real problems.

I felt sick with worry. How on earth was I going to persuade him to delete this video?

"I don't know why we couldn't stay in the warm," Marco said, sitting on the swing next to me.

"This video. Have you sent it to anyone else?" I asked.

"No. No one else. Why?"

I took a deep breath. "Marco, this is going to sound strange. But you have to delete that video and never mention it again."

He looked confused. "What? Why?"

"Just . . . trust me. No one can ever see that video. I need you to delete it," I said. "Please."

"Helen, you're acting strange. Tell me why I need to delete it. Why is it so important that—"

"I can't!" I snapped. "I can't tell you. You'll think I'm a liar."

We were getting dangerously close to the truth. I couldn't let myself reveal it.

Marco's expression changed from confused to hurt. "I would never think that of you, Helen. I meant what

I said earlier. You can tell me anything." He turned to face me, taking his gloved hands in mine.

"Can't you just believe me and delete the video?" I pleaded.

"That's not the point, Helen," he said. "We can't have secrets hanging over our relationship. We need to trust each other, and there's no trust without honesty."

We were both silent, his brown eyes wide and open.

"So you really don't trust me," Marco said, breaking the silence. "Helen, I don't think I can do this any more."

I felt sick. "W what are you saying?"

He sighed. "I'm saying I can't have a girlfriend who doesn't trust me."

It was the first time he'd called me his girlfriend. And I couldn't enjoy the moment, because I was too busy thinking about how I'd persuade him not to share Aphrodite's video. Once again, my family found a way to ruin my life.

I'd messed up my friendship with the girls. I couldn't lose Marco. We'd just started to get to know each other. It could have been the beginning of something special.

"I don't even know where to begin." I looked down at my feet, the black of my shoes indistinguishable from the tarmac. Marco didn't say anything. He was waiting for me to fill the gap.

"So the video, right? There's a . . . thing floating in mid-air. That thing was floating above my house. I'm surprised you didn't recognize it."

Marco's face was impossible to read. He nodded, as if to urge me to carry on talking.

"And the bright thing floating? It wasn't a thing, exactly. It was a person. Sort of," I said.

I felt my face go hot. Any minute now, Marco was going to call me a compulsive liar and dump me on the spot.

"Are you very sure about that, Helen?" he asked me slowly and carefully, as though he was talking to a small child.

"I'll prove it." I unlocked my phone and brought up the video Marco sent me a few hours earlier. I paused it at the bit when Aphrodite's face came into view. "Can't you see? That's a person's face," I said.

"I can *see* that, Helen. Which is why it's so weird. But that doesn't explain why I need to keep this secret," he said. "What's the connection here?" he added in a softer voice.

I opened one of Aphrodite's YouTube videos on my phone and showed Marco. "That's her, right?" I said.

Marco's eyes widened. "It's uncanny," he whispered under his breath. "Why was this person hovering above your house?"

I took a deep breath. "Because she's my sister. Well, half-sister. And she's not a person, exactly. She's a god."

"So you're saying that your half-sister is a god, Helen. Have I got that right?" Marco kept his face and voice neutral. He was impossible to read. Did he think there was a glimmer of truth to what I was saying?

"I know it sounds mental. I probably sound mental. But it's the truth," I said. "And if this video gets out, my family will get into serious trouble." Just the thought warped my stomach into knots.

"I don't care if you believe me," I lied. "But all I ask is that you delete this video and keep this secret. I'll lose them all if you don't."

"What do you mean by god? Like, someone with superpowers? Immortality? I just don't—"

"I've already said too much," I said. But if sharing this secret meant that Marco would delete the video, then it was worth the risk.

"I can see how important this is to you, Helen. And because I care about you, I'm going to delete the video," he said. "See?" I watched as he deleted the video file from his phone.

"Swear you won't tell anyone about this, Marco? If it gets out, I'll know it was you. And I'll never trust you again."

Marco stood up from the swing and pulled me close to him. "I swear," he whispered in my ear.

It started to rain and the tarmac turned slick, but Marco pulled me closer into his coat.

What had I done?

# THIRTY

I was woken up at one a.m. by what sounded like World War Three in the living room. I couldn't hear exactly what was going on. But it sounded like we'd soon get a knock on the door from the neighbours if my family didn't pipe down.

I crept out on to the landing and tried to make out what they were shouting. Then I realized I wasn't five years old, this was my house and I was part of this family. I didn't have to creep about and eavesdrop on their discussions.

I followed the voices to the living room. I was getting serious déjà vu vibes. What if Aphrodite had tried to mastermind another jailbreak? I couldn't deal with another night of *that*.

"What's going on?" I asked. We had a full house. Dad, Aphrodite, Eros and Apollo stood in the living room, deep in discussion.

There was someone else there, too. A man I'd never seen before. He was tall, head and shoulders above everyone else in the room, and totally bald. Even though he was dressed head to toe in navy-blue Lycra, I could tell straight away he was a god. He had that air about him.

"Unless someone's going to write me a sick note and let me have a lie-in tomorrow, I need you lot to keep it down," I said. "I've got school in the morning!"

Dad turned to look at me, but no one else reacted. It was like my voice barely registered. I was sick of this. What was so important that they could flat-out ignore me?

Their focus was on the tall, bald god. And he was looking annoyed at the interruption.

"This isn't one of your tricks, is it, Hermes?" Aphrodite said.

So that's who the towering bald guy was. Hermes, the messenger god.

Hermes smiled, and something about it didn't look right. It was the same smile someone gives you before they chuck a water balloon in your face or trip you up in the corridor at school. It was a smile that said "I know something you don't". If Hermes was here on the Council's instructions, I doubted that he had anything good to say. "Dearest Aphrodite," Hermes said, his lip curling into a sinister smile. "I'm only ever on earth for business. Rest assured that this is genuine." He held up a scroll.

Aphrodite swore under her breath.

"Oh, don't look so down," Hermes added. "You might enjoy coming back. Mount Olympus is lush and verdant all year round. Certainly nicer than this dump."

*Hey.* London might be dirty and drizzly and full of deformed pigeons, but it was my home. At least it was for now.

"That's my city you're talking about!" I said. Not expecting anyone to hear or notice me. Hermes raised one eyebrow. "Well. Enjoy it while you can, little girl. You may not be here for much longer."

He checked his watch. "If you'll excuse me, I have another delivery to make to the Underworld in just a few hours. And traffic on the River Styx is ghastly at this time of year."

"You can leave through the back door, Hermes," Dad said. "And please be inconspicuous," he added.

Hermes laughed. "I think it's too late for discretion, Father," he said, and walked towards the kitchen.

As soon as he left, Aphrodite sighed dramatically. "I cannot *stand* him. Did you see how smug he looked?"

"You know Hermes has wanted to see our downfall for centuries," Apollo said. "The guy is basically the Council's messenger boy. Surely he must be going out of his mind with boredom running their errands? I know I would be."

"Enough gossiping," Dad said in a quiet voice that somehow shook the whole room. Apollo and Aphrodite stopped chattering.

"Helen, come here and sit down, please," Dad said. "I was going to tell you in the morning, but you're up now." I perched on the edge of the sofa.

"I'll get straight to the point. The Council has ruled that we must leave London and return to Mount Olympus for judgement. Immediately."

I nodded, too terrified to ask why.

I had a sinking feeling I already knew the answer to that one.

"The Council found out about Aphrodite's destructive episode. It was the last straw, apparently," Dad said.

My heart beat so loud that I could hear it in my eardrums.

"Someone out for a quick buck recorded a video," Apollo said. "They caught the whole thing on camera and sold the video to a newspaper. Can you believe it?"

I tried not to cry. Had Marco done exactly what he promised he wouldn't?

"What's even more unbelievable is that the Council thought it was genuine," Aphrodite said. "Any runt with a laptop could've rustled up a fake video."

"Except it wasn't actually fake, was it, Mother?" Eros said sheepishly.

So it was happening. My boyfriend had just ruined my life. I wanted to be alone to sob and punch my pillow.

"The Council must have eyes everywhere," Eros muttered.

Dad sighed. "Everyone has a camera in their back pockct, these days. We should count ourselves lucky that no one recognized Aphrodite."

"But don't you think it's strange that someone just happened to be outside the house in the middle of the night?" said Apollo. "I wouldn't put it past the Council to send their spies to check on us."

"Apollo!" Dad yelled. I jumped out of my skin and everyone else looked stunned. Dad's rage went from simmering under the surface to exploding. "It would behove you to accept some responsibility for this. You and your sister."

Any moment now, they'd find out that Marco shared the video. They'd find out that my boyfriend, a regular mortal, knew our earth-shattering secret.

I had to tell them. The thought terrified me. But I wanted them to find out from me and not anyone else.

I took a deep breath, and burst into tears. Big, thick sobs. It was so embarrassing and went on for a good few minutes. Dad responded by leaping off the sofa and turning the kettle on. I think a few decades in Britain had taught him that tea is the cure for all distress. Aphrodite rubbed my shoulder with what I assume was meant to be tenderness, but felt more like a kneading motion. I'm pretty sure it left bruises. Eros got up to give me a cuddle and I instantly felt ten years old again.

"You don't have to say anything until you're ready," said Eros as I cried into his T-shirt.

By the time Dad came back with a too-milky cup of tea, I had calmed down enough to talk.

"Whatever you have to say, Helen, you won't be in trouble. You know that, don't you?" Dad said.

I nodded and braced myself. For all his understanding looks now, I knew he wouldn't like what

I was going to say next. There was no point trying to skirt around the truth. I had to be honest.

I decided to break down my announcement into a list. I could handle lists.

"I guess there are three things you should know. The first is that I've been seeing a guy called Marco. We've been spending a lot of time with each other since New Year's Eve," I said. "He's from Greece and taking a gap year in London."

Dad pursed his lips so hard that they practically disappeared. Aphrodite swore under her breath. Eros glared at her.

"Mother, keep your thoughts to yourself. This is Helen's announcement to make," he said.

"It gets worse," I said. "The other thing is that he filmed the video. He promised that he wouldn't show anyone. But," I said, holding back the tears, "he lied!" The reminder of Marco's betrayal made me cry even harder.

"You're not pregnant, then?" Dad asked.

"WHAT?" I shrieked. "Why the heck would you think I was pregnant?"

"Well, you looked so upset. And the first thing you did was tell us about your secret older boyfriend. I suppose, as a father, I just assumed the worst."

"I've got to admit, you had me worried there for a second too, darling," said Aphrodite.

"And me. Sorry," Eros said.

"Well, there's more. The third thing you need to know." This was the big one. Telling the truth was going to hurt, but I had to be brave. "I tried everything to stop Marco from sharing the video. So I thought that . . . that if I told him why he shouldn't share it, he wouldn't. I trusted him."

Four pairs of eyes stared back at me, waiting. But they must have known what I was about to say.

I took a deep breath. "So I told him the truth. About us. Where you're from and what . . . what I am."

Telling the truth didn't make me feel any better. I had betrayed them all.

I'd never felt more ashamed. The longer they were silent, the fiercer my cheeks burned with embarrassment. I wanted to slip out of the front door and never return.

"Aren't you angry at me?" I asked between sniffles. Anger I could take. Dad's rage or Aphrodite's spite was exactly what I deserved.

But I couldn't deal with their silent disappointment.

Dad nodded, his lips pursed so tightly they looked like a straight line. "Yes, I'm angry. I'm angry at my children for breaking the rules, including you, Helen," he said. "Above all, I'm angry at myself. Moving you in with us was a grave mistake."

I sniffed. "What's that supposed to mean?"

"My duty is to protect you and I've failed." Dad looked the most serious I'd ever seen him. It scared me.

"But it's going to be OK, isn't it, Dad? Marco didn't tell the newspapers that you were gods. He'd look crazy if he did!"

The gods exchanged glances and shifted in their seats. Eros put his arm around me and hugged me even tighter.

"I don't think you understand, Helen. The Council are serious about enforcing the rules. Deadly serious," Dad said.

What did that mean? The other gods were way too quiet.

Dad sighed. "The first rule: Gods must not reveal their immortal identity unless there are extraordinary circumstances. I'm afraid this counts as rule-breaking, Helen."

My heart pounded dull and heavy in my chest. "Yes, but Marco won't tell anyone else. He promised," I whispered pathetically.

"It doesn't matter, Helen. The Council already

know," Dad said. He produced a small cream scroll from his back pocket. The same one that Hermes delivered. "This is the official message from the Council." He unrolled the scroll at both ends, and we all leaned in to read ... absolutely nothing. The scroll was blank.

Suddenly, the paper flickered into life. Lines of handwriting appeared, floated off the page and hung in mid-air. The writing slowly expanded, becoming larger and larger, until it could be read from the other side of the room.

Devastated as I was, I couldn't help but feel impressed. It looked like something from a sci-fi movie.

The words said:

**The Rules were put in place in order to maintain harmony between gods and mortals.**

**To break these rules is to disrupt a careful balance designed to protect mortals from harm.**

**It has come to our attention that Rule One has been broken.**

**You must come to Mount Olympus and prepare for judgement.**

"I wouldn't be so sure he kept that promise," Apollo said grimly. He was the only one who looked angry.

"Apollo, not now!" Dad said.

"Do you realize what you've done, Helen? Thanks to your lover boy, we will never see earth again!" Apollo spat.

"W-w-what?" I stuttered.

Apollo smirked. "Don't you get it? Cranus and the Council will push for the maximum punishment. We will be banished to Mount Olympus for the rest of our lives. And that's if the Council are in a good mood. If they're not, then—"

"QUIET!" Dad roared, his face puce with rage. Apollo fell silent.

"Tell me. Then what? What happens?" I asked. Despite Eros having his arm around me, I suddenly felt cold.

"Then we'll be stripped of our powers and immortality. It will kill us instantly," Aphrodite said. Her eyes filled with tears. It was the most human she'd ever looked.

It terrified me.

"But that's not fair!" I gasped. "This was my fault. Why should you be punished for it?"

Dad smiled weakly. "The Council won't see it that way. You were in our protection, and we're all responsible for one another. We will be tried and sentenced as a family."

"How long do we have? Before the trial?" I asked.

"We leave for Mount Olympus on Friday night," Dad said.

Two days. I had just two days before my life changed for ever. The tears returned with full force, and I sobbed harder than ever before.

"I'm so sorry," I mumbled between sobs.

Dad looked at me sadly. "So am I."

# THIRTY-ONE

The morning after, I got ready for school in a stupor. My head swam with all the ways that I'd messed up in the past few days. I'd betrayed my family for a *boy*.

Plus, I'd have to tell my mates that Marco and I were over, too. That's if they were even still talking to me – I hadn't heard from any of them since our bust-up.

I didn't know how I was going to get through the day. My friends would definitely know that something was up, but what was I meant to say? *Sorry I'm not myself today – turns out that my dream boy betrayed my entire family for a bit of cash from the local newspaper.*

When I came downstairs for a quick breakfast and Dad was there, whistling to himself as he made his morning espresso, I thought he'd officially lost it. How could he act normal at a time like this?

"Having a day off work?" I asked. Dad was wearing jeans and a polo shirt. Hardly scruffy, but definitely not the sort of outfit he usually wore to the university.

"Helen, darling, how's your day looking? Any important lessons or assignments due?" he asked.

I shook my head. Homework was the last thing on my mind. How could he pester me about school at a time like this? Did I imagine Hermes giving us a warning from the Council last night? We had much bigger things to worry about.

"Excellent! Then get changed into your normal clothes and meet me back down here at nine thirty a.m., please. I'll deal with your school," Dad said, punching buttons on his phone. "We're going on a trip together."

Huh? Was this my dad actively helping me to skive off school?

I sent the girls a message saying I was off sick (which was technically true – I didn't have any physical symptoms, but my brain was mashed). I could tell them that Dad randomly decided on a surprise day trip, but then I'd have to explain why I'd been having such a tough time lately. The last thing I wanted to think about.

Gosh. Lying before I'd even left the house.

I went downstairs to find Dad waiting by the front door. We got the tube into Central London. I reminded Dad that I didn't have the chance to finish breakfast, so needed to eat some food. We stopped by a cool-looking coffee shop with wooden benches. To eat, I ordered three custard tarts (two for now, one for the road). Dad stuck to his usual order of an espresso. Dull as ever.

Being in town on a school day was such a novelty, but there was still a Mount Olympus–sized elephant in the room. I picked at my custard tart while Dad read the newspaper. Was he looking out for mentions of Aphrodite's video?

I went to take an Instagram photo of the cute pastries, but Dad reminded me that might not be a good idea. "Helen, please refrain from using social media for just one day. Not only would I like your full attention, but it may also well give away the fact that you aren't in bed recovering from a tummy bug," Dad said.

He was right. I'd have to save the Insta-brags for later. "Is that what you told the school?"

"I did. It should explain your absence for the trial over the next few days."

The trial. This weekend. It hovered over my

thoughts like a rain cloud. We'd have to talk about it eventually. But I didn't want to ruin our first day out together since . . . I couldn't remember when.

After our coffees we walked down Oxford Circus, past all of the shops. For a minute, I got all excited and thought Dad was going to take me on a wild shopping spree. But then I remembered that this was Dad. The only shopping spree he'd consider would be one in a dusty second-hand bookshop.

We carried on walking for about fifteen minutes, took a left turn and then I realized where we were headed to because the building was smack bang in front of me. The British Museum.

When I lived with Mum and had my monthly day trips with Dad, we nearly always went to this place. At the time, I thought Dad loved it so much because the entry was free and he was tight. Now, it made much more sense. The place is stuffed with ancient statues and paintings from all over the world. Including Greece. For Dad, it's the closest thing to a time capsule. He perked up as we walked through the grand columns towards the entrance.

"You know, darling, it's been years since I've been back to this place. I think the last time was with you," Dad said.

We both remembered the time well, then. It was the last normal day out I had with Dad because Mum had the accident not long after and everything changed for ever. I just nodded in response.

"Anyway, the best thing about coming back now is that I can give you one of my special tours! You wouldn't believe the gossip I have on some of these statues," Dad said with a wink.

The tour turned out to be our most fun trip to the museum yet. I got to drop by the unwrapped mummy, an exhibit that terrified me as a kid, and see that it didn't look quite as scary as I remembered. The thought of the trial didn't go away, but it wasn't all I was thinking about either. Anything had to be better than sitting in school and putting on a brave face.

When we reached the Parthenon exhibit, Dad seemed to get a bit emotional.

"You should have seen this temple in its heyday, Helen. Imagine a huge gold-and-ivory statue of Athena in the centre, surrounded by water pools sparkling in the sunlight," he said. "On feast days, the scent of roasted meat would fill the air. Athena's priestesses were the most powerful women in the city of Athens, you know."

"Just fascinating! You sure do know your stuff," said

a woman's voice with an American twang. We both turned to find an old couple hanging on to Dad's every word.

Dad even went a little wild in the gift shop: pyramid-shaped erasers for me and a book on the history of London's sewers for him. He insisted it was an intriguing subject. I said I'd just take his word for it.

Before we knew it, it was lunchtime. We walked around for a bit before deciding on a Japanese restaurant near the museum. I ordered my favourite thing to eat at Japanese restaurants: a plate of chicken katsu curry bigger than my head. Dad swapped his usual black coffee for a pot of jasmine tea.

"You're not eating anything, Dad?" I asked after the waiter noted down our orders.

"No, darling. I only eat so that my dining companion won't raise any eyebrows. It would look very strange indeed if, say, when I took Lisa to dinner, I sat there and ate nothing."

"Nothing like Apollo, then," I said smirking. Maria still complained about the size of his appetite. "Where does that food even go?"

"Food does much the same thing to you as it does to us," Dad said. "Some foods can boost our energy, and too much of other foods can affect us too. The only difference is that food isn't essential for our existence."

So Aphrodite really was on to something with those organic green smoothies every morning.

"While I very much enjoy the tastes and smells of food, and the joy of sharing meals with the people I love, it feels somewhat distasteful to eat something I don't need. Especially when so many people go without," Dad continued. I'd never thought of it that way.

"Anyway, one of the many benefits of the modern world is that far fewer people are hungry. It's heartening to see humanity improve and develop over the centuries."

I put my chopsticks down. It annoyed me so much when Dad brought up this conversation. Humanity may have "developed" since the days of no soap or plumbing, but there are still some terrible things going on in the world.

As if he predicted my incoming rant, Dad held up one palm to stop me from interrupting.

"Yes, yes, I know. Humanity is far from perfect. Fewer people may be starving, but inequality is rife the world over. Helen, you don't have to tell me. I've seen it all," Dad said. "But I have to give credit where it's due.

The world is a far kinder place to live now than it was three thousand years ago."

While Dad flagged down the waiter for the bill, I wondered what would have happened if Mum had never jumped on her bike. Or if that driver had never knocked her over, or if she'd held on until the ambulance arrived. Would she be here with Dad and me, tutting because I decided to eat meat even though she raised me vegetarian? Would I even have a relationship with Dad beyond monthly trips to museums? No Maria, Aphrodite or Eros. No creaking house filled with ancient artefacts. No gods interfering with my life.

No trial. It didn't take long for my thoughts to return to that. The restaurant was practically empty after the lunchtime rush. My questions couldn't wait any longer. But where to begin?

"Dad. I've been meaning to ask. Why does Cranus have it in for you?" I phrased my question carefully. Even though the restaurant was practically empty after the lunchtime rush, I didn't want to risk being overheard.

Dad sipped his tea. "Some years ago, Cranus's wife came to me for counsel. She was desperate for a separation, and he wouldn't agree to it," he said.

"I overruled Cranus and assisted her in starting a new life far away from him. Unfortunately, he remains bitter about it to this day."

"So he blames you for stealing his wife?"

"Something like that, yes," he said. "Ever since, Cranus has been looking for the perfect opportunity to pounce."

My heart sank. "And Cranus is on the Council, right?"

Dad nodded. "He's their most powerful and long-standing member. Ultimately the Council strives for fairness, but Cranus holds a good deal of power. It will make our trial . . . challenging."

I started to wish I hadn't asked. Was it better to go into the trial knowing what to expect?

I was dreading it either way.

"I don't know how best to prepare you for the days ahead, Helen," Dad said, as if reading my thoughts. "But I'll answer any questions you have."

"What will I have to do? At the trial?"

A waiter brought a fresh pot of jasmine tea for Dad and took my empty plate. We were quiet until he disappeared back into the kitchen.

"A trial – especially one involving us – is quite the event back home," Dad said. He was also being careful with his words. "Many people will be interested in the trial. And interested in you, too."

"Why?" I didn't have immortal life or special powers. I was just another half-mortal child of a god. There have been plenty of those in history.

Dad looked surprised at my question. "Because you're a child of Zeus." Did he realize how pompous he sounded talking about himself in the third person? "But there's another layer of intrigue. You are on trial. I imagine it's the most exciting news to reach that sleepy little realm in centuries."

The idea that I was known on Mount Olympus was too surreal for me to grasp. "So I'm, like, famous there?"

Dad nodded.

"So how will we get to Mount Olympus, anyway?" I asked. I imagined whirling portals to another dimension, or winged horses flying us to a cloud-topped mountain.

Dad snorted like I'd said something silly. "We don't, my dear. Mount Olympus will come to us. Our technology allows for the trial to happen in both realms at the same time. None of us want to visit Mount Olympus unless it's strictly necessary, Helen."

Oh. I felt slightly deflated. "Right. So where do we go?"

"The trial will take place in a court of mortals, somewhere in London. Where exactly will be determined shortly."

In just a few days, I'd be in a court room facing the Council. It began to feel less like something happening in a crazy fever dream, and more like real life.

I wanted to be as prepared as possible, even if talking about this trial made me feel sick with nerves. "Dad, what else can you tell me about this trial?"

"Forgive me. I forget that you know nothing about the legal system back home," Dad said. "We will face the twelve Council members. Now, an interesting fact about them is that their gowns signify their rank. The longer they've been serving, the darker the gown."

Here we go with the not-so-interesting facts. I should have asked Athena.

"Stop there, Dad. Can you tell me stuff that's, you know, relevant?" I asked.

"Right. Of course. The trial will last for two days and we can't leave the court at all while it lasts. So be prepared for an overnight stay, as well as a dinner with some of our most senior officials."

"Fine," I said, nodding. Usually the thought of a dinner with Mount Olympians (who I can only assume are as stuffy as Dad) would have me rolling my eyes.

But it didn't feel important.

"And we gods need to submit a written testimony, which is our statement of defence," Dad said.

"And what about me? How do I submit my testimony?"

Dad put down his cup of jasmine tea. "It's a bit trickier for you, Helen. We've discussed it as a family, and feel your testimony would have more impact if it was a speech."

It was so typical of the gods to have a family discussion and decide the best course of action without asking me. Was I a member of this family or not?

I folded my arms. "Care to explain why?"

"The Council may take more pity on you, and the family, if you're able to present a powerful speech."

Me? Give a powerful speech? I can't even read a poem in English without stumbling over a line.

"Dad, I'm not sure I'm the powerful-speech-giving type," I said.

He sighed. "I'd like to say you have a choice in the matter. But this is the most peril our family has faced in centuries. To be frank, it's a matter of life or death."

"Is this your way of trying to take the pressure off?! Believe me. Not helping!"

"Helen, I wouldn't ask you if I didn't think you

weren't capable. Can you trust me?"

Dad could be eccentric and strange and up-in-the-clouds, but I did trust him. I nodded.

"Good thing I've got you all on my side," I said, trying hard to be positive. "I could definitely do with some help putting together this speech."

Dad shook his head. "We can't help you, Helen. You must prepare everything on your own. We can't be seen to favour you, or anyone on trial. It could result in a much harsher sentence."

The whole conversation felt like being in a boxing ring. Blow after blow rained down.

But we hadn't got to the worst bit yet.

"And if we're found guilty. Something really bad happens, right?" I tried to sound calm, but I was a bag of nerves. The rich meal churned in my stomach.

"We could be banished to life on Mount Olympus or stripped of our immortality, which would prove fatal eventually. Honestly, I'm not sure which is worse."

"Is Mount Olympus that bad?"

"I can't begin to explain how banal immortality is. There's no stimulation or challenges of any sort on Mount Olympus. Being consigned there for eternity is a fate worse than death," he said quietly.

I wanted to ask what that meant for me, someone with

no powers to strip. But Dad was on to the next subject.

"Right!" he said with a loud clap. "I think we should walk off that lunch, and catch a movie. Do you know, it's been years since I've been to the cinema?"

I somehow moved my legs and made it to the cinema. The action film Dad chose was packed with explosions and special effects but I couldn't concentrate on the film.

All I could think about was the trial. And what would happen if the Council found us guilty.

The movie zipped by, leaving me with a headache from the extra-large screen and booming speakers. Luckily Dad did most of the talking as we walked to the tube station.

I was more than happy to be Dad's therapist for half an hour. It was the least I could do. Goodness knows he must be feeling torn-up after finding out his own offspring betrayed the family for a shot at fame.

Or to keep from getting dumped.

"I wish I could say that Eros's love spell on Lisa was the worst thing they've done," Dad said, linking his arm with mine as we walked over Waterloo Bridge. We took in the landmarks: the London Eye, Big Ben and the River Thames. The view was stunning, but the iconic buildings aren't part of the London I love. They're not home to me.

"Worse than what I did?" I asked.

"The Council will believe your crime to be the worst," Dad said. I flinched at the word "crime". "But interfering with matters of the heart can cause untold harm."

"You must be so angry with them," I muttered.

"They are the only family I have, and we must endure this together. I only hope the experience hasn't interfered with Lisa."

"Have you spoken to her recently?"

"No, and I probably never will. Once the enchantment wears off, her memories of me will appear very dim until they vanish altogether. If I contact her now, it could be very confusing for her. I've made that mistake before."

Dad stopped walking and turned to take in the view. "I've been in London for nearly seventy years, and I still think it's a breathtakingly beautiful city. Enjoy it while you can," he said with a sad smile.

The thought that I may never return to London terrified me. I appreciated Dad taking me on one final day out. But all it did was remind me of how much I stood to lose.

"Do you think we'll be found guilty?" I asked. It had been playing on my mind all day.

"It's impossible for me to say, Helen," Dad said. "It's

not a feeling I'm used to having. This uncertainty."

That didn't fill me with confidence. "I don't like uncertainty either," I said. "I'm really, really sorry, by the way. About . . . everything."

Dad tightened his jaw. "I'm sorry too. I should have been there for you, Helen."

I couldn't bear to think about it. Having to stand up and tell a courtroom how I naively trusted Marco with my family's secret was bad enough.

But what if it didn't work? My family could be stripped of their powers. And I'd be banished to Mount Olympus.

I'd lose my friends, Grandma Thomas and everything else I'd ever loved. The gods would be destroyed.

I'd be completely alone.

The realization filled me with an intense, grief-like pain. Only sharper and more urgent.

Dad wiped away the tears streaming down my face and wrapped his coat around me while I cried into his jumper.

I wanted to dissolve into a thousand pieces and be whipped away by the freezing wind, never to be seen again.

# THIRTY-TWO

Dear Mum,

Most fourteen-year-olds get into trouble for skiving PE or forging a sick note. But me? I betrayed my family.

This weekend, I'll be facing the Council to fight for our right to live on earth. In the case of Dad and the gods, it's the right to live at all. To say I'm jittery would be an understatement. I'd take a month of detention over this in a heartbeat.

At least I won't have to deal with travelling to Mount Olympus on top of everything else. In fact, we won't be travelling any further than a *few stops on the tube. Instead, the trial will take place in the Royal Courts of Justice. It's famous, apparently. Have you heard of it, Mum? I'm not sure if I'm relieved or disappointed. Obviously, I'm happy every day that my feet stay in the mortal dimension. But a part of me was looking forward to seeing this enchanted place I've heard so much about.*

*No matter where the trial is, I still have the humiliating task of talking about my betrayal. In front of everyone. I'll have to tell an entire court room about the way Marco manipulated me into revealing my family's secret. I'll look like a naive little girl. My embarrassment levels will be off the chart! It'll be a miracle if I don't collapse into a ball of sweat and shame right there on the witness stand.*

*I know that it isn't all my fault. Aphrodite went ballistic and nearly destroyed the house. Apollo got himself on national TV. Even Eros broke the rules by messing with Lisa's head. But I was the only one stupid enough to share our secret. With a boy. And telling Marco about the gods broke the most important rule of all. It could cost them their lives.*

At least the fear of being banished to Mount Olympus and losing my family for ever outweighs the pain of heartbreak. I've cried my body weight in salty tears, but not one of them was sadness at losing Marco. He showed his true colours by betraying my family.

But what if the worst happens? That I do all of the above and we're found guilty anyway. The gods could have their powers stripped, which would be fatal. I'd lose them for ever.

It would make me an orphan. And I'd be forced to live out the rest of my days on Mount Olympus.

The thought makes me want to hide under the nearest table and wait until the trial blows over. But I know that's impossible.

There's nowhere I can run. Nowhere to hide.

All I can do is focus on my testimony. It's the only thing in my control. If I can persuade the Council that we still deserve to live on earth, there's a shot I won't end up losing everything.

And it's not just my future at stake. If I'm banished to Mount Olympus, I'll never see Grandma Thomas again. She's already lost one daughter. I don't know if she could bear the pain *of losing her granddaughter, too. In a few days, the trial will be over and my fate will be sealed.*

*I can do this. I have to do this.*

*I'm sorry this letter isn't quite so cheerful this time, Mum. Maybe next time I write to you I'll have something good to share. I wish you were here.*

*Love for ever,*

*Helen xxx*

# THIRTY-THREE

Pants. Toothbrush. Hair gel. Testimony notes. I ran through the checklist in my head as I packed. It all seemed so pointless. So what if I didn't have spare socks? The trial was going ahead and my fate would be decided in a couple of days.

I rooted through the back of my wardrobe to find my overnight bag, and saw something I'd long forgotten. It was the memory box that Mum and I made together.

Whenever we went somewhere special, we kept a memento and tucked it into a shoebox. I flicked through the contents. Seashells and grubby coins nestled alongside passport-sized photos and ticket stubs. I fished out a small sheet of green paper – it was a printed flyer for the *Bugsy Malone* show I put on while at drama school one summer holiday.

I hated every minute of it. I hated having to do drama while my school friends went to the same play centre. I hated being the only black girl in the class. And I hated having to do anything that drew attention to myself.

But Mum's friend was a teacher at the school and got me a heavily discounted place. For Mum, it was a no-brainer.

The only good thing about that show was the outfit Mum made for me. I was one of the lowly chorus girls, which, to be quite honest, suited me just fine. No lines to remember, just a rendition of the Charleston that we choreographed during lunchtimes.

Mum wouldn't go to the costume store for the flapper outfit, like the other girls in the show. "Why spend good money when I've got a perfectly fine sewing machine at home?" she said.

I knew better than to argue with Mum but I was dreading it. "Why spend good money when I've got a perfectly fine oven at home?" was something she said whenever we passed Pizza Hut and I begged for a Hawaiian. Mum would roll up her sleeves when we got home and present me with her version of a pizza. Just for the record, broccoli and chickpeas should never be on a pizza.

So when Mum decided my dress was going to be a DIY job, I got a little nervous. But I had no reason to be. It was the most beautiful dress in the show by far. The sequinned fabric shimmered purple and blue in the light. I'm sure the fabric had higher aspirations than to grace a clumsy eight-year-old, but it did the job. With a touch of scented roll-on body glitter and a matching shawl over my spaghetti-strapped shoulders, I'd never felt more glamorous.

I can't remember much about the play or my performance (other than vomiting with stage fright). I got ketchup from the after-play hot dogs on my shawl and the dress was dispatched to the bottom of a cupboard. It probably got lost in the house move, after Mum's accident.

Looking through the box made me feel a strange mix of happy and sad. Weirdly, it made me feel just as connected to Mum as writing the letters did.

A knock on the door interrupted me, and I rushed to put my memory box away. I didn't want anyone else to see it – this was between me and Mum.

"Come in," I yelled, once the box was hidden away.

Aphrodite poked her head through the door. I'd

barely talked to her since she destroyed our house. But now was as good a time as ever to break the wall of silence between us.

"Did Father tell you about the dress code for the trial?" she asked.

There was a dress code? Just another one of the crucial details he forgot. What else had he forgotten to tell me?

I shook my head. "Nope. I was just going to wear one of my old church dresses."

"Typical," she muttered. "Unsurprisingly, the fuddie-duddies at the Council prefer if those on trial wear traditional attire. Luckily, I have a few gowns in your size."

Aphrodite placed a bundle of cream cotton on my bed. They turned out to be three maxi-dresses in a toga style.

"Um, thanks and all. But it might be a bit cold for this?" I said. Those old courtrooms looked like they might be draughty (or at least they did on TV).

"I can assure you that the court will be temperature-controlled, Helen." Aphrodite smiled. "Sometimes I forget that this all must be extremely strange for you."

Was she showing empathy for another living being? Now *that* was strange.

I shrugged. Strange, inconvenient, so terrifying the thought made my heart pound: all of the above applied.

"You should know that I . . . well, I think you're very brave. Braver than you realize," she said.

"The Council summoned me so I kind of had no choice. You do know that, right?" I said, rolling up the gowns to fit into my suitcase.

Aphrodite nodded. "I know. And I also know that you're taking this trial very well."

"Are you forgetting that this is my mistake to fix? If I hadn't said anything to Marco, then—"

"You were trying to save us, Helen. If Apollo and I hadn't been so foolish, this would never have happened. Believe me when I say that this isn't your fault."

When she said that, the guilt I'd been lugging around didn't seem to feel so heavy.

I sighed. "Thanks. I hope the Council feel the same way."

# THIRTY-FOUR

"Helen? Are you up? It's time to get ready for the trial." It was Eros, nudging me awake at an ungodly hour. At least he had the good sense to come armed with a cup of tea.

I showered, got dressed, nearly tripped going down the stairs (note to self: watch out for the toga), and met my family in the kitchen for breakfast.

Their ability to look fresh-faced at all times was especially grating at seven a.m. Aphrodite's long dark hair cascaded in blow-dried waves over her shoulders, and Apollo's skin glowed radiantly. I, on the other hand, could do nothing more than scrape my hair into a bun. Apollo, Eros, Dad and Athena all wore traditional togas, too. Unlike me, they didn't look as though they were playing fancy dress. The togas suited them.

The kitchen was strangely quiet. Everyone seemed absorbed in their own world. Apart from Athena, who was in bossy-pants mode.

"Good morning, Helen," she said as I poured myself a bowl of cereal. "Do eat quickly. I'd like to take you through the itinerary before the cars arrive."

"It's too early to be this organized," I muttered under my breath.

Athena didn't say anything. Instead, she slapped a printout on the table in front of me. I cast my eyes over it as I crunched my cornflakes.

## Helen's Trial Itinerary

### Friday a.m.

Depart from home in chauffeured cars for the Royal Courts of Justice.

Arrive at Royal Courts of Justice. Entry through the side entrance *only*.

The audience, Council and judge are seated. The trial begins promptly with a review of the charges.

Lord Zeus, Lady Aphrodite, Lord Apollo and Lord Eros provide their testimony.

Lady Helen provides her testimony.

**Friday p.m.**

**The trial resumes for cross-examination from the Council.**

**Closing dinner with Mount Olympus officials.**

"Now, Helen, it's crucial that you arrive at the correct entrance for nine o'clock," Athena said. "We wouldn't want you getting lost and starting the trial late. The judge, like all of us, will appreciate punctuality."

"Why would I get lost?" I asked. Did she really not trust me to go through doors on my own?

Athena did that tight fake smile again. "You won't! But you will be travelling in your own car, so might not enter the court at exactly the same time as us."

I narrowed my eyes. "Why do I get my own car?"

Dad cleared his throat. "It's just something the Council have insisted on, Helen. Perhaps they prefer that the key witness not travel with the defendants. It may look a tad strange."

My spoon landed in my cereal bowl with a sharp rattle. "But they know we live together, right? And we're related?"

"Like Father said, it's just a formality," Athena said. "I wouldn't dwell on it too much, Helen."

No, of course she wouldn't. Athena, Dad and the rest of the gods had no idea what it felt like to be an outsider in their own family. It made seemingly unimportant things (like, I don't know, not even being allowed to travel in the same car) feel like a way bigger deal.

I didn't have much longer to simmer because the cars soon arrived at our door. I collected my overnight bag, put my parka over my thin cotton toga and climbed into the first of two sleek black cars with tinted windows. Sore as I was about travelling alone, it did feel kind of exciting to have my own chauffeur-driven car.

Unfortunately Dad insisted on triple-checking my seat belt and waving at the car until it reached the end of our road. You know, just in case I was feeling too much like an adult.

The car wound its way through to the centre of London, pausing from time to time in rush-hour traffic. I stared out of the window, wishing I at least had the distraction of my phone (strictly forbidden in the courthouse apparently, so I'd left it at home).

What would I be doing if this was a normal day?

Probably meeting Yasmin, Noor and Daphne at our spot near the gates and chatting on the way to double English. If they didn't hate me. I hadn't seen them since I'd abandoned them for Marco, and I felt like such an idiot. Was it weird that I wanted to be at school? I pushed the thought out of my head. The trial was happening whether I liked it or not. It wouldn't help to fantasize about being somewhere else.

"Miss? Where would you like to get out?" the driver asked, interrupting my pity party.

I looked out of the window and saw the historic building towering above me. A black-and-gold coat of arms glinted on the wall, with the words "Royal Courts of Justice" beneath it. I had arrived.

"Miss? I can't stop for long," the driver said.

"Um, here's fine." I grabbed my bag and got out. The car wove its way back into the stream of traffic and was out of sight in seconds. I looked up at the building. With its turrets, arches and sandy-grey stone walls, it looked more like a fairy-tale castle than a courthouse.

The gods were nowhere to be seen, so I had to find this side entrance myself. I took my crumpled itinerary out of my pocket. But it didn't offer any more clues about where this side entrance would be. I hitched up my toga and decided to circle the building. At this point

I became aware that I looked ... strange. Wearing a parka over a white floor-length toga on a cold February morning was definitely an attention-grabber. A few people in sharp suits and winter coats glanced up at me from their phones as they power-walked along the pavement.

I walked for what felt like ages before I saw it. A side entrance! Bordered by the Royal Courts of Justice and the pub next door, it was dark and dingy-looking. At the end there was an iron gate leading on to a courtyard. I dashed through it, the cobbles slick and grimy underneath my trainers, before anyone noticed me.

I pushed the gate open, expecting to meet resistance from a lock, but it swung open with ease. I stepped into the courtyard and gasped.

Where was I?

# THIRTY-FIVE

It was the strangest thing. I could still hear the roar and beeps of rush-hour traffic from the main road. But the winter chill and grey skies had gone. Instead, the sky was powder blue and the air was warm. I felt the sun on my face and took off my parka.

I was in a courtyard surrounded by the Royal Courts of Justice. It seemed like the same building that, a minute ago, my car had dropped me in front of. Maybe Dad was right: Mount Olympus had come to us. I could feel it in the air.

A church bell chiming in the distance reminded me that it was nine o'clock. Wasn't that the time the trial was meant to start? I hitched up my toga and jogged towards the entrance, where I could hear voices and chattering.

"Helen! You're here, just in time." It was Athena, waiting by the entrance. I had run past her on my way in. "I trust you found the entrance all right?"

I didn't answer. Athena could be so smug sometimes – did she know I nearly went into panic mode trying to find the entrance?

"Anyway, you're here and that's what matters. There's someone I'd like you to meet," Athena said. She put her arm around me and walked me over to a tall, thin man with skin so pale it was tinged blue. I thought that I'd better get used to this: two whole days of pointless introductions.

"Helen, I'd like you to meet your Uncle Hades."

Hades was the only ugly god I'd ever met. His skin had a moist, clammy sheen and when I shook his hand it felt like stroking a toad. Gag. I wondered if the myth about his wife Persephone was true – that he'd kidnapped her and tricked her into being his wife. It wouldn't surprise me in the least, now that I'd met him.

"It's a pleasure to finally meet you," he said. He clasped both hands over mine (gross gross gross). "We must arrange a visit to the Underworld sometime. The

River Styx is beautiful at this time of year," Hades said, cackling at his own joke. No one else laughed.

"Come, let us take our seats," Athena said. I followed them both inside the courtroom. But it was like no courtroom I'd ever seen on TV.

It was huge. There were hundreds of people packed into benches facing a podium the size of a stage. I imagined this would be where my family, the Council and the judge would stand. And me, too.

I followed Athena and Hades to a reserved bench in the front row. The chatter from the people seated in the rows behind us hushed slightly as we took our seats.

My body was seized with fear. How was I going to say a single word in front of all these people?

Then I noticed the windows. On one side of the room, the windows looked out on to the main road. I saw grey pavement, traffic lights and double-decker buses. But the windows on the other side of the room? They had a completely different view. I saw blue skies laced with wispy white clouds and a glittering blue ocean. It looked so vivid. Was it real?

"Athena, what's out there?" I asked her.

"Why, Mount Olympus of course."

"For real? So are we on earth or Mount Olympus?"

Athena smiled. "Neither. Or both. Depends on how you want to look at it."

I rolled my eyes. Classic Athena, but today I wasn't in the mood for a riddle.

"Think of this courtroom as a halfway house of sorts," she continued. "Honestly, Helen, I would think you have more important things to worry about."

I couldn't argue with that.

Suddenly the courtroom hushed completely. Aphrodite, Dad, Apollo and Eros took to the stage.

I couldn't get over how different they looked. The warmth in Dad's eyes, Apollo's cheeky grin and Aphrodite's perma-smug pout had been wiped from their faces. They looked as rigid and stately as the statues in the British Museum. They sat on throne-like chairs in the centre of the stage, not a single trace of emotion on their faces. I hoped that my nerves wouldn't betray me and show on mine. I felt like a quivering wreck.

The second all four of the gods sat down, I watched as four guards came to the podium bearing heavy terracotta pots filled with soil. They placed two pots in front of the chairs and two pots behind, forming a rectangular shape. The guards sprinkled a handful of what looked like ashes into the pots, then backed away.

Suddenly, vivid green stalks and leafy tendrils shot through the soil like giant octopus tentacles. They grew and grew, towering above the throne-like chairs before interlinking to form a tight canopy. The stalks whipped around one another, snapping and groaning, until the gods were encased on all sides by this plant-like prison.

"Don't worry, Helen," Athena said when she noticed the shock on my face. "Those on trial are fixed in place by the Bough of Demeter. It's tradition."

It was a tradition I didn't like the look of. Imagine being surrounded on all sides by snake-like vines? Just the thought made me feel claustrophobic.

The trial would start in any minute. It could have been my nerves, but I suddenly had a dry throat.

"There's a little water fountain just by that archway." Athena pointed to the corridor we came through. "Move swiftly. The judge won't take kindly to latecomers."

I made my way to the fountain in record time and glugged the cool water. I was still a bag of nerves, but at least I didn't have a dry throat. As I walked through the archway and came out of the other side, a man dressed in a sharp black suit and sunglasses appeared out of nowhere, blocking the archway. He was at least seven foot tall, so I have no idea how I'd missed him before.

"I believe you need the entrance on the other side of the auditorium, miss." He didn't even look me in the eye.

"No, I'm sitting there," I said, pointing to the front bench.

Athena was chatting to Hades and couldn't see me trying to get her attention.

He laughed, flashing a row of teeth sharpened to a point. Suddenly, I felt even more nervous.

"You must take me for a fool, child. Everyone knows those seats are reserved for the gods of Mount Olympus. You will have to take your seats at the back, just like everyone else."

I wanted to be assertive, but I felt like throwing up.

"I know who it's reserved for: my family. The trial is going to start soon, and I need to go back to my seat," I said, trying to sound confident.

It annoyed me how tiny my voice became, betraying my nerves.

He bent down, inches from my face. I suppressed a gulp. "By Jason's Fleece, if you do not leave immediately then I'll knock you from here to Tartarus!"

I didn't doubt that he would do it. He looked like he just wanted any excuse to get me out of there. Like when security guards in the shopping centre see you in a big group, and they're just waiting for a reason to pounce. Before I could answer, a middle-aged man in a dark grey gown walked past us. He must have been important because the guard took a break from snarling at me to bow his head.

"What appears to be the problem, Leon?"

"There is no problem, my lord. This silly little half-lifer was trying to sneak her way into the courtroom."

That is when I lost it.

"I've already told you, that is my seat. My family are sitting right there! My dad is Zeus, and I'm on trial with them! I'm his daughter Helen, as he will prove to you any way you like if I can just get to my seat."

The man in the grey gown peered down his nose at me. "Absurd," he spat. "Who do you think you are, impersonating a daughter of Zeus?"

*What?* I couldn't believe it. This strange man thought I was lying, too. "N-n-no. I *am* Helen," I stuttered. "You have to let me in. The trial can't go on without me!"

The older man laughed and it sounded like rocks tumbling down a cliff face.

"Is that right? Well, I can see the judge taking to the stage. That means the trial is starting now," he said, with the same twisted smile on his face. "Leon? Have this urchin removed at once." Then he walked down the corridor towards the courtroom.

Was this really happening? I shouted and screamed for Dad, Athena, *anyone*. But the judge's voice boomed around the courtroom, drowning me out.

"Quiet, half-lifer," Leon yelled. "Don't make me have to carry you out," he growled, pushing me through the corridor.

I broke down into sobs. What if I missed the trial altogether? It had to look bad if I was late for my own trial. Would I be found guilty by default?

As Leon pushed me further down the corridor, I heard the booming cheers of a crowd. Where did they come from? I didn't notice anyone in front of the courthouse.

The guard opened a heavy wooden door and I was thrust into daylight. I squinted in the light of the sun and made out hundreds of people held back behind dozens of guards dressed just like Leon.

Somehow I'd ended up in Mount Olympus.

# THIRTY-SIX

My humiliation was complete. Hundreds of people were going to see this.

I wiped the tears from my face and walked out of the auditorium with my head held high. The cheers became louder as the crowd noticed me walk out. I smiled and waved, pretending I was there on purpose. No one had to know I was being escorted from the premises.

"Helen! Helen, daughter of Zeus!" the crowd chanted. It got louder and louder. I could have sworn I heard a few people yell "Half-lifer!" too. Whatever they were saying, it was clear they knew who I was.

I turned around to face Leon. "Don't you see? They recognize me!" I yelled above the rising swell of the cheers.

The look on his face said it all. He knew he'd made a terrible mistake.

Leon dropped to one knee and bowed his head. "Forgive me, Lady Helen. I was acting on orders and—"

"Um, hello? There's no time for this! I need to get to the trial!"

"Of course, right away. Follow me," he said. I legged it down the corridor and into the courtroom.

I was so relieved at being let back into the trial, even if it meant interrupting the judge. She stared at me hard as I took my seat next to Athena (who didn't look too pleased either).

"I'll explain everything later," I mumbled.

The judge wore a white gown that seemed to glow against her brown skin. Her hair was in a short black Afro streaked with silver. Like the gods, she seemed both ageless and ancient.

"The twelve elected members of the Council will now take the floor," the judge said. I let out a sigh of relief. I couldn't have missed much if the Council weren't there yet.

The twelve Council members filed on to the stage to take their seats on three rows of benches. They seemed to be a mix of men and women of different ages and races, wearing gowns in various shades of grey and dark grey. Goosebumps ran down my spine. I recognized one of the Council members. I don't think I'd ever forget that face.

I nudged Athena. "He's the man who made me late! The one in dark grey."

Her eyes narrowed. "Ah. I suppose it was only a matter of time before you met Cranus."

*That* was Cranus? No wonder I'd caught some serious nasty vibes from him.

"For anyone new to the Mount Olympus Court of Law," the judge began, "let me take a few moments to explain the proceedings. Firstly, we will establish what rules have been broken. We will deal with the gods, followed by Lady Helen's offence. Please note that Lady Helen is both a key witness and on trial herself." I heard gasps from the crowd at the judge's last sentence. "We will culminate proceedings with the judgement and punishment, if deemed suitable by the Council."

It was going to be a long day.

# THIRTY-SEVEN

"First, let us go through the charges," the judge continued. Her voice resounded across the courtroom but there was no microphone to be seen. "The Rules were put in place to maintain harmony between gods and mortals. To break these rules is to disrupt a careful balance designed to protect mortals from harm. All immortal beings residing in the mortal realm swear to follow these rules. Very little good has come from mortals being aware of our existence."

Huge swirls of coloured smoke appeared behind the judge, rising and expanding until they could be seen from any seat in the room. As she spoke, the wisps of smoke curled into words and sentences.

"Rule One," the judge said, "gods must not reveal their immortal identity for any reason."

The smoke mimicked her words, twisting like snakes. It was mesmerizing.

"Rule Two: gods must not use their powers to interfere with the fate of mortals," she said. "For any reason."

Again, the smoke obeyed the words spoken by the judge.

"I trust we are all clear?" She turned to face the gods. They gave tiny nods in response.

"Now, the Council are quite aware of the charges laid against the gods today. But I'd like to recap them for the audience," she said. *Audience.* This trial was beginning to feel more like a show with every passing minute.

"The first offence: Lord Eros used his powers to cause a mortal to fall in love with Lord Zeus," the judge said.

I gasped. The smoke words cleared and what looked like a giant hologram flickered into life. It was seriously cool. Like a film reel, it showed clips of Dad and Lisa together: having coffee in a cafe, drinking in a pub and walking hand in hand in a park. They looked so happy.

How did they get this footage? Was Apollo right – did the Council have spies everywhere? The thought that our family was being watched at all times made me shiver.

I glanced at Dad but his face didn't betray any emotion. "I should add," the judge continued, "that with Lord Zeus distracted by a mortal, Lady Aphrodite and Lord Apollo were free to pursue fame. It remains unclear if they used their powers to facilitate this."

The huge hologram flashed through a different set of clips: Aphrodite's TV interviews and YouTube videos, and Apollo on *House of Stars*.

"The gods have chosen to provide their testimonies in writing. However, they are still invited to give a short statement in their defence," the judge said. "Should they wish."

Dad stood up slowly and regally, like a ruler surveying his kingdom. The Bough of Demeter arched and bent to make space for him to stand up. He seemed nothing like the person I knew at home. He looked more like a god with every passing minute.

"Citizens of Mount Olympus," he began, his voice filling the courtroom, "I can't begin to describe how good it feels to see familiar faces. I only wish it was under better circumstances. We have nothing to say in our defence. I trust that the Council, a legal institution that I established aeons ago, will make the right choice."

Good thing Dad stood up and not Apollo or Aphrodite. Their line of defence might not have been so diplomatic.

"Thank you for your succinct words, Lord Zeus," the judge said. "Now, let us begin with the main event. Lady Helen, please come to the floor. It is time for the courtroom to hear your testimony."

My robe was sticky with sweat and my eyes still sore from crying. I wished I had just a few more minutes to pull myself together. My argument with Cranus and the guard had left me in a complete state.

I rose and walked towards the stage. Wait. Where were my testimony notes?

"Go on, Helen," Athena said under her breath, motioning towards the stage.

"But . . . my notes! I need my notes."

The judge cleared her throat. "It would be appreciated if you didn't waste any more of our time, Lady Helen," she boomed.

"Helen, you're holding them!" Athena whispered hurriedly.

I looked down and she was right. My notes were

scrunched tight into a sweaty ball in my right hand. My nerves had got the better of me already.

I stepped out of our box, down towards the stage, and a guard motioned for me to stand in the centre of the stage. The gods were to my left and the Council were to my right. The air in the courtroom seemed to stand still. I was too hot, and the toga felt too tight around my shoulder. Sweat pooled down my back.

"Thank you for eventually joining us, Lady Helen," the judge said.

I gulped. She was like the sternest teacher I'd ever had, multiplied by fifty.

"Council members, I urge you to pay close attention to Lady Helen's words. You may ask any questions you see fit. Her testimony will be key to your deliberations."

And to saving our lives.

My hands trembled as I smoothed out my page of notes. The moment I'd been dreading was just seconds away.

It was time. This was the chance I had to undo my mistake and make things right.

# THIRTY-EIGHT

A Council member in a light grey robe stood up. He looked young, not much older than me, but his voice circulated the room effortlessly.

"Lady Helen," he began. "Can you tell us, the Council, why the gods should be free to live in the mortal realm?"

I cleared my throat. "I know how it looks. The evidence makes it look like the gods are spoilt, selfish and arrogant," I said. Gasps and mutters came from the audience. I definitely had their attention.

"But after living with them for just a few months, I truly believe they make the world a better place. A world without love, beauty, music or sunshine is not one worth living in. Yes, they came a bit close to getting too much attention. But they are gods, after all. Isn't that what they're used to?"

Just like the Council member who spoke before me, my voice filled the courtroom. I instantly felt less nervous.

"Take Aphrodite," I continued. "I mean, Lady Aphrodite. The point of her very existence is to make things more beautiful. She didn't use magic to invent her wonder cream. She used centuries of knowledge. I saw it for myself. Aphrodite earned her fame and fans. Not through powers or potions or spells, but from her own wisdom."

I thought about the care Aphrodite had put into her career recently. How excited she got over gross ingredients and different chemical formulae. "Don't get me wrong. She loved the attention that came with fame and adoration. Who wouldn't? But that wasn't her goal. She just wanted to sprinkle the world around her with beauty. And why should the world be denied that?

"It's the same with Lord Apollo. His music is pure joy. He's dedicated centuries to his craft, and it shows. His music is the closest thing to sunshine I can think of. Whether he's tutoring kids or playing in a nightclub, Apollo is in his element. His charisma and talent were what got him on TV. He didn't need to enchant anyone into thinking he's an incredible musician. He *rocks*."

I wished that I could turn around and see the looks on my family's faces. I don't think I'd ever told them how awesome they were before.

My hands had stopped trembling and the air in the room didn't feel so oppressive. I had the full attention of the courtroom.

It didn't feel terrifying. It felt seriously good.

"As for Lord Eros, I know first-hand how important his presence is in my life. I'm a teenager. We think about love, like, a lot." A few people chuckled in the audience, giving me a last-minute confidence boost. "Eros has been there for me when I needed it the most. As someone without a mum, this means the world to me. He's much more than just a matchmaker. I feel like he expresses love in all forms."

"Lord Zeus, my dad, has lived on earth for years as a professor. He doesn't let his status as head of the gods interfere with his disguise. He's rational, humble and if I'm being honest, a bit dull." A few brave people chuckled in the audience. Even the judge looked like she was suppressing a smile.

"What I mean is, you'd never in a million years think that this man was a god. He's perfected his mortal disguise and has close contact with students on a daily basis. They never suspect a thing. They have no idea how lucky they are."

My eyes flickered up to steal a glance at the Council members. It was so hard to tell if I was getting anywhere with them. Their poker faces didn't betray any emotion.

"It's clear, to me at least, that the mortal world would be worse off without the gods. I know that it would destroy mine." My voice cracked with emotion. I'd made it this far without crying. I couldn't break down now.

I took a deep breath and continued. "My life would be deprived of love if my family were banished to Mount Olympus. Or, worse yet, stripped of their powers. I'd lose the love of siblings, cousins and a parent. My only living parent, for that matter. To be robbed of that, the closest link to my immortal heritage, seems so unfair."

Tears filled my eyes. I hated the thought of crying in public. But maybe it would work in my favour? The audience were here for a show, after all. I let tears trickle down my face.

"The last few months have been such a challenge. My mum passed away when I was ten. She was my world. I've been trying to find a new family ever since.

I hope the Council will see how important the gods are to me. They are my family now. Please, don't take them away from me."

Murmurs filled the room, followed by sombre applause. I even saw a few people in the audience wipe their eyes. If I'd won them over, was there a chance I'd convinced the Council?

I turned and began walking towards my seat in the gods' box.

"Just one second, Lady Helen." The familiar oily voice stopped me in my tracks. I turned around to see a Council member in a grey robe standing up.

It was Cranus.

"Touching as that was, I'm afraid I have a few . . . niggling doubts. Doubts that your testimony failed to lay to rest."

I wanted to wipe the smug smirk off of his face.

"May I have the floor, Judge Themis?" Cranus asked.

The judge nodded and he descended from the Council benches. We were now face-to-face.

"Lady Helen. You insist that the gods improve the world. That they make it a brighter place for mortals. Is that correct?" he said.

I nodded.

"Speak up, Lady Helen," said the judge.

"I mean, yes. That's what I think, anyway," I added.

"And apart from Lord Eros's love spell, the gods have never used their powers to interfere with mortals? To your knowledge?"

"Not to my knowledge, no," I stammered. I longed to be off the stage and away from this horrible man.

Cranus's smirk stretched into a cruel smile. He relished every minute of my discomfort.

"Well, I beg to differ. We have it on good authority that the gods did use their powers in the presence of mortals," he said. "Perhaps this will jog your memory."

The giant hologram flickered into life again, and a moving clip came into focus. I could hear music and chatter, and see people crowded into a small room.

My living room. It was the New Year's Eve party. The party I'd managed to hide from Dad.

Until now.

My stomach lurched but I managed to keep my face smooth and expressionless. I couldn't let Cranus have the satisfaction of seeing me scared. Not again.

The video clip showed Apollo turning off the music pumping from the stereo, picking up his guitar and diving straight into a song. The effect on the crowd was instant. They went from yelling at Apollo to swaying gently or sitting cross-legged on the carpet.

How on earth did the Council get hold of that? They must have had spies parked outside the house at all times. Wasn't this against our human rights or something?

"Where did you get that?" I demanded. The rest of the courtroom seemed to disappear. It was just me and Cranus.

"Unimportant," he said. "This is clear evidence that Lord Apollo enchanted a room full of mortals. No musician, no matter how skilled, could have that effect on so many people. They're like putty in his hands."

"But that's not the whole story! A fight was about to start, and Apollo calmed them all down. He stopped them getting hurt!"

Cranus's eyes flashed bright. "So you admit it?" he shouted. "You admit that Lord Apollo did enchant an entire room full of mortals?"

My heart pounded. My mouth was dry. Cranus knew he had me in a corner.

"H-h-he did. But if it wasn't for Lord Apollo, someone would have been seriously hurt."

"I will concede that Lord Apollo acted with noble intentions. This time. But we all know our history. We know that the gods haven't always been quite so high-minded."

I couldn't argue with that point. If the myths were anything to go by, they had acted terribly in the past.

"It was my fault, anyway!" I blurted out. "It was my party. Lord Apollo didn't even know about it."

Cranus raised both eyebrows. "It was your party, eh? And can you tell me where this party was?"

"My house," I said, wary of his questions.

"Is this the same house you share with Lord Zeus, Lady Aphrodite and Lord Eros?"

"Yes," I said through gritted teeth.

"You had several dozen mortals gallivanting around a house of the gods?" Cranus shook his head. "I don't like the sound of this. It's reckless behaviour, through and through."

"But Dad, I mean Lord Zeus, didn't know! It was my party, and I made the other gods promise to keep it secret," I yelled. "It was my fault, not theirs." My eyes filled with tears. I hated that I was practically pleading. But I couldn't let Cranus win this and destroy my family.

"I know just how much your family means to you, Lady Helen," Cranus said in his smooth, oily voice. "However, the evidence speaks for itself." He paced around me like a tiger circling its prey. "It is pure selfishness that compelled you to testify here today. That much is clear."

His brown eyes bored a hole in mine. "I have nothing else to add, Judge Themis," Cranus said.

"Thank you, Cranus," said Judge Themis. "Between Lady Helen's testimony and this startling new evidence, the Council have much to think about. Lady Helen's trial will continue tomorrow."

I could have collapsed with relief. After Cranus's gruelling questions, I was in no state to defend myself.

# THIRTY-NINE

I stepped down from the podium and sat back on the front bench. Athena put her arms around me but said nothing. She didn't have to.

"Cranus always was a miserable turd," Hades said loudly enough for half the courtroom to hear. Athena glared at him.

"You did well, Helen. Honestly," she said. I shrugged. I wasn't convinced.

"Now, I'm afraid we have a gathering of Mount Olympian officials to look forward to," Athena continued. "Let us make our way to the dining hall."

"Will Dad be there?" I asked. The gods were still on the stage, bound by the canopy of green vines.

"But of course! We're dining in his honour," Athena said. "Now, upstairs."

We left the courthouse and trudged our way up a dark spiral staircase. Eating was the last thing on my mind (I must have been *really* upset) but I did want to sit down with my family. I wanted to hear about the trial from their perspective and tell them all about my run-in with Cranus.

We reached a windowless candlelit room, all wood panels and tapestries. A long table ran through the middle, with enough place settings for fifty people. Dozens of men and women, dressed in togas like us, stood beside the table. Everyone looked up as we entered. They were waiting for us.

Athena raised her hand to silence the room. "Greetings, fellow Mount Olympians. It's good to see you, albeit not under the greatest of circumstances. My father and family will join us shortly. Please, do be seated."

The Mount Olympians checked the place settings to find their names on the table. The older men and women seated nearer the front were closer to the gods, and didn't half look smug about it. I squinted in the candlelight to find my place name, but it became clear I wasn't going to be sat with my family. Was this an admin error? Or just another "formality" the Council insisted on?

I finally found my place name – and it was nowhere near my family. I was surrounded by a few other people my age. Sons and daughters of the Mount Olympus officials, I assumed.

I smiled at the girl and boy sitting opposite me. They had to be related. They shared the same long faces, and silvery-blond hair fell in wisps around their shoulders. They responded to my smile with a curt nod. They didn't look too thrilled to be sitting close to me.

I turned my attention to the table. No plates or cutlery, just bronze goblets and jugs. Weren't we meant to be eating? Then the people around me began helping themselves to whatever was in the bronze jugs. The liquid pouring into the goblets glinted gold in the candlelight. It looked like . . . honey?

The ghost twins filled their goblets and sipped, like drinking syrup was a perfectly normal thing to do.

"Um, why are we drinking honey?" I asked.

The boy smirked at me. "You mean you've never had ambrosia before?"

Ambrosia! I'd heard about this before, mostly from Aphrodite raving about how much she missed it at home. It was a food unique to Mount Olympus. Only those with immortal blood could eat it.

I ignored his unkind smile and poured a small portion of the thick ambrosia into my goblet. I took a sip and I suddenly realized why this stuff was such a big deal.

Oh my gosh. It didn't taste like honey at all! The first sip tasted like hot chocolate with whipped cream. Then the second sip tasted like hot chips with salt and vinegar. The third and final sip was the most delicious of all: it tasted exactly like mum's chicken stew with rice. It was like nothing I'd ever experienced before. I drained the goblet and poured myself an even bigger glass.

"It tastes like all of my favourite meals in one!" I said.

"Ambrosia is a divine food of the immortals," the girl said. "It couldn't possibly compare to any dreadful mortal food."

The ghost twins radiated nasty vibes. It was obvious that they had nothing nice to say to me. They chatted in a language I didn't know, never looking in my direction. It wasn't until their mother fixed them with a few short, sharp words that they looked at me. Why was she so keen for us to talk?

The girl gave me a bland, watery smile that couldn't be faker if she tried.

"My name is Phaedra, and this is my brother Flavian," she said with the same fake grin fixed on her face. It didn't reach her eyes.

I decided to give them the benefit of the doubt. It couldn't hurt to make new friends from Mount Olympus.

It could end up being my home.

"I'm Helen. Nice to meet you both," I said, returning the smile with all the social energy I could muster.

Flavian snickered. "Oh, we know who you are." He leaned in across the table. "Mother hasn't stopped talking about you for some reason." His gaze flickered across my face in a way that made me feel instantly judged.

"Quiet, Flavian," Phaedra said, but she smirked all the same.

She punched him playfully in the ribs. I noticed the band, silver and delicate, wrapped around her upper arm. It was shaped like a snake, with diamonds for eyes.

"Ooh, sick armband," I said. And I meant it. It was beautiful in a dark, twisted way.

"Sick?" Phaedra said, looking as though I'd spat in

her ambrosia. "I think the word you're looking for is 'exquisite'. This is the most valuable thing I own. It's the exact replica of an armband that Hephaestus gave to Aphrodite. It is of great significance to *our* culture."

"Oh, you don't get it. Where I'm from 'sick' means good. It's, like, slang," I said.

"Where we come from, slang indicates a lack of refinement," Flavian said, looking like he'd sucked on a lemon.

Phaedra continued to look as though my "insult" caused her physical pain. "I would never have believed that she was a daughter of Zeus unless I saw it with my own eyes." She spoke to her brother but glared at me.

Phaedra muttered something I couldn't understand, and her brother sniggered. They both looked at me. Just so that I knew for sure that was why they were laughing.

I drained my goblet of the last sip of ambrosia, but the bitterness I felt didn't budge. So far, Mount Olympians were rude and dismissive. I couldn't wait to get away from them.

The gods were all present and seated, but they were deep in conversation with the people surrounding them. Why hadn't Dad or Eros checked in on me yet? And why were they having fun? I wanted them to be miserable like me. Maybe it was the ambrosia or spending time with immortals for a change, but they didn't look at all unhappy to be there.

That morning, I'd felt a small comfort knowing we were all in this trial together. But there I was, sitting at the other end of the table near people who thought I was beneath them. I was an outsider again. A feeling I knew all too well, whether it was in London or amongst Mount Olympians.

We couldn't be found guilty at the trial. My testimony *had* to persuade the Council. Or else I'd have a lifetime with nothing but awful creatures like Phaedra and Flavian for company.

# FORTY

The feast felt like it went on for hours. Long after the novelty of the ambrosia had worn off, I was still sat there. The ghost twins blanked me for the rest of the gathering (I guess even tormenting me got boring after a while). Athena introduced me to a few dry-looking officials with greying beards and cold eyes. Another formality. Mount Olympians seemed to be dead keen on those.

Just as the feast was winding down, the door opened. In walked a young woman in a toga flanked by two guards. Thanks to my encounter with Leon, just the sight of the guards set my pulse pounding.

The young woman cleared her throat, commanding the attention of the room.

"Lords and ladies of Mount Olympus. I come bearing a message from Councilman Cranus and Judge Themis. It's come to our attention that Lady Helen is residing in the Gods' Quarters," she said. "As a key witness, this is in clear contravention of the Dikastian Code."

Athena jumped to her feet. "Are you suggesting that I, Athena, goddess of justice, would break Mount Olympian law?" Her voice boomed around the room. Even the messenger looked shaken for a split second.

What was going on? And what was this code all about? I didn't want to ask what it was and betray my ignorance.

"The gods must not be seen to favour anyone on trial. Especially if they are kin. Judge Themis has ruled that it would be inappropriate for Lady Helen to share quarters with the gods during this trial."

They were tearing me away from my family before the trial was even over.

"We have prepared lodgings in the basement, several floors away from the Gods' Quarters," the messenger continued.

"Unacceptable!" Athena said in a clipped tone, the scariest I had ever heard her. "A daughter of Zeus cannot sleep in the basement."

"Lady Athena, may we remind you that no one is above the law," the messenger said. Then she turned to me. "The basement is a much more suitable alternative, and guarantees fairness. Lady Helen, you will remain in your new lodgings until the trial tomorrow."

Wait, what? "Athena, can they do this?" I said, running towards her.

My heart was pounding. I hated the thought of being alone. This could be my last night with my family. And I was going to spend it in a dingy basement cell under the courthouse.

Athena nodded. "Cranus is right. It's written into our code. But it's just one night. We'll see you bright and early tomorrow for the trial." She squeezed my hand gently.

I looked back at the gods, frozen at the dinner table. Their faces were blank slates, but I could have sworn that Dad's eyes flashed bright as lightning for a second.

Two guards shuffled me out of the dining hall before anyone had a chance to see my tears.

The guards escorted me down a stone staircase slick with damp, down into the belly of the courthouse. It was dark and deathly silent, like a medieval dungeon.

Was this a glimpse into my future? If I was found

guilty the next day, would I be imprisoned somewhere like this?

Being a daughter of Zeus didn't stop me from being harassed by a guard or from spending the night in a prison cell. How much worse would it be for me if I didn't have that status? What if the gods were stripped of their powers? A life in Mount Olympus with no one looking out for me seemed unbearably grim.

The guards stopped outside a wooden door. The one in front of me unlocked it with a key from a brass ring shaking with dozens of other keys. How many people were down here?

"Your new lodgings, my lady," the guard said. I could hear the laugh in his voice. He was enjoying this.

The door creaked open. My eyes adjusted to the darkness as I stepped shivering into the cube of grey stone. Flame lamps lining the wall flickered into life, illuminating the room. A narrow cot-like bed sat in the corner. And absolutely nothing else. I'd seen rabbit hutches more welcoming. I couldn't have imagined a more dank and depressing place.

I hated Cranus and his meddling. If it wasn't for him, I'd be in the Gods' Quarters. I'd probably have hot, running water, a soft bed, and a few more precious hours with my family.

"We will be outside, Lady Helen," the other guard said. "As instructed, you will be released in time for your trial at sunup."

"Wait!" I shrieked. "Can I get some hot water or a book or ... something!" I couldn't be alone with my thoughts all night. It would drive me crazy.

But the guards ignored me. The wooden door slammed shut and I heard the clack of metal bolts.

I'd never felt more alone.

My cotton toga was no match for the icebox cell. The stone walls radiated cold. I climbed in the bed, bringing the rough hemp-like sheets up to my shoulders. It felt itchy, but I was a bit warmer at least.

To be alone at a time like this felt unbelievably cruel. I wished more than ever that I could speak to Mum.

*Dear Mum,* I thought. *I know I messed up. But I don't deserve this. Why is my life so unfair? I can't think about that, or else it'll lead to a downward spiral of despair.*

*And the gods, my family, have it much worse really. Whatever happens tomorrow, I'll live. I might be alone and banished to Mount Olympus. But I'll be alive.*

*They could be stripped of their powers. It would be a death sentence.*

*Mum, I'm so scared about tomorrow's verdict. The Council have to find us innocent. They have to. I won't survive otherwise. How much heartache and loss can one person take?*

The emotional exhaustion of the day seeped into my bones. Every sinew of muscle ached with fatigue. I was too tired to even cry.

I fell asleep with the next day weighing heavily on my mind. What other tricks could Cranus have up his sleeve?

# FORTY-ONE

I woke up with a pain in my shoulder after a tense sleep on the narrow bed. The rough hemp sheet was tangled around my waist.

I sat up straight. My trial would start any moment.

The toga I wore yesterday clung to my skin. *Gross.* Did I have to testify in front of an entire courtroom wearing this? I looked around. The room seemed less dark and dim, somehow. I knew that morning was near. Then I noticed a table in the opposite corner of the cell. On it was a large basin, cloth, jars and a brush.

That wasn't there last night.

I climbed out of bed and peered into the basin. The water was hot! Perfumed steam rose from the surface, scenting the room with lavender. I splashed my face, wiped it clean with a cloth and felt a million times better.

I turned around and noticed a fresh robe laid on my bed. That *definitely* wasn't there last night. The objects must have arrived there courtesy of the gods. That was a much nicer thought than a guard creeping in while I slept.

I inspected the robe. On the inside, barely-there silver stitching glinted in the light. It read: *May the scales of justice tip in your favour.*

I smiled. It sounded like something Athena would say.


A guard unlocked my cell door and escorted me up to the courtroom. My eyes adjusted to the late morning sun pouring through the windows. Was it this bright yesterday?

The courtroom was just as crowded as the day before. The crowd even cheered when I made it to the stage. Their applause made my stomach turn. My fate was their entertainment.

My heart leapt to see the gods all seated in the front row. They smiled weakly and waved as the guards steered me towards a single throne-like chair on the stage.

Just like yesterday, the guards followed with huge

terracotta pots of soil. Once activated by the handful of ash, the Bough of Demeter snapped into life. After a few moments, I was trapped by a network of stalks and leaves. The Council soon shuffled on to the benches in their monochrome robes.

Judge Themis took her spot on the podium. "Welcome, citizens of Mount Olympus. I won't waste any time. Today we will hear about the second offence of the trial," she said. "As you may know, Lady Helen broke our cardinal rule. She revealed her family's immortal heritage to a mortal."

Gasps reverberated around the courtroom, and my cheeks burned. For a horrible moment, I thought there'd be a hologram film of Marco and me. Maybe kissing on the bus or sitting in the playground.

It was something even worse. A familiar voice boomed through the courtroom.

*"Why was this person hovering above your house?"*

It was Marco. That was Marco's voice.

*"Because she's my sister. Well, half-sister. And she's not a person, exactly. She's a god."*

And that was my voice. I wanted to collapse with shame.

It was an audio recording of the moment I told Marco our secret. Somehow, hearing the evidence was a million times more humiliating than hearing Judge Themis talk about it.

If I'd been standing, my knees would have buckled. How did they get hold of that? The Council really did have spies everywhere.

I couldn't let my emotion show on my face. I couldn't give anyone the satisfaction of seeing how humiliating this was.

The crowd murmured and chattered, shocked at the obvious betrayal. Hearing it all over again brought back the heartbreak. I'd trusted Marco and he had betrayed me.

I stole a glance at Cranus, who looked immensely satisfied. My hatred for him was overwhelming.

"Lady Helen, you may give a short statement in your defence," Judge Themis said.

My defence? I'd hardly thought about my defence. When I prepared for the trial, it was all about saving the gods.

I forgot to think about saving myself.

"I can't deny the recording. I did tell a mortal about our heritage. But I had a good reason! He had a video of Aphrodite using her powers, and he was going to share it with the world. I had to tell him the truth. To stop him from sharing it and revealing the truth to millions of people."

The auditorium was silent. We all knew it was a pathetic excuse. It was going to cost me my freedom.

"Did it work, Lady Helen?" It was Cranus. He was probably giddy at the thought of questioning me. "Did revealing your secret stop this young man from sharing the footage of Aphrodite?"

"No. It didn't." There was no point in dodging the inevitable. "But no one recognized Aphrodite. They have no idea about the identity of the gods!"

"That is because we, the Council, had to step in and nip this video in the bud. We used our powers to ensure that the video never went any further than a few mortal websites of ill repute," Cranus scoffed. "Lady Helen, your naivety is extremely troubling. Combined with your family's recklessness, I'm surprised the entire mortal realm doesn't know of your heritage."

"Please save your comments for the deliberation, Cranus," Judge Themis said. Cranus sat back down on the bench, looking satisfied. "Lady Helen, you may finish your statement," she said.

"When I said what I said . . . it was in a moment of weakness. I really did think I was doing the best for my family. I was only thinking of keeping us together," I said. "It's no excuse, but it *is* the truth."

"Thank you, Lady Helen," Judge Themis said. "This

is an uncharacteristically short trial, but in the face of irrefutable evidence, I see no reason to delay the deliberation.

"As is customary, the twelve Council members will have twelve minutes each to present their views followed by twelve minutes to confer and decide on the appropriate sentence. We will reconvene here in precisely one hundred and fifty-six minutes to hear the verdict. In the meantime, I've been informed by Lady Athena that ambrosia awaits everyone in the dining hall upstairs."

That was it. The only shot I had at defending myself had slipped through my fingers. Suddenly, the Bough of Demeter began to wither and shrink, reversing until the roots slumped back into the terracotta pots. I was free.

I ran to the gods' box and hugged Dad, crying into his gown as his arms came around me in a big bear hug. He didn't say anything, but his arms and hands shielded my face from view. I didn't care if Cranus or the Council or the auditorium full of people saw me howling like a toddler.

In one hundred and fifty-six minutes, my life would be over.

# FORTY-TWO

The minutes zipped past. Before long, the courtroom was again full of people and I was back in the Bough of Demeter. This time with Dad, Apollo, Aphrodite and Eros. I put my icy hand in Eros's warm one.

"Many thanks for returning promptly," Judge Themis said, addressing the audience. She turned to face the rows of Council members. "Have you arrived at a verdict?"

An elderly woman in a mid-grey gown stood up. "We have arrived at a verdict, Judge Themis."

Judge Themis nodded. "The first offence: Lord Eros used his powers to cause a mortal to fall in love with Lord Zeus. What is your verdict, Council members?"

I squeezed Eros's hand so tight that my knuckles

went white. Every millisecond that passed seemed like a year. Why were they torturing us with silence?

"We conclude that the evidence points to Lord Eros using his powers of romantic persuasion on a mortal," the Council member said.

I knew it. The evidence was all there. I glanced up at Eros and saw his eyes welling with tears. It was the first time I'd seen him cry. It made me want to cry too.

"However," she added. "As the romance lasted for a very short period of time, it could be attributed to infatuation. Ultimately, as there is not enough evidence either way, we cannot be entirely sure. The Council will not pass punishment."

Tears of relief flooded down my face. I turned and hugged Eros.

"Interfering with the lives of mortals has led to wars and bloodshed," the Council member continued. "In this case, no harm has been caused by the gods being on earth. We will therefore allow the gods to remain in the mortal realm, provided they continue to abide by the rules. Lord Zeus must continue to fulfil his role as custodian of the gods on earth."

Polite claps from the audience punctuated the air. Anyone watching for drama and distress seemed to be missing out.

"Thank you, Council members, for your sound judgement," Judge Themis said. "Now we must come to Lady Helen's verdict."

My head shot up when I heard my name. My stomach fluttered, but I was way less nervous than I was a few minutes before. I was so happy and relieved that my family were free.

"Lord Zeus, Lady Aphrodite, Lord Apollo and Lord Eros. You are free to go," Judge Themis said.

The vines in front of them withered and crumbled to dust as they rose from their seats. They each gave me a squeeze on the shoulder before leaving and taking their seats in the god box. The vines grew back into a cage of greenery. I was alone on the stage to hear my fate, trapped in a living prison.

"The second offence: Lady Helen revealed the gods' true identity to a mortal," Judge Themis said. "What is your verdict, Council members?"

"We conclude that the evidence points to Lady Helen revealing her true identity to a mortal. This breaks the most important rule of all." The Council member's clear voice rang like a bell through the courtroom.

I waited for her to say "however".

But it didn't come.

"Lady Helen claims to have had good intentions, but revealing one's immortal heritage is a serious crime," she continued. "It is possible for half-mortals to balance separate identities while living in the mortal realm. But it appears that Lady Helen cannot."

The audience rumbled. My heart pounded in my eardrums.

"We, the Council, propose that Lady Helen lives out the rest of her days on Mount Olympus. This sentence will begin immediately."

I shot up from my seat. "No!" I screamed. I tried to climb through the nest of plants but the Bough of Demeter wouldn't budge. I pushed and pushed, but the vines kept me in their iron cage.

The audience gasped and sighed. They were getting their show all right.

The Council seemed unmoved by my show of emotion. Apart from Cranus. His lips curled into the slightest of smiles.

"Thank you for your verdict, Council members," Judge Themis said. She turned to face me from the podium. "Lady Helen, this may seem like a harsh sentence, but. . ." The judge's voice trailed off. I couldn't absorb anything, not with the deep sadness springing up inside of me.

I'd never have another sleepover with Yasmin, Noor and Daphne. I'd never sleep in my own bed or take the 43 bus over Waterloo Bridge. I'd never see Grandma Thomas again.

I hung my head and let the tears fall. My life wasn't worth living.

My grief was interrupted by shouts and cries from the audience.

"Judge Themis! Judge Themis, I need your attention!" A man's voice cut through the clamour. I looked up and saw a young man with dark curly hair and tanned skin approach the stage.

It was Marco.

# FORTY-THREE

I wiped my eyes. Were tears blurring my vision? Was I having a sleep-deprived hallucination?

No. It was definitely Marco, wearing the same traditional robes as everyone else in the courtroom. He was close enough for me to see his smoky brown eyes and the mole just above his lip.

"Marco?" I stuttered. "Is that you?"

Nausea mingled with shock. I never expected to see him again.

Least of all at this trial.

Had he followed me here and snuck in past the guards? I didn't understand how he had found his way into our trial. Only those with immortal blood could be here.

Marco ignored me and marched up to Judge Themis, dwarfed by the podium.

"Judge Themis, I have to tell you the truth. Helen is innocent!"

A flicker of hope leapt inside me. Was he here to rescue me? But then I remembered our last conversation. This trial would never have happened if it wasn't for him. He'd betrayed me.

So why was he telling Judge Themis that I was innocent?

The auditorium gasped. The gods rose from their seats in shock, but Dad held them back from approaching the podium.

Judge Themis looked as though she recognized Marco. "Makario! This is most unorthodox. What is the meaning of this claim?"

My tummy twinged. Makario. Maybe it wasn't Marco after all. Just someone who looked and sounded exactly the same?

*Wake up, Helen.* I'd know that face anywhere. It was him all right. But I still didn't understand how he'd got into the trial.

"Helen, I mean Lady Helen, didn't reveal her secret to a mortal." The entire auditorium waited with bated breath. My pulse quickened. "She revealed it to someone who already knew everything. An immortal. Me. I'm the person in the recording."

My hands shot to my face as I gasped. It was all too much to take in. Marco wasn't a normal guy. He was immortal. He was more like me than I ever could have imagined. No wonder we'd connected.

Any small joy I felt at knowing Marco had immortal blood disappeared. The true realization of what this meant flooded through my head.

Marco would have known I was half-mortal. He pushed me into a confession by threatening to dump me. Then shared the video with the world anyway. He would have known the consequences.

My confusion turned into rage. His betrayal was even worse than I thought.

Judge Themis raised one eyebrow. "You may take the floor."

He walked to the centre of the stage, just metres from me. "My father instructed me to spy on the gods while they lived in the mortal realm. I was to gather any evidence of rule-breaking. When I couldn't find enough compelling evidence, he told me to persuade Lady Helen into revealing her heritage. I coerced her into admitting it, which is what you hear on the recording."

It was all a trick. Every goodnight text message. Every email filled with kisses. Every lingering hug. How could I have been so stupid? I felt like a spider trapped under a glass, exposed and imprisoned at the same time. I wanted to slip down into my basement cell, far away from the crowd's yells and cries.

Shouts of "Retrial!" and "Free her!" rang through the air. Judge Themis raised her hands and the audience simmered down.

"Makario, this comes as a huge surprise," she said. "You're one of the most diligent young legal minds in our land. And your father, Cranus, is our longest-standing Council member."

Cranus was Marco's dad? I imagined having such a cruel parent and my heart throbbed with pity.

Marco held his head up high. "I'm ashamed to say that it's true," he said.

Judge Themis turned to the Council benches. "Cranus, can you confirm this is true?"

But Cranus wasn't sitting on the benches. He was nowhere to be seen. While we were all distracted by Marco, he must have slipped off.

Judge Themis motioned a pair of guards forward. She muttered instructions that we couldn't hear. The guards jogged out of the auditorium.

"Judge Themis, you must overturn Helen's punishment!" It was Athena. She stood up and glided over to the podium.

While they talked, Marco turned around to face me. Seeing his face jolted the anger out of me, but only for a few seconds. It must have shown on my face because when I turned to him, he stepped back. Like he was scared of me.

Good. He had every reason to be nervous.

"Do you have any idea how much you've put me through?" I said through gritted teeth. "I've lost everything. All because of you and your snake of a father," I spat.

"I can't apologize enough, Helen. That's why I'm here. I want to put things right."

I didn't care about his apology. He'd left it until the very last moment to have a change of heart.

"You targeted me, gained my trust. You betrayed me." I sniffed, not bothering to hold back the tears.

"That's not exactly how it happened," Marco stammered. "I didn't target you. You didn't feature in the plan at all. Not at first. But you caught my eye, and I couldn't *not* approach you."

I wiped away the tears pooling under my chin.

"What's that supposed to mean?"

"When Father found out that I met you, he suggested that I should get to know you better. That you might let your secret slip. To me."

Cranus knew I was the weak link. The half-mortal. I hated that I had proved him right, even if I was tricked.

"It's the worst thing I've ever done. I hate myself and will continue to hate myself for a long time to come."

I could feel my cheeks burning. Just thinking about the sweet emails and kisses and longing glances that we shared, that he must have faked. Shame consumed my entire body. I couldn't stand to think how desperate I must have looked. All Marco had to do was fake the slightest interest in me, and I was putty in his hands.

I looked up to meet his eyes. I had to ask.

"Was any of it real?"

"I wasn't truthful about my background or motives," he said. "But nothing else was a lie. How I feel about you ... it was never a lie. I couldn't live with myself, knowing that your life would be turned upside down. Because of me. No one deserves that fate. Least of all you, Helen."

I knew he was telling the truth, but nothing stirred inside of me. He had betrayed my trust, and worse, my family. What he did was unforgivable.

"Your attention, please," Judge Themis called from

the podium. "This new evidence from Makario is quite startling. Lady Helen did not reveal her family's immortal status to a mortal after all. Therefore, I hereby overturn your sentence," Judge Themis said.

The Bough of Demeter withered and crumbled before my eyes. I ran to the gods' box and hugged Dad. I was free!

"Well, well," Hades said with a chuckle. "That was a lucky escape, Helen."

My tears soaked Dad's robe. "I thought my life was ruined!" I said between sobs.

"It was a close call," said Eros.

Aphrodite looked murderous. "I could strangle Cranus with my bare hands. To think I once gave him fashion advice!"

Judge Themis cleared her throat. She wasn't finished. "However. Makario, you must face punishment," she said. "You knowingly assisted your father. You were aware of his deceit."

Marco nodded. "I was, Judge Themis. I knew what I was doing."

"Oh dear," Dad muttered under his breath. I looked around at the courtroom, which had turned silent. What was about to happen?

The judge sighed. "Very well. You know the

punishment. You are sentenced to a lifetime on Mount Olympus. You may never enter the mortal realm again," she said. "I'm very disappointed in you."

I'd never watch him sip espressos in Cafe Gio's or show him my favourite bus routes around London. We'd never go ice skating under the stars or eat sticky food until our bellies hurt.

He'd sacrificed that for me.

I knew he was making up for his lies, but tears still sprang to my eyes. I'd probably never see Marco again. His sentence made sure of that.

Before I could catch one last look at his face, Dad put his arm around me. We left the courtroom through arched entrances. I couldn't wait to go home.

"Now, Helen, I must ask something else of you. We're having a little party at home to celebrate. Are you too tired to join us?"

A nap was the last thing on my mind. My nerves were on edge and my head swam. Did that just happen?

In the last hour, my immortal ex-boyfriend had appeared out of nowhere, admitted that he'd tricked me, and secured my (rightful) freedom. With the whirlwind events of the last hour, I felt like I'd never sleep again.

I sighed. "I can deal with a party. But can I have a shower first?"

# FORTY-FOUR

We bundled into taxis (no chauffeur-driven cars this time) and drove home together, as a family. I never thought I'd be so happy to see the house. It felt like weeks, rather than two days, since we'd left for the trial.

I immediately went upstairs to get changed. Hopefully I'd never have to wear that cotton toga again. After I showered and dressed, I came down to the living room. Dad, Aphrodite, Athena, Apollo and Eros were there, laughing, chatting and singing. They made enough noise for thirty people. I didn't mind, though. It was the warmest and liveliest the house had ever felt.

I found a space on the sofa next to Athena. I don't know what I would have done without her guidance that weekend.

"Gosh," I sighed. "Imagine if Marco didn't do the right thing today? My life would be over."

"There are worse punishments, believe me. A lifetime on Mount Olympus is nothing compared to Hades or Tartarus," Athena said. "There, you'd have pure air, wholesome food and a top-notch education."

I shuddered at the word "wholesome". Athena made Mount Olympus sound like a Swiss boarding school. I'd never swap that for North London, even if the air pollution was asthma-inducing.

"And would I be accepted? Even though I'm half-mortal?"

"Mount Olympus has moved on quite a bit since my day," Athena replied. "It's true that at one time half-mortals were looked down upon. But no one really thinks like that. Not any more."

I remembered the look that guard gave me when he called me a "half-lifer", and the frosty reception I got from Phaedra and Flavian at the feast, but I decided not to argue. Athena wasn't going to get it. She was 100% goddess, after all.

"Anyway, Helen, shouldn't you be getting to bed soon? We can't have you miss any more school," she said.

"Nope," I said grinning. "It's half-term tomorrow. No school for a week!"

It was good to see my family smiling and laughing together for what felt like the first time in for ever. But I couldn't quite enjoy myself. Despite everything, a part of me felt sorry for Marco. If only he'd told me he was immortal instead of following Cranus's orders, I would have had someone to talk to. I wouldn't have had to deal with the madness of my family alone.

A familiar wave of sadness reappeared. I couldn't cry here, not when everyone was having a good time. I decided to slip upstairs for a bit of peace and quiet.

I switched my phone on and several days' worth of notifications sent it into a frenzy. I was only interested in one update. Were my friends worried about me? I nervously opened the group chat and saw several "get well soon" messages. So they had worried about me. That was a relief. I wasn't sure I deserved their sympathy after how I'd treated them.

I had to make sure things were OK between us. I typed into the group chat:

*H: Hey lovelies! I'm feeling much better now. I miss you. Want to come over for a sleepover tomorrow night? Xx*

I went back downstairs and joined the family, still celebrating our lucky escape.

"Hey, Dad? I have a favour to ask."

# FORTY-FIVE

The doorbell buzzed as I put the salted caramel cupcakes in the oven. I'd woken up early on a school holiday to begin Operation Forgive Me and make my friends smile. I'd even roped in half the family. The gods agreed to leave me home alone for the night, and they'd even helped with a few other surprises. I hoped it worked.

I opened the front door to let in Yasmin, Daphne and Noor. They'd arrived together. We all hugged and they asked if I was feeling better after my tummy bug. They were smiley and friendly but things weren't the same. There was a definite tension between us. I had to be brave and address the issue.

We sat down in the living room. "Listen, I know that I've been a bit distant lately," I said.

The girls went silent and exchanged glances. But they didn't deny it.

"Moving back in with my dad, getting to know my new family . . . it's been a lot of change for me. And I'm not very good at talking things over," I continued.

"You've been kind of weird since DJ Sunny was on TV," Noor admitted.

"And since you met Marco," Daphne added. "You wouldn't tell us anything!"

"We thought you went quiet on us because we weren't as cool as Marco. We had a few theories," Yasmin mumbled.

I thought about how much weirder my life had been, and how that looked from their perspective. My friends only saw the random days off school, my family's fame and me being withdrawn. I never let them in.

"No way! Meeting you all has been the best thing about moving back to London. That first day in Miss Bloom's English class . . . I was so nervous it was unreal. And you guys made me feel at home. It meant the world to me," I said.

"Then why the disappearing act?" Daphne asked.

There was no easy way to answer that honestly.

"Things have been weird lately. I'm still adjusting to

this new life with my dad." I took a deep breath. "Also, Marco and I broke up."

The girls gasped.

"When?!"

"Why?!"

"Do you need me to get Isaac to jump him?!"

"Slow down with the questions! It was never going to work out between us anyway," I said. "And I'm doing OK."

Daphne went over to my side of the sofa and put her arms around me. "I really wish you'd told us, Hels."

"We just want to be here for you, babe," Noor said.

"Sometimes I just can't talk about things that easily," I said. "I'm working on it, though."

"Um, Helen," Yasmin said. "Is something burning?"

The salted caramel cupcakes failed miserably (and Maria was going to kill me for ruining her baking tin). Luckily, the other surprises I had planned didn't rely on my cooking skills.

As we waited for our pizzas to arrive, I told the group about their surprises.

"So you know how I'm really sorry for being a crap friend? I want to make it up to you properly," I said.

"Aw, Hels, you don't have to do that!" Yasmin said.

"Seriously, Helen, you don't. No one needs to try your baking for the second time," Noor said, laughing.

I raised my eyebrows. "You sure about that, Noor? Because I can always find another home for this." I pulled a cardboard box from behind the sofa. "My big sis deleted her YouTube channel. She doesn't need her state-of-the-art webcam any more. Plus there's a load of untouched make-up in there. She's assured me it's good stuff."

"Whoa, Noor, this is awesome!" Daphne said. "Now you've got no excuse not to start that YouTube channel."

"Helen, this is sick!" Noor said, rooting through her box of goodies. It felt so good to see her happy.

"Daphs, this is for you," I said, pulling out a huge shopping bag. "I remembered you saying you love all things vintage. Right?"

Aphrodite (reluctantly) let me choose a couple of old dresses from her vast wardrobe for Daphne. I picked the fifties-style dresses with full skirts.

Daphne pulled out a crimson number and unfurled it. "Where did you find this?! It's beyond perfect," she squealed.

"Don't worry about that. If you love it then it's yours," I said. I turned to Yasmin. "Yas, I haven't exactly got you a gift."

"Oh please, Helen," she said. "I owe *you* one for saving my life on New Year's Eve."

I gave her a look. "Yeah, yeah. Anyway, you know that my other sister works in a law firm, right? She says you're welcome to shadow her for work experience whenever you're ready. And she'll write you a reference, too!"

Yasmin's jaw dropped. "Helen, are you for real?! This'll help me so much when I'm applying for sixth-form colleges."

"Honestly, girls, it's the least I can do," I said.

"Awesome as all of this is, you know it's not necessary. Right?" Daphne said.

"Innit," Noor said. "Just talk to us next time, dummy."

I nodded. "Sounds like a deal."

# FORTY-SIX

I opened my front door and could hear arguing. Great. We'd been back home for less than two days but my family were already bickering.

"Eros, you're getting ashes on the floor!" Maria said. I rushed into the kitchen and gave her a massive hug. I was so happy to see her.

"Helen! You must tell me all about this dreadful trial. Right after Eros gets rid of his flaming herbs."

"Maria, it's a sage cleanse," he said. The acrid smell wafted in my face. Gross. "This house has seen a lot of . . . energy recently. This'll sort out the atmosphere."

I sat at the kitchen table while Maria shooed Eros out of the kitchen.

"My Snail Slime Serum arrived over the weekend!"

Aphrodite dumped a package on the kitchen table. "You'll help me test it, right, Helen? It's the only hope for that spot on your forehead."

Before I could answer, a DOOF-DOOF-DOOF sound boomed from the ceiling. Apollo was reunited with his DJ decks.

"Happy to be home, darling?" Dad wandered into the kitchen with his coffee mug.

I waved the sage smoke out of my face and grinned. Home.

Dear Mum,

I can start the letter with something positive, for once. I'm doing much better since I last wrote to you. To try and describe the last week in one letter would make my hand ache (and I'm sure you'd prefer I save that energy for my French homework).

Mum, I think I would have made you proud. I never in a million years thought I could be so brave. But I just kept putting one foot in front of the other like you taught me. I guess I'm much more like you than I thought.

Even though today is Valentine's Day, the only card I'll be getting is one from Eros. Marco is well and truly out of my life. It's for the best. I think I'm going to swear off boys for a while. At least for a couple of months anyway. . .

Things are back to normal now. Or as normal as they'll ever be. Apollo and Aphrodite are staying far away from fame. Dad is as *passionate about junk sales and probiotic bacteria as ever, but he comes out of his office every now and then. We're even going to try visiting somewhere other than a museum.*

*Let's face it: I was never going to have a "normal" family. My life with you never fitted into that category, but that didn't make it any less wonderful.*

*One good thing to come out of this whole trial? Dad actually trusts me. I'm allowed to have friends over for sleepovers and everything! And Aphrodite is way easier on me. She doesn't flip if I take too long in the bathroom, and she hasn't tried to transform my hair in ages.*

*My family aren't perfect, but they're mine and they've got my back. Wherever you are, you don't need to worry about me.*

*Love for ever,*

*Helen xxx*

# Q&A WITH THE AUTHOR, ALEXANDRA SHEPPARD

**What inspired you to write *Oh My Gods*?**

*Oh My Gods* was inspired by a comedy-musical from 1946 called *"Down to Earth"* – my sisters and I watched it with my mum one Sunday afternoon, back when families typically had one TV per household so were forced to spend time together (ahh, the noughties). The film starred Rita Hayworth as a Greek muse, who, after finding out that a Broadway producer is about to spoof Greek mythology in his next play, comes down to earth disguised as a mortal actress in order to intervene. The film, truth be told, is forgettable. But the idea of Greek gods on earth has stuck with me ever since. This idea, combined with my evergreen love of angst-filled teen confessionals, was the source for *Oh My Gods*.

## Have you always been interested in Greek mythology? What's your favourite myth?

I've been interested in myths, folklore and legends for as long as I can remember – Indian, Egyptian and Caribbean stories are amongst my favourites. But Greek mythology's impact is unrivalled, and the stories were constantly repackaged throughout my childhood. From Disney's *Hercules* (yaaaas, gospel-singing goddess babes!) to *Percy Jackson*, I couldn't get enough of the retellings.

My favourite myth? It's impossible to choose just one. But the myth that I first remember reading over and over again is the story of Arachne, the skilled weaver who was turned into a spider by the jealous goddess Athena – and condemned to weave for ever! It's a creative origin story combined with vengeful, petty behaviour. I love it.

## If you could be the Greek god/goddess of anything, what would you be?

I'd be the Goddess of Travel. I know it sounds dull, but hear me out. Seeing new places is my favourite way to spend time but I cannot stand long journeys. I get carsick, trains are expensive and airports are a special type of hell. Imagine being able to cut all of that out by, I dunno, teleporting or whatever? It would save time, money and boredom. I wish more than anything it could come true.

## What were your favourite books growing up?

I loved teen diaries like *The Princess Diaries*, *I Capture The Castle* and *The Secret Diary of Adrian Mole*. *The Confessions of Georgia Nicolson* series made me and my friends weep with laughter. Despite being an avid reader, books by Malorie Blackman and Zadie Smith were the first time I read black British women in literature. And I loved vampire stories like *Dracula* and *Blood Sinister*, which was set in Highgate Cemetery – minutes from where I grew up.

**If you could tell your teenage self anything, what would it be?**

The world won't end if someone dislikes you. When I was a teen (and well into my twenties, if I'm being honest), I couldn't bear the thought of someone disliking me. It would stop me from speaking my mind, expressing my true thoughts and generally being myself. Now, I care a good deal less. It's so liberating. Try it.

# ACKNOWLEDGEMENTS

It's easy to believe that books are a solo endeavour, but that couldn't be further from the truth. This story would be nothing but a few hundred words in a battered notebook if it weren't for the people in my life supporting and uplifting at every turn. I'm very lucky.

Thank you to my dream of an agent, Leticia, and the rest of Team Pontas, for your guidance and publishing smarts. Thank you for welcoming me to the global Pontas family!

I'm certain that I lucked out with my editors. Eishar and Sophie, it means the world that you understood Helen from day one. Thank you for making the editing process a joy from start to finish. Scholastic is the perfect home for my story, and I'm so grateful to everyone there who has worked to make my dreams come true. Huge thanks to Paul and Liam for the beautiful and eye-popping cover of my dreams.

A HUGE thanks must go to Kerry and Write Like A Grrrl. Kerry, your incisive and loving critique made this book a reality. The course changed my life and introduced me to the kindest, smartest and most talented writer gang a grrrl could ask for. All of the thanks to Equal Writes (especially Charlotte, Elizabeth, Naina, Grace, Sara, Flo, Renginee, Sarah and Kitty) for pushing me to get on your level. You make me a better writer.

Nineteen Newbies! This whole author thing is much more fun with your rants, puns and GIFs. I pray our Twitter DMs never see the light of day.

Thank you to #TeamSocial: Laura, Caner, Sam and everyone else at FCB Inferno for accommodating my writing alongside my day job – it's so, so appreciated.

Thank you to Mel and Nat for the tidal wave of

support, and for bringing Black Girl's Book Club into my life. With every event, I feel eternally grateful for the space you've created. You are the epitome of #BlackGirlMagic. Love and thanks to the many hilarious, smart and beautiful women I've met through BGBC. Thanks again to Tito for catching my best side.

Thank you to my family and friends, especially Beth, Nathan, Zaire, Antonia, Shakana, Zion, Christine, Max, Hannah, Adam, Marie Anne, Aiss, Robin and Howard. Extra special thanks to the women I'm lucky to call my aunties – Abigail, Sonia, Monica and Jackie – and my beloved grandparents.

Endless love and thanks to Michael, my sidekick for life. Thank you for everything, but especially for putting up with my 5.30 a.m. alarms.

Above all, thanks to Mum and Dad for bolstering my creative confidence since before I could write full sentences. Thank you for calling me a writer from childhood and treasuring every short story and poem. This book would never have happened without your unwavering belief in me.